MADE IN
London

BOOK 6 IN THE LONDON ROMANCE SERIES

by Clare Lydon

custard books

First Edition October 2019
Published by Custard Books
Copyright © 2019 Clare Lydon
ISBN: 978-1-912019-86-1

Cover Design: Kevin Pruitt
Editor: Kelli Collins
Proofreader: Gill Mullins
Typesetting: Adrian McLaughlin

Find out more at: www.clarelydon.co.uk
Follow me on Twitter: @clarelydon
Follow me on Instagram: @clarefic

All rights reserved. This book or any portion thereof may not be reproduced or used in any manner whatsoever without the express written permission of the author.

This is a work of fiction. All characters and happenings in this publication are fictitious and any resemblance to real persons (living or dead), locales or events is purely coincidental.

Also By Clare Lydon

London Romance Series
London Calling (Book One)
This London Love (Book Two)
A Girl Called London (Book Three)
The London Of Us (Book Four)
London, Actually (Book Five)
Made In London (Book Six)
Hot London Nights (Book Seven)
Big London Dreams (Book Eight)
London Ever After (Book Nine)

Standalone Novels
A Taste Of Love
Before You Say I Do
Change Of Heart
Christmas In Mistletoe
Hotshot
It Started With A Kiss
Nothing To Lose: A Lesbian Romance
Once Upon A Princess
One Golden Summer
The Christmas Catch
The Long Weekend
Twice In A Lifetime
You're My Kind

All I Want Series
Two novels and four novellas chart the course
of one relationship over two years.

Boxsets
Available for both the London Romance series and the
All I Want series for ultimate value. Check out my
website for more: www.clarelydon.co.uk/books

Acknowledgements

This book wouldn't be in your hands without the help and cheerleading of so many people. Here's where they get a shout-out.

Thanks to Denise Murphy for chatting with me about being a solo lesbian mum. All power to ya! I'm also indebted to Melita Falzon and Nicki Brown for their stories of sick and poo. I love kids, but if anything's going to put you off having one, it's listening to those. In case you were wondering, that poo story from the pub? Yes, it really happened.

No book of mine would be in the world without my first readers who tell me if it's any good, and point out where it could be better. Thanks as always to HP Munro for her initial thoughts. Buckets of gratitude to Tammara Adams for running my ARC team with grace and style. Plus, of course, thanks to every one of my early readers who picked up those last-minute typos and missing words. Especially to Hilary and her proofing superpowers. You help make the book as polished as it can be, and I'm beyond grateful.

Oodles of plaudits to my cover designer, Kevin Pruitt, for another fabulous cover. He also keeps me supplied with great wine, so is forever my best friend. Thanks to my editor Kelli Collins for the initial feedback and thumbs-up; also to Gill

Mullins for taking a final chammy to my words and making them shine. Plus, of course, cheers to Adrian McLaughlin for making this book look so pretty in your hands. You're all brilliant and I couldn't do any of this without you.

Thanks to my wife, Yvonne, even though she hates being thanked. I believe her words on this one went something like: "It's actually pretty good and not nearly as bad as you're making out." She was right, too. She usually is.

Finally, thanks to you for buying and reading. The London Romance series is one that I intend to keep going, mainly due to reader feedback that they want it to continue. The London Romance ladies were the women who started it all for me, and as such, I'm forever in their debt. However, it's you reading my books that gives me the impetus to keep going, and that means the world. I hope you enjoy this book, and want more London tales. I already have another one lined up, expect that in 2020!

If you fancy getting in touch, you can do so using one of the methods below. I'm most active on Instagram.

Twitter: @ClareLydon
Facebook: www.facebook.com/clare.lydon
Instagram: @clarefic
Find out more at: www.clarelydon.co.uk
Contact: mail@clarelydon.co.uk

Thank you so much for reading!

Chapter One

Heidi Hughes lowered her driver-side window and leaned out. A barrage of fat raindrops hit her cheeks. She pulled herself back into the car, glancing at the bright blue digits of her dashboard clock.

"Fuck." Who got stuck behind a florist's van on Valentine's Day when they'd been single forever?

The florist gave her a what-ya-gonna-do smile as she got back into the van, the massive bouquet and garish red-and-white teddy bear safely delivered. There were plenty more squashed against the van's back window.

Heidi ground her teeth together. "Fuck, fuck, fuck." Swearing wasn't going to teleport her to the photography studio for her annual family photo any quicker, but it made her feel better. Fuck was her very favourite swear word. Perhaps even her favourite word, full stop. It got people's attention. However, now her daughter was talking, she was trying to curb her enthusiasm for it. It wasn't easy.

The van moved finally, and Heidi pressed the accelerator. She eyed the clock again, guilt settling in her stomach. She wasn't just late. She was *next-level* late. The kind of late that needed to sit in a chair and think about what it had done. The kind of late that made her mum talk about *disappointment*.

The original Maya Hughes was a laid-back woman. She'd had to be, having given birth to Heidi and her sister, Sarah. The only thing she didn't tolerate was bad timekeeping. Mum always said it was a reaction to her upbringing, where timekeeping was non-existent.

Heidi had been on board until she'd had her own daughter, Maya. Now, she had no idea how anyone with children got anything done on time. With her work and her daughter, Heidi's life was one constant race against the clock, and the clock normally won. That excuse held no truck with her Caribbean matriarch mother, though.

Fifteen minutes later, Heidi parked and pulled the sun visor down. When she clocked the full extent of her makeup fail in the tiny square mirror, she shook her head. It had been perfect when she'd left her flat this morning. However, this morning's engagement photoshoot — which had massively overrun — had also involved her clients' cats, Laurel and Hardy. Who Heidi was massively allergic to. Hence now she looked like she'd been sobbing for a century. Her waterproof mascara hadn't stood a chance.

Heidi flipped up the visor and got out of her silver Audi. She'd fix her face once she'd said hi to everyone. She pulled her coat up over her head in a bid to keep out the rain, inhaling the thick, damp air.

Heidi's tardiness didn't matter to her daughter. Maya greeted her with a shriek as she walked into Pippa's studio. Heidi felt the heat of her mother's glower, so decided not to look up and face it just yet. Rather, she was going to enjoy giving Maya a cuddle because she hadn't seen her for four hours. The way Maya was grinning, it might have been four years, because that's how kids measured time. Whenever Heidi was away from her daughter for anything longer than an hour, it was like she'd been on expedition to the Arctic for months.

"Hello, my little munchkin!" She picked up her daughter and spun her in the air, much to Maya's delight. Her dark curls framed her face, her brown eyes sparkling as she let out her adorable cackle. At times like these, Maya was the perfect Sunday supplement child. "Were you a good girl for Aunty Sarah?"

Heidi glanced her sister's way as she walked towards her. Maya wrapped her arms around Heidi's neck, her hot cheek sticking to Heidi's own. When she reached Sarah's side, Heidi brushed her lips against her sister's cheek.

"She was a perfect little girl for me, weren't you?" Sarah gave Maya's side a tickle and she wriggled in Heidi's arms. "She went into Albert's room and messed up his cards, which he's still getting over. But I told him to clear them up, so he's learned a valuable lesson." Sarah paused. "And then we made cupcakes and Maya helped to mix the dough, didn't you?"

Maya nodded, her smile slick with dribble. "Cakes!" She clapped her hands, before wriggling too much. Heidi put her down. Maya ran over to her cousin, Max. Heidi glanced back to her sister.

"What happened to your face? You didn't look like that when you dropped Maya off earlier." Sarah wasn't one to beat around the bush. It was a family trait.

"I meant to sort it out in traffic, but I gave up. It was too stop-start. Let's just say this morning's photoshoot involved cats." Heidi nodded towards the bathroom. "Let me go and fix it before Mum frowns at me."

She was going to do just that when her sister's husband, Jason, arrived at her side. "Happy Valentine's Day!" He studied her face.

"If you say I look like a panda, I'll give you a different kind of black eye."

Jason opened his mouth to speak, then promptly closed it.

"How about a raccoon?" Sarah offered, flashing her trademark grin.

"A sad badger?" Jason followed up, gaining momentum.

Heidi let a smile invade her face. "Fuck off, the pair of you."

Both Sarah and Jason turned up their grins.

"By the way, I've made a decision about my birthday weekend." Sarah paused for added effect. "I've found a festival we can go to, so that's what we're doing. Jason's going to be the at-home dad to look after all the kids — Maya included — while we go and listen to music and get drunk. Sound good?"

"Free childcare and booze? Count me in."

Footsteps walking across the laminate studio floor signalled Heidi was too late to move, and her heart deflated like a balloon. She'd failed at avoiding her mother. She blamed her sister.

"You're late, Heidi Ray."

Her mum was using both her names, so it must be bad. "I know, I'm sorry." Even though she was 41, she still felt 12 at times like these. "The shoot ran over, and then I got stuck in traffic. The rain didn't help, either."

Her mum peered closer at her face. "Have you been crying?"

"Allergic reaction. The clients had cats."

Her mum waved her away. "Go sort yourself out before the photo, then. We're already far too late, so let's get things going."

Heidi gave her mum a nod, obeying immediately. She walked towards the bathroom, knowing exactly where it was because they'd been coming to this studio for their annual family photo for as long as she could remember. However, this year was special, because it was to be Maya's first where she knew what was going on. Last year, she'd been eight months old. This year, she was approaching the grand old age of two.

Heidi rearranged her face the best she could, a sparse single radiator on the far wall not really doing enough to heat the space. She shivered as she balanced her makeup bag on the edge of the white porcelain sink, wiping away the mascara on her cheeks, touching up her foundation and lipstick. She put a comb through her hair, practised her family-photo smile, then rolled her eyes. She'd have to do. Maybe Pippa could touch her up in the post-production. She'd have a word.

When she got back outside, Pippa was waiting. She gave her a hug. Heidi had always been close to Pippa. What's more, her mum's oldest friend had been an invaluable source of advice when Heidi had become a wedding photographer some years ago. Now she was older, Pippa mainly stuck to studio work, referring any wedding clients to Heidi. Without Pippa, Heidi wouldn't have the thriving business she did.

"Come on, eldest child. We haven't got all day!" That was Dad, his tone soft, his smile wide. Her dad never drove her as hard as her mum.

Heidi walked towards her family. Sarah and Jason standing behind their three children, Albert, Alex and Max. Her parents, Maya and Robert, to their left. Up until last year, she'd always been alone in the family photo. Just Heidi, year after year. None of her girlfriends had ever been permanent enough to make the shot. She'd never dreamed her child would make it before a partner, but life had a funny way of surprising you.

Now Maya was nearly two, Heidi was thinking about dating again. She missed sex. She missed romance. She missed regular adult conversation. She missed all of it. Maybe next year, she'd have a partner as well as a child. The full set.

Maya already had both hands in the air as Heidi scooped her up, kissing her curls as she settled in her arms. At times like this, she never wanted to let Maya go. Her dad squeezed her shoulder as Heidi settled next to him.

"You look lovely," he whispered, giving her a smile. Heidi wanted to find someone just like her dad. But perhaps with more hair and less stubble. And female.

"Alright, everyone! Jason, could you scoot in a little. Get closer to Sarah, act as though you like her." Pippa was in full-on directing mode.

Jason did as he was told.

"On my count, look at me, best cheesy smiles, and say Valentine's Day!" Pippa held up a hand. "Three, two, one!" The camera clicked, and Heidi gave the best smile she could.

"Valentine's Day!"

Maybe next year, she'd have someone standing to her left, too.

Chapter Two

"You're 40. It's a big deal. We're going away. End of story."

Eden Price raised a single eyebrow at her flatmate, Lib. "I've told you before, I may be 40, but it's also just another Saturday in March."

Lib didn't even react to that. "What about Lithuania? I've heard it's gorgeous and the wine is less than a quid a bottle, so it gets the thumbs-up from me." Lib was clutching a glass of Chablis as she spoke, neck crooked to look at the screen of Eden's tablet. "Tammara went last year and said it was gorgeous and unspoilt, so long as you avoided the stag parties around the main square at the weekends."

"We don't have to go away."

Lib let out a long sigh and turned to face Eden, putting down her wine and the tablet. She got hold of Eden's shoulders and squeezed, looking her in the eye. "How long have we known each other?"

"That one's easy. Ten years." They'd met through a friend of a friend, dancing in a club in King's Cross. Lib and Eden had hit it off right away. When Eden bought her Camden flat five years ago, Lib had moved in the following weekend. She hadn't been able to shake her since.

"Exactly. In that time, I've taken a holiday every single year." Lib furrowed her brow. "Tell me, how many holidays have you taken in the past decade?"

Eden wriggled under Lib's glare. She knew the answer, but she didn't like to say it out loud. It sounded bad when she did that. "I've been to Scotland to visit my uncle and aunt."

"That was ages ago. Plus, seeing family is not a holiday. You've taken precisely none of those. You either stay in London, or you work and take the money. You never have an adventure, never put yourself out there. It's why you get those tension headaches, too much staring at a screen. You need to stop working all the time and take a break."

Eden swiped her hand through the air, doing a 360 of the lounge. Lib was right about the migraines, but she didn't miss holidays. She'd rather work. Going away on her own wasn't much fun. "Take a look around. I might not have gone on holiday this year, but the money I saved, I spent on new furniture and redecorating. You must admit the place looks pretty cool." Eden was still revelling in its newness. The couch was stone-coloured and a dream to sit on. The walls were dapper in olive green with crisp white cornicing and skirting. Her carpet was a lush grey that cushioned your feet. Eden especially loved her new coffee table – a retro gaming machine with a glass top.

"It looks amazing, I told you that. But I still think for your 40th we need to mark it with something special. And don't tell me it's just another Saturday in March, or I might clock you over the head with your tablet."

"You should see someone about that anger, you know."

Lib shook her head, a wry smile invading her face.

Eden sat up. How could she convince Lib she was okay

staying local? "I can go to Barcelona or Madrid or wherever when I'm 41 or 42. Even 40 and a half. But going away on my birthday isn't an option, you know that. It doesn't work. You've got your mum, plus Issy and Kath have their kids. I don't mind postponing."

"But I do." Lib's mum was terminally ill, and she'd put her job as a web developer on hold to be there for her. Her mum had gone downhill fast in recent weeks, and Eden knew she wouldn't be comfortable going away. Lib kept telling Eden 40 was a big deal, a milestone birthday, one to celebrate. But that was the story Lib believed, not her. To Eden, she was just another year older.

She picked up her tablet and did a search for events on her birthday, March 2nd. An ad popped up for a festival on her birthday weekend: Year Awakening. What's more, the headliners were a band she wanted to see. She sat up a bit straighter. A one-day local event could be the solution to their issues, and then she could drag her mates away for something further afield when it suited them all.

"What about this?" Eden pointed at the screen.

Lib peered closer, before glancing up at Eden. "But will you be happy celebrating your 40th in a wet field rather than sunning it in Barcelona?"

Eden nodded. "So long as I'm with my nearest and dearest, I don't care where I am."

Lib raised a single eyebrow. "You sure you won't regret not going away for your big birthday? I know you said it's 'just another Saturday in March', but still." She used her fingers to put quotes around her words.

"I'm positive," Eden replied.

Lib flopped back on the sofa, wriggling deeper. "This is bloody comfy, I'll give you that." She glanced at Eden. "You promise me you'll go away this year? When I can come, too?"

Eden didn't like to think about the reasons why Lib would be free to come, too. "I promise. A long weekend somewhere exotic."

Lib picked up Eden's glass of wine and passed it to her. "In that case, let's book it. I'm going to make sure your 40th is the bomb, whatever it takes." She took a gulp of her wine. "If it helps, even though you're the oldest in our group, you don't look it."

"True. Taylor wins that one, going prematurely grey. Plus, Issy and Kath have aged about ten years since they decided to have kids. Message to self: don't have kids, they make you old."

Lib smiled. "I thought about it once, but seeing as I'm 40 in two years, it's getting a bit late."

"Thirty eight is still young to have a kid. Plenty of lesbians are doing it." Eden shivered. "But you know my thoughts on kids. You have to be really certain you want them, and then be prepared to put time and patience into raising them. Even then, it's a gamble — for the children and the parents." She cast her mind back to her childhood, but it was dark. Some things were best left in the shadows.

Eden stretched her arms over her head, before leaning forward and snagging a couple of salt-and-vinegar crisps from the bowl Lib had set out. "You know what I have been thinking about getting for my birthday?"

Lib turned to her. "Twins?"

A chill whipped through her. "No, thank you." She paused.

"I've been thinking about getting some pussy. A small, furry one, to be precise. The key to me embracing my middle years is to get a kitten and truly be a lesbian. What do you think?"

Lib put down her wine and hugged Eden, before holding her at arm's length. "This flat has been crying out for some pussy action for a while now." She held a finger in the air and drew her mouth into the shape of an 'O'. "You know, there was something about kittens on Facebook yesterday. Somebody Sheila knows was looking to home some." Lib pulled up Facebook on her phone. "You want me to see if I can find the post?"

Eden gave her a wide grin. "Yes please." She leaned over Lib. "Imagine if I could get a tiny baby kitten before my birthday." That truly would be her birthday wishes coming true.

"Wait till you see them, they were so cute." Lib glanced up from the screen. "Plus, it goes without saying that tiny baby kittens work wonders on the hearts of women, doesn't it?"

Eden shook her head. "You are fixated on my love life, or lack thereof. I'm perfectly happy, I've told you before. Concentrate on yourself before turning the spotlight on me."

A blush rose up Lib's cheeks as she studied her screen. "Too soon for me." Lib was still getting over her last break-up. "But I'd love to see you meet someone. Don't you want to give your new little kitty a two-parent household?"

Eden sat back. "They always say you turn into your mother, don't they? If I get a cat, I'm heading right down that path, being a single parent. Let's hope I don't go the whole hog and turn into a self-obsessed, selfish arsehole, too."

Chapter Three

"Did I tell you I've got someone else who wants their wedding photographed?" Heidi's best friend Cleo threw a packet of bistro salad into Heidi's shopping trolley to go with the ham-and-mushroom pizza with dough balls they'd just selected. Their no-carb diet could wait for another day.

Heidi held up a hand. "I've told you, don't tell me this shit in the supermarket. I won't remember. Send me an email and I can reply. But you should know I'm pretty booked up. Plus, doing weddings with a toddler in tow is no picnic. Last year, everyone wanted to babysit Maya, because she couldn't walk and she slept a lot. This year, my little hellion is a walking weapon of mass destruction. Aren't you, sausage?"

As if sensing she was the star of the conversation, Maya held up both arms and let out a high-pitched squeal, which caused a woman to Heidi's left to crash her trolley into a display of kitchen rolls. They tumbled to the ground one by one. Heidi wheeled the trolley away sharpish. Behind her, Cleo snorted.

"I love your daughter, have I told you that?"

Maya applauded herself. Heidi didn't blame her.

"I don't know where she gets her headstrong vibe from, do you?" Cleo gave Heidi a grin. "I'll email you, no problem."

They turned into the wine aisle, with Heidi pulling up her trolley and depositing two bottles of Malbec into it.

Maya leaned over to the shelf and tried to grab a bottle herself, but Heidi stopped her just in time. "Mummy's breakfast!" she shouted.

More snorts from Cleo as the woman beside Heidi turned to her, eyes wide. "She's joking," Heidi told her, her head filling with noise, her cheeks with blood. "I don't drink it at breakfast. Just in the evening." She was oversharing, wasn't she?

The woman edged away.

Heidi glanced at Cleo. "Don't say a fucking word."

"Fucking!" Maya repeated.

Cleo couldn't hold in her laughter any longer, clutching the trolley as she shook.

Heidi brought her face level with Maya. "What have we said about chatting in public?" She could never be mad with her daughter for long, though. Plus, she shouldn't have sworn in the first place. It had just been a very long day. She kissed Maya on the cheek.

In response, Maya slapped her in the face.

Heidi took a moment, then pushed the trolley down the aisle, hoping for silence till they made it out of Waitrose. "Remember when I said my child would never do this or that? I hear new parents say that now, too, and I laugh."

Cleo chucked some sweet popcorn into the trolley, before massaging Heidi's shoulders. "You seem a little wound up today. What have you been up to?"

Heidi gave Cleo a look. "One word. Aquababy."

"Oh no, not the dreaded Aquababy with the standoffish dads. I thought I told you to stop going?"

Heidi shrugged as they passed the bakery. The smell of cinnamon wafted into her nostrils, and it took all her effort not to scoop the whole display into her trolley. She was trying not to eat too many carbs. "Maya loves the water. But I'm looking into other options. Tell me about your day, take my mind off it."

Heidi's oldest friend had a big job that was taking her to Boston for the next six weeks, with a view to taking her there permanently in the not-too-distant future. Heidi wasn't looking forward to that. Their bi-weekly pizza and wine evenings were her lifeline.

"I had boring back-to-back conference calls. The corporate life isn't all it's cracked up to be."

"Whereas I had an Aquababy class with a load of dads who were giving their wives a break for a couple of hours."

Cleo began to load their haul onto the shopping belt as Maya began to clap again. Cleo tickled Maya's tummy as she set the wine on its side, the glass clinking together as the belt moved in jerky fashion. "Was the lesbian there again today, too?"

"She was." Heidi frowned as she thought about it. "But she kept her distance. Again. What does she think I'm going to do? Jump her at the first opportunity? Honestly, being the single lesbian mum is the hardest job of all." Heidi shook her head. "The husbands think I want their sperm; the lesbians think I want *them*. I never realised what a hard job single mums have until I became one."

She put the pizza on the belt. "Plus, they're all white, while I'm mixed race. So they see me as the black single mother, which makes me even more other." Heidi put the words 'black single mother' and 'other' in finger quotes. "Even though my mum has lived here for over 40 years, and my dad is Robert Hughes from Surrey." She pushed the trolley to the end of the checkout, sighing. "But I'll survive. It's nothing some pizza and wine won't fix." Her fingers hovered over the display of chocolate by the till, but she resisted picking up a KitKat Chunky. Such self-control.

Heidi turned her smile on the cashier, a woman in her fifties with a severe fringe.

"Didn't you say you'd met one nice lesbian couple? They've been babysitting for you?"

The cashier began to scan the groceries, twitching as she heard the word 'lesbian'. Heidi ignored it. "Yes, Kate and Meg. They're from the lesbian parenting Facebook group, and I'd be lost without them."

"Fuck the Aquababy crowd, Heids." Cleo flashed her smile at the cashier. "Excuse my French." She waved away Heidi's attempt to pay, tapping her card on the paypoint. It declined.

"You have to insert your card, madam. It's over £30." The cashier's tone was firm, her look stern.

"It's Waitrose, babe, not Aldi," Heidi told her, laughing. "You need me to get this?"

"I got it." Cleo clicked her tongue against the roof of her mouth, before keying in her pin.

"I'm just going over to the pharmacy. I need some help with my period pains. They've gone batshit crazy since I had Maya."

The cashier looked up at Heidi.

"Sorry again," Heidi said. Then to Cleo, "See you back at the car?"

Cleo nodded as Heidi handed over the keys. "We're going to try not to eat all the crisps before Mummy comes back, aren't we?" Cleo told Maya.

Satisfied her daughter was in safe hands, Heidi strolled along the end of the line of checkouts, her stomach churning. She knew the drug she wanted that would settle her stomach.

Heidi was level with the final checkout when a tall woman in a natty blue jacket came careering past the cashier and straight into her.

Heidi had no time to process anything as her body took the brunt of the woman's weight. Her shoulder crunched as she toppled left, staggering into a line of three chairs. They were meant for a breather after a marathon shopping session. They saved Heidi slamming into the shop window.

"Fucking hell!" More swearing, this time from the mouth of the speeding woman. "Where did you come from? You materialised out of thin air!"

Heidi took a moment before she responded, standing up straight, grabbing her shoulder which was already throbbing. She tested her elbow. It hurt to move, which wasn't a surprise. Was this the sort of thing she could call one of those daytime accident helplines for?

Heidi refocused on her assailant. She was still tall, and when Heidi looked closer, she saw deep blue eyes under a head of styled, streaked-blond hair. Did Heidi know her from somewhere? Her face looked familiar. She flicked through her mental notebook, but quickly gave up.

If she did know her, it probably wasn't because of anything good. She was probably one of those women on Tinder who said they were up for 'fun and good times'. She looked exactly the type. She probably got her way all the time, spending her days running into people in her workplace, on the phone, via email. The woman wasn't quite sure what to do. Her facial expression was flicking between concern and 'I don't have time for this.' This chick had some fucking nerve.

"I came out of nowhere?" Heidi put a finger to her chest, pulling herself up as tall as she could get. She was still a good few inches shorter than Mrs Sprint. "Me? Who was just walking over to the pharmacy? I wasn't the one practising my 100m in Waitrose, was I? Were you planning to hurdle the flowers by the door? Roll across a few car bonnets outside?"

The woman was shaking her head. "I'm sorry, it's been a long day." She clutched the bridge of her nose between her thumb and forefinger. "I've got a splitting headache and was on my way to get something for it."

Now Heidi looked closer, she could see the woman's eyes were watery. She looked tired, too. Still, it was no excuse.

"And I'm on my way to get something for my period pains." Possibly oversharing again, but there was only so much brushing aside Heidi could take in one day. This woman had piqued her annoyance. "You're not the only one having a bad day. Just look where you're going next time." She rubbed her arm, which was still smarting.

"Sorry again." The woman checked her watch. "I've really got to run." She gave Heidi a pained smile, then sprinted off.

Heidi shook her head. At least there was wine in her near-future.

Chapter Four

Eden couldn't get out of Waitrose quick enough, but she was careful to look where she was going this time. She popped two Migraleve into the palm of her hand and swilled them straight, no water required. A practised move.

She blamed her boss, of course. If Caroline hadn't agreed to take on this account, she wouldn't have been under so much pressure, and therefore had to spend hours and hours in front of her screen. It was days like these she wondered why she wasn't working for herself by now. However, she knew the answer: the job had perks, paid well, and she loved it. It was the pace and the pressure that made Eden tick. Mainly because she was good at it. Only lately, her body was saying otherwise.

She rolled her wrist and thought about the woman she'd run into. She'd just appeared out of nowhere, but Eden had nearly pitched her through the supermarket window with the force of her blow. It would have been a terrific offensive play on an American football field, not so much in real life.

Still, she hoped the woman was okay. She'd been raging mad at her, but Eden kinda liked that. Nobody was going to steamroller her. When the woman had pinned Eden with her maddened stare and started ranting at her to slow down — not anything she hadn't heard before — Eden had noticed her eyes. Rich, nutty brown, the colour of the sherry her grandmother used to like on a Sunday.

She blinked. She hadn't met a woman who made her think about her gran before. Although 'met' was a strong term to use for this instance. Bumped into? Let's go with that. However, it was undeniable this woman's eyes had brought her gran to mind. At least she hadn't been wearing geranium perfume, too. That would have been too strange.

Eden took a deep breath as she glanced up at the cloudy sky, the chill of the February evening scratching her airways. The story of her bumping into this woman was something she would have told her gran when she visited her on Sundays. She used to do so most weeks when she was alive. It'd been seven years since she'd died, and it still hit Eden hard some days. Her gran would have told her it sounded like the plot of an old Hollywood movie, a great meet-cute. Her gran had loved the movies. She'd never had an issue with Eden's sexuality, only with her lack of a partner to share her life.

Her gran had been adamant you needed romance for a happy, fulfilled life. Whereas Eden was pretty sure she could survive without it. Romantic love meant being in a relationship you counted on, and in Eden's world, those didn't work. Her life was simple and straightforward, with her friends and her work. That was just the way she liked it.

On the agenda this evening was some food and a spot more work. She had a presentation she needed to finish.

Eden checked her phone. Another message from a friend saying they could make her birthday the following weekend, which was awesome. She might not be coupled up, but she was feeling the love. Eden liked to have her life planned out in weekends, and she was now busy for the next few. Her friend's wedding this weekend, her 40th the following, and a Camden night out the one after that. So long as her head didn't explode beforehand.

She walked across the car park as lightning struck in her skull. Her phone pinged again and she looked down. It was then she heard some car wheels squeal.

She looked up and saw a car inches from her waist. Where the hell had that come from?

She held up her hand in apology. However, it was only when she looked through the windscreen that she saw the same deep brown eyes staring back at her, quickly followed by a brisk shake of the head.

Shit, it was that woman again.

The woman wound down her window. "If you've got a death wish, you're going about it the right way. Next time, I'm running you over."

Eden's eyes widened in surprise. This woman had verve. Her gran would have liked her. "Sorry." Eden put her phone in her pocket as her head boomed.

She needed to get home and have some food. Then lie in a dark room and hope this headache didn't develop into something more.

But she knew the whole way home, she was going to be recalling those eyes even through the pain. Eden hadn't been stirred by eyes quite as large as those in a very long time.

Chapter Five

"Just go. She's going to be fine." Kate held Maya in her arms, but it didn't stop her daughter's face crumpling. "Mummy's off to work and we're going to play. Me, you and Finn. What do you say, Maya?" Kate was putting on her best singsong voice, but Maya was having none of it, holding out her hands.

Heidi checked her watch. She had to go, otherwise she was going to miss the bride putting on her makeup, and that would never do. Wedding start times were getting earlier and earlier. Soon, the bride was going to want the photographer to sleep with her the night before so she wouldn't miss a single thing.

"Bye, sweetheart." Heidi placed a kiss on Maya's cheek, her nose snotty as always. "Be good for Kate! Mummy will see you later." She squeezed Kate's hand. "Thanks for this. I owe you."

"You owe me nothing," her friend replied. "Now go shoot some gorgeous photos."

Heidi hadn't thought she'd be one of those mums who went to pieces when she had to leave a crying child, but nothing pulled on the heartstrings like your own child's tears. She got into her car and took a moment, gripping the steering wheel. She had to work, but some days were harder than others.

At least today's wedding was super-close to Kate and Meg's flat, which meant she could pick Maya up as soon as she was done later. Without Kate and Meg, she would have been stumped today.

Heidi started her car and braced herself for the Old Street roundabout.

***

Heidi had noticed a growing trend for London weddings lately. People had got bored with the idea of trekking to stately mansions in the home counties, wanting instead to get married in the heart of the city. Today's ceremony was taking place in a disused church, with photos afterwards just around the corner in Soho Square.

The wedding went off without a hitch, which pleased and disappointed Heidi in equal measure. Pleased because that meant happy, smiling faces for her photos, and happy clients who paid on time. Disappointed because, just once, she wanted to be at a wedding where someone got jilted at the altar, or where someone spoke up to declare their undying love for one of the leads. She guessed maybe that only happened in films and books, but she lived in hope. Last year she'd done 35 weddings, so the chances for her were higher than most of the population.

The bride and groom were now leading the crowd out of the church that wasn't a church, confetti and laughter coating the air. Heidi loved this part of weddings. The most optimistic part, where everything was still new, like virgin snow. However, one glance up at the dark clouds told Heidi they might have an issue. The wedding party had provided large umbrellas that were being carried by the groomsmen, but a torrential downpour was the mortal enemy of any wedding party. The clock was ticking, and it was time for Heidi to get shouty. They not only had to battle the impending rain, but also the fact the photos were being taken in a public park.

"Okay, listen up, wedding party! The clouds overhead look ominous, so if we could get a wriggle on to Soho Square to get our outdoor shots done before the heavens open, that would be awesome. Remember, nobody gets a drink until we get to the venue. The quicker you walk, the quicker I can snap, the quicker you get champagne."

A murmur went around the crowd at that. Heidi knew how to press buttons and get people to do what she wanted.

Luckily, Soho Square wasn't quite as packed as Heidi had been fearing, the Tudor building in the centre drawing excited chatter from the wedding party. They selected the nearest corner of the grass-covered square and asked people already there to move. If they were annoyed, they didn't show it. Weddings held a magic nobody wanted to pop.

It only took five minutes to get everyone in place, and then it was time for Heidi to work her particular brand of magic. She might be only five foot six, but what she lacked in height she more than made up for with the boom of her voice.

"Okay, well done on making it here. One step closer to the champagne. Let's have a little cheer for the champagne!"

The crowd cheered, as did the growing group of onlookers behind her.

"What I need you to do is organise yourselves so you can see me. Remember, if you can't see me, I can't see you. Everyone make sure you can see my ugly mug before you settle."

Just as she said the final word, a fat drop of ice-cold rain hit her nose.

Shit, she needed to get this done quick, otherwise she'd have a drowned bridal party and that was never a good look. She looked through her lens, then dropped her camera. "Can everyone see me? Even those at the back?"

There was jostling and laughter as a few women on the left rearranged themselves.

She checked the lens again. One of the women — tall, in a jaunty floral trouser suit that Heidi had admired from the back earlier — was outside her view. Heidi waved her hand. "I need you to scoot in a bit more, lady on the left in the floral suit." The woman shifted, but not enough.

The rain began to fall that little bit more, and the crowd murmured.

"Madam, please move in and we can get this done and go inside!" Heidi's tone was firmer, because she could sense a revolt on her hands. The woman shifted out of sight.

"Can you see me?" Heidi was shouting now.

The woman moved a fraction.

"For fuck's sake," Heidi muttered under her breath. She needed to take this. She snapped a few shots, but knew she'd lost the crowd.

"Okay!" She held up her hand. "Let's get going before we get soaked!"

* * *

The wedding party were on to their main course, speeches done and photographed. Heidi was taking a well-earned break, due back in the main room after the desserts were eaten.

She sat in the bar, which looked over Trafalgar Square and London beyond. She sipped her glass of white and stared at the London Eye going round so slowly that its movement was almost imperceptible. She'd just finished her steak and chips when a noise startled her.

She looked up to see the woman in the floral suit walk in, her phone stuck to her ear. She glanced up and caught sight of Heidi looking her way.

When their gazes locked, Heidi's lips parted.

Fuck, it was *her*. That woman who'd crashed into her this week. Waitrose Flo-Jo. She'd thought she looked familiar earlier, but hadn't seen her close up. Now, with just the two of them in this bar, all other distractions were gone. The woman's mouth curled into a smile of recognition as she hung up her call and walked over.

"We meet again." Her golden hair was like a ray of sunshine, swept back from her head, the back just touching her collar.

"Seems that way." Heidi still hadn't forgiven her. "A bit early to escape the wedding, isn't it?"

The woman smiled, revealing a pristine set of straight white teeth. "Just doing a bit of work."

"At a wedding?"

The woman shrugged. "I never stop working." She held out a hand. "It's about time we introduced ourselves. I can this time, seeing as I'm walking at a steady pace. I'm Eden."

"Which makes your floral suit all the more apt." Heidi shook her hand. Eden's handshake was firm, sure of itself. She oozed cool. Heidi bet she worked in the media. A journalist, maybe. Although journalists couldn't usually afford such expensive-looking suits.

Eden sat down opposite her.

"I'm Heidi."

"I know." Eden crossed one leg over the other, her gaze settling on Heidi's empty plate, and then Heidi. "Did you enjoy your steak?"

Heidi nodded. "For wedding food, above average."

"I suspect you would know." Eden's gaze pinned her to the spot. "You know, when you were shouting at me earlier, I wondered if this was your default with me."

"Only when you deserve it." Heidi cleared her throat. "You weren't in shot, so you deserved it."

"Apparently so."

Heidi regarded her again. Her eyes weren't so watery today. They were bluer, more steady. "How's your head?"

Eden nodded. "Better. How are your period pains?"

"Better also." Heidi tried and failed to stop a blush rising to her cheeks. She picked up her wine and took a healthy slug. "You certainly look more relaxed than when I first met you."

"Not hard." Eden smiled. She had a piercing smile. She should use it more often.

"You look familiar, though. I thought that last week when you crashed into me."

Eden shook her head. "I thought the same, but I can't pin it down." She cocked her head, went to say something, then shook her head.

"What?"

"Nothing." Eden's gaze met hers, then dropped sharply.

"Tell me what you were going to say." Heidi's tone was firm.

Eden flicked her gaze back up.

Damn, her eyes were blue.

"Okay, you asked for it. This might be a bit out there, but are you gay?"

Heidi's heartbeat picked up as she nodded. It always happened when she was asked that question. It was rarely uttered without consequences, good or bad. "I am. Why do you ask?"

Eden put a finger to her chest, raising her square chin. "I am, too, so maybe I've seen you around. I know the scene's bigger in London, but the six degrees of separation thing still counts."

"Very true. Although I don't get out on the scene so much these days. Blame my job. It doesn't leave a lot of time for weekend socialising."

"I guess not." Eden tilted her head. "Is this time of year that busy? Do people get married in February?"

Heidi laughed. "We're at a wedding, aren't we? Although I do have next Saturday off. I'm going to a festival with my sister. I haven't been to a gig in years and I'm really looking forward to it." She glanced out the window. "I just hope the weather's kinder than today."

Eden's mouth curled into a grin. "It's not the Year Awakening festival, is it?"

"It is. Why?"

Eden nodded. "I'm going, too. So we get to spend two weekends in a row together. Isn't that something?"

"Something good, or something bad?" Heidi gave her a measured smile to go with her comment. Eden was attractive, and kind of annoying. Knowing she was a lesbian had raised the stakes.

Eden lifted her impressively styled left eyebrow. "I guess

we'll find out soon enough." She drummed her fingers on the table. "I'm looking forward to seeing the headliner. Are you a fan?"

Heidi nodded. "I am. I love her latest. She's got the energy of PJ Harvey when she launched."

"I love PJ Harvey." Eden's eyes lit up.

"Me, too." Heidi sat forward. "I've seen her in concert five times. I had a signed copy of her debut album on vinyl. My mum threw it out, thinking it was rubbish."

Eden put her head in her hands. "No!" She peeked through her fingers. "Do you still speak to her?"

Heidi smiled. "She's my mum. It's kind of in the contract."

"Not necessarily." Something crossed over Eden's face, but Heidi couldn't place it. "I'm going to the festival with friends for my 40th birthday. If you see me, please stop me to commiserate."

"I'll try to remember," Heidi replied. "I turned 40 last year, and you want to know the difference?"

"Love to."

Heidi sipped her wine. "Here's the difference. If you die in your 30s, it's a tragedy. The papers will write it up as such. But if you die in your 40s, you just die. It's not tragic anymore. Once you turn 40, you're officially old."

Eden exhaled before replying. "Aren't you a ray of sunshine? You're telling me I've got one more week of youth?"

Heidi nodded. "Use it wisely."

Eden pushed her chair back. "My first wise move is going to be to go back to the wedding and eat my sticky toffee pudding. I'm not sure my personal trainer would say that was wise, but if my death's not going to be tragic anymore, I don't need to worry, do I?" She stood up, smoothing down her trousers, her hand gliding over the petals of a red rose.

Her hands looked strong, capable. Heidi's gaze settled on them for a brief moment.

"Are you coming, too?"

Heidi pressed her phone, then shook her head. "Fifteen minutes till I'm back on duty. They're bringing my dessert here."

Eden hesitated. "You want some company for it?"

Heidi shook her head. "You go and make the most of your last week of youth. Don't waste it on the aged."

Chapter Six

Eden picked up the post from their shared mailbox by the front door, flicking through it as she walked back up the stairs to her first-floor flat. Her stomach was tumbling, even at her age. Why did she do this to herself every year? She knew the rules, she'd learned them the hard way. But clearly, there was still a sliver of her that hoped 40 might be different.

It wasn't. Her stomach duly rolled and pitched. She took a deep breath before she went back into the flat.

A gas bill, a mailer for a new gym, something from the tax office, a card from her friend Evan and one from her aunt. But nothing from her mother. Deep down, she'd known there wouldn't be. Why would her mum even know where she lived?

It didn't stop it hurting, though.

When Eden walked into their kitchen, Lib was standing wrapped in her baby blue dressing gown, her short red hair all over the place. She was wearing a grin that didn't cover up her sleepy eyes, holding an elaborately decorated cupcake with a single candle stuck in the top. "Happy birthday! You want me to light this now, or shall we have it drunk later?"

Eden took a deep breath and slapped a smile on her face. "Later. And thank you."

Lib put the cupcake down and gave Eden a hug, squeezing her tight. "I love you, have I told you that lately?"

"Only when you're drinking yet more of my gin."

Lib gave her a grin. "I love you the most then, it's true. But I love you on your birthday all day long, like any good friend should. Was there much post?"

Another scratch to her heart. Eden shook her head, busying herself filling the kettle. "The usual, plus a couple of cards for me." Eden could still taste the disappointment on her tongue. What would her gran do? She'd tell her to take no notice of her mother, that no good could come of it.

"Who are the cards from?" Lib picked up the pile. "The tax office sent you a new tax code. That's nice of them."

"They think of everything." Eden made the tea. She was determined to focus on the cards she had, not the ones she didn't. Like she did every year.

"Come to the lounge and I'll show you the card I bought you. If it doesn't win best card ever, there's something seriously wrong in the world." Lib raised both eyebrows. "And then you know what we're going to do?"

Eden smiled, ignoring the echo of disappointment in her heart. Lib's enthusiasm was infectious. "What?"

"We're going to the festival and giving you the best 40th birthday ever!"

Eden gulped. She was going to try. Put this out of mind and focus on making today the best last day of her 30s possible.

"By the way, did you hear back about the kittens?"

That brought a genuine grin. "I did, and I got one. A little black-and-white one. I get to pick it up in six weeks."

Lib hugged her. "Awesome. Soon you're going to be a 40-year-old with a fur baby. Who'd have thought it?"

* * *

The grass was already soft underfoot when they arrived at the festival at just after 2pm, the sweet, fresh smell of wet earth hanging in the air after last night's downpour. The sun was trying to break through, but the forecast was for more rain later. Eden had come prepared with a cagoule in her bag, but she was also ready to get wet. This was exactly the sort of thing she was determined not to stress about; tomorrow she turned 40, so what was a little rain between friends?

Plus, the organisers had clearly read the forecast. Though the main stage was open to the elements, the two smaller stages were inside red and blue-striped circus tents. What's more, most of the bars dotted around the space were under cover, with a large amount of seating available at the wine bar, its sign already brightly lit. It was a festival squarely aimed at their age group. This was further hammered home by the number of gourmet food trucks lined up to their right. Eden had her eye on the taco truck already. Straight ahead, a massive banner proclaimed this was the first festival of the year.

It was a good omen: Eden was kicking off her next decade with a bang.

However, when she turned to her friend Issy, Eden was pretty sure she wasn't thinking the same thing.

"Perhaps Barcelona would have been the wiser choice." Issy's face had been set to grimace-mode ever since they'd stepped onto the damp grass.

"But this was the greener choice. Far less of a carbon

footprint, you have to admit." Eden knew Issy would have to concede that point. Ever since she'd had her twins, Issy was all about being green.

"Yes, but it's 29 degrees in Barcelona."

"No moaning, that's my birthday orders. Sweetness and light all day, okay?"

Issy went to reply, caught herself, then gave Eden a wide smile. "Let's find the bar. Sweetness and light will surely follow hot on its heels, agreed?" She threaded an arm through Eden's, grabbed her wife Kath, who in turn was hanging on to Lib, and they began to march towards the bar in a row. Up ahead, the crowd was patchy; they were some of the first to arrive.

* * *

Halfway through the second set on the main stage — a Cuban rhythm band — the rain began to fall. Eden pulled on her cagoule as the rain spat down in random patterns, not quite enough for umbrellas, but enough for furrowed brows.

She was taken back to the wedding last weekend, and to Heidi, who'd had to deal with the rain while she was taking her photos, and had done so with aplomb.

The thought of her made Eden smile. She wasn't sure what it was, but in the short time they'd spent together at the wedding, Eden had placed Heidi in the 'want to know more' box and that didn't happen often. In fact, it never happened.

Eden had been happily single for the past seven years, and bizarre as it seemed to her friends, she was settled in her solo life. So much so, she couldn't imagine it being any other way. Eden was happy with her lot. Content. Even though her friends didn't believe it and so wanted to trip over themselves to make sure she didn't feel lonely on her big birthday. Eden had endured a lifetime of lonely. She was used to it.

She'd looked for Heidi after the wedding meal had finished, but she hadn't found her. A different photographer had appeared for the dancing portion of the evening, and the hum of disappointment inside her had been strange. Eden had wanted to wipe it away, but she had to admit: Heidi had something about her. Verve. Drive. Piercing sense of humour. Or perhaps it was the way she shouted at people that made them pay attention. Eden liked her no-nonsense attitude.

She was here today, too. Eden had looked for her, but hadn't seen her yet. They could do with Heidi's crowd-management talents now. All around her, faces were pinched as people tried to work out how to handle the rain. Eden had already decided. She was going to stay exactly where she was and embrace it. The feel of the rain on her skin, the semi-warmth of the muted sunshine on her face. She was outside for a change, with live music, her friends, and a drink. Life was good, and a little rain wasn't going to stop that.

However, when the rain began to cascade in steady sheets half an hour later, it was a different story. Umbrellas were popped, coats embraced. Torrential rain wasn't in the script. But she was determined not to let it dampen her mood, even though she might be damp herself.

She glanced left and saw her friends' sad faces, trying to make the most of it. The wind whipped up and the hairs on the back of her neck began to complain. Eden leaned down and put her mouth beside Lib's ear. "Shall we head to the wine bar and see if we can get a drink and a seat? At least until this passes." As if to back up her decision, rain cascaded off the end of her nose, her head like an overflowing gutter.

"Yes please," Lib replied. "And once we're there, I'm buying a bottle of red because we need to heat up." She hugged her wet jacket, then winced. "Whose idea was it to have a birthday in March, anyway?"

* * *

"Don't you just love springtime?" Sarah was seated at one of around 20 wooden picnic tables under the wine bar's canopy, staring at the festival crowds. The rain was hammering down now, but most people were embracing it. A steady stream were also heading towards them, their feet slipping in the mud as they raced for a spot of cover. "Remember that time my birthday was super-hot?"

"It's called global warming." Her sister had selective memory. "Remember last year when you had that barbecue? Jason ended up cooking everything inside, and you had 30-odd people crammed into your lounge."

Heidi remembered it well, because Maya had been eight months old and the star of the party. She'd been passed around like a parcel and hadn't moaned once.

"I had forgotten. Funny the stories you tell in your head, isn't it?" Sarah paused. "Sometimes, I pretend I'm not married with three kids. It feels liberating."

Heidi eyed her sister. "To other people or just to yourself?"

"Mainly to myself. I'm never anywhere without my husband or children to get away with it. Maybe I'll try it today. Not identify myself as a wife and mother first. Instead, I'll just be me." She pointed at her chest. "If anyone asks, I'm single, okay?"

Heidi furrowed her brow. "If you're planning to cheat on Jason, I'm not on board."

Sarah punched her upper arm with her fist. "Oh, relax! It's just a game, nothing more. I'm not going to *do* anything. I love my life, just sometimes I'd like to step off it. Today seems like as good a time as any. Especially since I came to soak up the sun at a festival and we're stuck in a dripping-wet tent freezing our tits off."

"You were being hopeful with the sunshine." Heidi let her gaze wander the bar. Calling it a tent was pushing it; far more people than intended were now sheltering under the canopy. Was it built for such a downpour? Heidi glanced up uncertainly. If it collapsed, they might drown. The rain had been playing havoc with her wedding bookings of late, but she was becoming an expert at manoeuvring crowds at speed when she had to.

She glanced at her watch: 4pm. She pitied any photographers dealing with this weather today. She'd done a wedding this week and had shouted so much, she'd left hoarse. That day, the weather had included thunder and lightning, too, and she'd got a fabulous shot of the bride and groom in the storm.

This time last week, she'd been shouting at Eden. Heidi had only met her twice, and both times had been brief but impactful. She'd even enjoyed chatting with her at the wedding. She'd found her intriguing. Even a little hot. Was she in the crowds getting soaked now? They'd only arrived half an hour ago and she hadn't spotted her. There must be at least a few thousand people here, so the chances were low. Still, it might make the day more interesting if she did. So long as Eden wasn't in a hurry.

Sarah nudged her with her elbow. "So, are you in? If anyone asks, we're both young, free and single?"

Heidi frowned. "Do I have to play along?"

"Yes. You know why?"

"Because it's your birthday?" Heidi knew the rules.

"Bingo! We can keep our real names, I'm not asking you to go too far. I know what a stickler for rules you are." Sarah poured more wine. "Anyway, let's get drunk and dance in the rain. That's what single people do with their weekends, isn't it? What do you say?"

Heidi looked at Sarah, before topping up her glass. "I might need to catch you up before that happens."

Chapter Seven

Eden threw herself under the bar's canopy. Her short blond hair was plastered to her face, and her cagoule so wet, it was like another skin. She peeled it off, trying not to think of the time her uncle skinned a rabbit in front of her. She hadn't been able to eat rabbit since.

Lib grabbed Eden's cagoule and took off her 'I am 40!' badge, handing it over with a grin. "We wouldn't want anyone thinking you were 39, would we?"

But she *was* still 39 for the next eight hours. She was just about to tell Lib that, when her arm was yanked. Before she knew it, Eden was sat at a wooden bench, undercover, her friend Issy looking triumphant.

"Don't say I never do anything for you," Issy said. "I had to fight off three groups of people for this table."

"Thank you," Eden replied, giving Issy and Kath her drinks order. When she turned to Lib, her friend was frowning at her phone.

"Everything okay?"

Lib shook her head. "Not sure. I just have to give Mum's carer a call, okay?"

"Of course. Take your time." Eden wished there was

something she could do, but there wasn't. The only thing she could do was be there for her.

When she looked to the next table, she did a double-take. Sitting there, laughing with a woman who looked like her twin, was Heidi. She'd been easier to find than Eden had thought.

When their gazes snagged, Heidi's face betrayed the hint of a smile.

Eden raised her hand in greeting, then shifted to the end of her table, which was nearly touching theirs. "I was just thinking when I was getting soaked, we could do with your crowd management skills. It's carnage."

Heidi gave her a measured smile. "Bit of a big crowd. I'm focusing on my wine-drinking skills today." Her eyes raked Eden. "Good to see you again, even if you do look a little… damp."

"I prefer moist." Eden paused. And then wanted to stick her fist into her mouth.

Heidi raised a single eyebrow her way. "I'm sure you do. This is my sister, Sarah." She held out a hand. "This is Eden. Who's rapidly turning into my stalker."

"A terrible stalker. Grade-A awful. I need to be more stealth."

"Agreed." Heidi stared at her for a beat too long, then back at her sister. "Eden and I have met twice briefly, the last time at a wedding I did."

Heidi's sister sat up straight. She looked from Eden to Heidi, her interest piqued.

"We had a post-dinner drink at the wedding," Heidi continued, "and I gave Eden some advice on turning 40." She pointed at Eden's badge. "Is it today?"

Eden touched the badge. "Tomorrow."

"Happy birthday for then." Heidi's stare was heated, in stark contrast to the rest of the day. "Did you plan on spending it in a field in the rain?"

"It was top of the list."

"We're here for Sarah's birthday, too. She wanted to get away from…" Heidi paused, glancing at her sister, the words stuck for a moment. "From her life for a day. So here we are, drinking wine in a downpour."

"Happy birthday, fellow Pisces." Eden cast her gaze to the sky. "Our star sign is kinda apt with all the rain. When my wine eventually arrives, we can cheers our birthdays." Eden turned her attention to Heidi. "And we can also cheers the universe, because it clearly wants us to keep meeting, doesn't it?"

Heidi nodded, her gaze still firmly on Eden. "Seems that way, doesn't it?"

When she said the words, their gazes locked and anticipation danced on Eden's tongue. It'd been a while since that happened. She frowned as she stared at Heidi, thoughts forming in her brain that hadn't been allowed to for quite some time. Like, was she interested in Heidi?

Eden gulped. Was this what happened when a big birthday approached? All her usual rules went out the window. Was she having some sort of midlife crisis?

She shivered as some wind whipped through her wet clothes. Eden shifted on the bench, Heidi's big brown eyes still focused on her.

She took a deep breath. Heidi probably had a girlfriend, anyway. Or a wife who loved PJ Harvey like she did. She could just ask, but that seemed a little forward. Also, she'd never hear the end of it from Lib, who'd just hung up her phone call and was leaning across, holding out a hand for introductions. She was never one to stand on ceremony.

"I'm Eden's flatmate and best friend, Lib. Lovely to meet you."

Heidi and Sarah agreed the same, just as Issy and Kath returned with wine.

Cheers all round.

Lib filled their glasses, and they all crowded together for a toast.

"Happy wet birthday to Sarah, and to Eden." Heidi increased the wattage of her smile when she said Eden's name. "But mainly Eden, seeing as she is 40."

"In eight hours," Eden added.

"Having turned 40 last year, I'd say not to be too judgemental of your life on such an occasion," Heidi told her. "People make a big deal of 40, but it's just another day. It's like New Year: nobody wakes up on the first of January a new person. It just takes some time to get used to your new status, and then you slip into it naturally. I know many of my friends took stock of their lives, working out if they were happy. I was, even though nobody believed me because I was single."

"I'm single and happy, too." Eden's gaze was focused on Heidi. "Some of my friends don't believe me, but it's true. I have freedom. I can do what I want, when I want. That's the best feeling, wouldn't you agree?"

Heidi glanced at her sister, who was giving her a look Eden couldn't decipher. "Sure," Heidi replied. "Most of the time."

"Your life might be calm, but it's also predictable," Lib said. "We all think Eden should pep up her life with a bit of romance, but she lives to work, and that's it. Forty is going to be your year of shaking things up, isn't it?"

Eden sucked on her top lip. "I'm planning to live a little more dangerously. I might even go on holiday, confound you."

"I would love it if you did." Lib paused, turning to Heidi. "Are you still single?"

Eden could have cheerfully strangled her.

"She is," Sarah replied, making Heidi shut her mouth. "So am I. And up for a good time!" Sarah followed that statement with a whoop and a fist pump. "Talking of which, who wants a shot? I've got my husband's credit card, so let's put a dent in it."

Sarah got up, taking orders.

Beside her, Heidi rolled her eyes.

***

A few hours later and Sarah was down the front of the festival with Eden's friends, all of whom had consumed far more alcohol than Heidi or Eden. After agreeing this band wasn't their favourite, the pair made their way back to the bar. It was far less crowded now the rain had let up. Heidi bought a carafe of red wine and brought it back to Eden. She insisted on paying as it was Eden's birthday.

"You sure you don't want to be in there, dancing away the last of your 30s?" Heidi reorganised her bum on the bench. It was going to take days to warm her bones after this.

"Not to this music. Maybe when the main attraction comes on, then you can show me your killer moves."

"Deal." She smiled at Eden, unsure when she'd become so relaxed around her. Especially after their first less-than-stellar meetings. It didn't happen often with people she'd only just met.

Did she like Eden *that* way? Heat crawled up her chest and into her throat. Yes, she'd *said* she was ready to date again. But this time around, it wasn't just about her. This time, she had cute, complicated, curly-haired baggage. But she wasn't going to worry about that right now.

"So do you have big plans for your 41st year?"

Eden shook her head. "I like my life how it is, so no midlife crisis here." She paused. "Did you change yours much?"

Heidi shook her head. "No. I set up my business five years ago, so that's already established. Plus, I made big changes in other areas when I was 39, so I left 40 alone. You need some uneventful years, too."

"Lib would say they're my favourite type. She thinks I work too hard and don't play enough."

"Is she right?"

Eden shrugged. "Maybe. But perhaps I like work and being in control." She smiled. "Thanks for the wine."

"You're welcome." Heidi stared into Eden's crystal-blue eyes. They reminded her of the sea.

Eden shifted under her gaze as the rain picked up again, drumming once again on the canopy.

They both stared upwards, then out to the field where a crop of umbrellas were blooming under the bright stage lights.

"This reminds me of last weekend's wedding," Eden said. "I've thought about you this week, but I didn't think we'd meet again. I'm glad we did, though."

"Me, too." Something flipped in Heidi's stomach. "I got some good ones of you and your friends later on when you were chatting. Very natural." She wasn't going to tell Eden she'd been staring at the photos all week, marvelling at her hair. It wasn't looking quite so salon-ready today thanks to the rain.

"I'd love to see them sometime. Maybe we could meet for a drink first." Eden's face was pensive, like she was expecting the worst.

Heidi let her words sink in before she replied. "Did you just ask me out?"

Eden blew out a long breath. "Apparently I did. I'm not sure what happens when I'm around you, but I either trip you up, annoy you or ask you out. I don't have any beige settings." She leaned in. "If we're honest, I already swept you off your feet the first time we met in Waitrose, right? So the groundwork was laid."

"Totally laid."

Eden tilted her head, letting time slip by for a few seconds before she crinkled her nose. "I notice you haven't answered yet, by the way. I pay attention to this stuff."

"I do, too." Heidi's body and heart were leaning forward, wanting nothing more than to say yes. But in the back of her mind, one word was lit up: Maya.

Eden liked her, but she didn't know she had a child. Would she have asked her out if she knew?

"You're taking too long now. Do I need to remind you it's my birthday, and I'm putting myself on the line here?"

Heidi's insides churned.

Eden wasn't finished. "I mean, this isn't a difficult question.

Would you like to go out for a drink with me? I'm not asking you to go horse-riding or skydiving."

"I'd say no to both of those, just so we're clear." Heidi hated horses with a passion ever since one had galloped off with an eight-year-old her on its back. "But I'm not going to say no to this. It's just, there are some things you should know first. I come with baggage."

But shit, this was awkward. How should she phrase it? Would Eden think that just because she had a child, she'd once had a partner and they'd split up? Most people did. Most people assumed you wouldn't voluntarily make yourself a single parent.

Heidi wasn't most people.

Eden reached over and grasped her hand. "Don't we all have baggage? You're overthinking it. And just for the record, you make me very nervous, which I'm pretty sure is a good thing if you read those dating books. Which I don't, by the way, but my friends do and they fill my mind with useless information for picking up women."

"You can chat, you know that?"

"It's been said before. Especially when I'm nervous. Have I mentioned you're making me nervous?"

Heidi was staring at Eden's mouth, imagining it on hers. She shook herself.

Focus.

Because Eden was still talking. It was like some kind of valve had been opened, and then she was off like a horse that had been caged. A little like the one that had thrown a tiny Heidi.

"Anyway, what I'm trying to say is, don't tell me everything.

Save some mystery. I'm all for mystery. In fact, I think we should promise not to stalk each other online before we meet up. Save the family photos till at least the third date."

"I haven't even agreed to a first date and we're having a third?"

Eden made Heidi laugh, which counted for a lot. Eden was funny and attractive. Perhaps that was all Heidi needed to know for now. They could go on one date and get to know each other *before* she dropped the Maya bomb. Then, she'd be 'that woman Eden liked who happened to have a child'. It made complete sense. Plus, she'd be sticking to her sister's rules for the day.

She'd been quiet for too long again, hadn't she? "Sorry, I was lost in thought for a moment. But sure, let's keep some mystery. And let's go on a date, why not? I haven't been on a date for nearly two years, so I should warn you, I'm a little rusty."

Eden licked her lips, before dropping her gaze to Heidi's mouth. "I'll bring a can of oil. Extra virgin, of course." Then she blushed at her own joke. "Is this a 40-something thing, you think? These terrible sentences that keep slipping from my mouth?"

"You're not 40 yet."

Eden's blue eyes smiled. Heidi didn't even know eyes could do that.

"I like you. You're very perceptive. And you listen, which is a very underrated trait in a person."

"I agree."

Eden shifted closer, casting her eye out to the field, then back to Heidi. Heidi could smell Eden's perfume now, something musky. It made her stomach flip-flop.

"So we're going on a date."

"Looks like it."

"I don't date."

"Neither do I." Heidi grinned. This was absurd. She turned to Eden. "Aren't we a pair?"

Eden's stare dropped to Heidi's lips. "You could say that."

A tingle of anticipation ran down Heidi's body. "But even though we don't date, I'm glad we ran into each other again."

"Not literally, this time." A quirk of Eden's mouth.

"This time is much better." Heidi's heart rate kicked up a level, banging in her chest. "I'm not normally this forward, but you bring it out in me." Her gaze fell on Eden's lips, then moved back up to her eyes. Desire flared red in her vision. Heidi hadn't kissed anybody in nearly two years. Not romantically. But Eden's hot, wet lips were now inches from hers. She hadn't planned this today, but her body was showing her the way. Every fibre of her being wanted to kiss Eden.

She lifted a finger and ran it down Eden's cheek. The sensual curve of Eden's mouth made Heidi's insides curl. "Happy birthday for tomorrow." Then, just as the encore finished and a cheer went up from the crowd, Heidi pressed her lips to Eden's. The release made her soar.

Eden's lips spoke a language she'd forgotten, and she knew right away it was a language she wanted to practise over and over again. She wanted to perfect the vowels, roll the consonants. She wanted to lose herself in its soft, undulating rhythm. Eden's soft, firm lips transported Heidi far away from this damp field, from London, from her life. Now, she was in another world altogether.

As Heidi deepened the kiss, her mind tumbled, spinning

round and round with abandon. This kiss was making her kick off her shackles. She wanted to lay back and bask in its splendour.

Eden's fingers gripped her waist, then snaked up her neck.

Something fluttered against Heidi's rib cage. Something she'd long forgotten. Eden's tongue led her down new paths, and Heidi gripped her arms to steady herself. Ground herself in the moment. When she slipped her tongue into Eden's mouth, and Eden groaned, Heidi felt it *everywhere*. If she'd been chilled before, her body was now a roaring furnace.

However, it wasn't set to last. Their impromptu birthday kiss was shattered by a loud whistle from nearby that made Heidi's ears prickle.

Eden's muscles stiffened under Heidi's fingertips, their kiss paused.

They'd been rumbled. The two self-professed, happily single women had been caught snogging each other's faces off. If Heidi wasn't so damn proud of her behaviour, she might have been embarrassed. But the pleasure flooding her body left no room for that.

She pulled back, shooting Eden a quick glance. Her face sported a satisfied grin.

"What do we have here?" Lib's voice was raised and scratchy from too much singing. "Was that a kiss I spied taking place?"

Eden sat back, shaking her head. "Nope, no kissing here. Have you had your eyesight checked recently?"

Heidi could take the ribbing, it was worth it. Plus, she hoped she might get to kiss Eden again soon. She knew jackshit about her, and Eden knew even less about her, but they could deal with that another day. For now, sitting here in this field with steam rising from them, she knew two important facts: Eden was a mighty fine kisser, and they were going on a date.

Chapter Eight

Eden spun her black biro between her thumb and index finger, a practised move. If there was ever an Olympics for pen spinning, she'd enter immediately.

She was in her happy place: her office. It was housed in an old building in Soho, above a delicious Italian deli, which came in very handy at lunchtime. The floorboards creaked, the windows let in gusts of air, but she adored the character of the building, which dated back to sometime in the 1800s. In her downtime, when she wasn't people-watching out of her second-floor window, she liked to imagine all the lives that had passed through these walls. If only they could talk.

Eden also loved working in the centre of town. Hell, she loved working, full stop. She was the creative director at Quote Media Communications and she was good at her job. Her feelings at work were always between two invisible lines; tethered, secure. When she was at work, Eden was untouchable. She came up with plans to make companies surge ahead and glow, and she loved doing it. Eden was good at making products and services desirable, which meant Quote Media was in demand.

Today she was meeting her client for the new Chocolate Delight account. She hoped they weren't too old, or a man.

Eden could deal with most people, having been client-facing for most of her career. However, she got the shortest shrift from men over the age of 55, who assumed she was younger than she was and far less capable. The sooner that breed died out, the better. Give Eden a young, enthusiastic millennial any day. Or, at the very least, a woman who didn't dismiss her automatically.

Forty-something women were her speciality. One 40-something in particular kept popping into her head today, sparking a series of smiles to grace her lips. Heidi. Where had she come from? And who would have thought that, after such a terrible beginning, they would now be going on a date? Not Eden, that was for sure. Eden didn't date. All her friends knew that and had long since stopped setting her up with their friends and acquaintances. But there was something about Heidi. Something she'd connected with. That hadn't happened in a very long time. Not since her gran died. Seven years of nothing.

Eden shook her head. She rarely thought about the past. What was the point? Especially *her* past. The future was what interested her. Not that Heidi was her future. But Eden was entertaining a date with Heidi, which showed Heidi had broken through her shiny veneer. Heidi was a special case.

Eden didn't date because relationships didn't work. People left, died, or broke your heart. Love of any sort — romantic or family — was risky. However, she and Heidi seemed to be on the same page. Happy being single. Willing to go on a date. If it didn't work out, no hard feelings.

That kiss, though. That had been something else. The feel of it had stayed with Eden ever since: dazzling, electric. Something she wished they'd started at least five minutes earlier, so it could have lasted longer before their friends got back and called time. Hopefully, when they met up again, they could pick up where they'd left off.

She tapped her keyboard and pulled up the client they were seeing. Stable Foods was an established brand and trusted producer, but they had a new chocolate spread they wanted to sell to the masses. If her company could come up with a new ad campaign and a PR schedule for it, they'd land Stable Foods' whole suite of brands, many of which were household names.

This was a big deal for Quote Media, Eden's employers. They'd spent the past decade working with media clients, but budgets were being cut in that industry, and her bosses had decided to branch out into other areas. Food was an arena that always had money to spend, and this was a great opportunity. Get this right, and Eden could see her stock rise even more.

She smoothed down the lapel on her Ralph Lauren jacket and patted her fingers on top of her hair. She'd styled her blond cut earlier, and it was set solid. Her office manager, Pixie, had told her she looked glowing this morning. Wasn't that normally reserved for pregnant women? Perhaps it was because a light switch had been pushed inside her, which was all down to Heidi.

Eden couldn't focus on that this morning.

Her colleague Johan walked up to her desk, giving her a grin. "Ready to be charming?"

Eden grinned back. Johan was the perfect mix of gorgeous and catty, all rolled up in one colossal charm offensive. With him in the room, their chances of scoring the account doubled.

"Charm and me went to school together." Eden stood up, grabbing her laptop and phone.

***

Johan was showing her a dick pic on Grindr when Pixie knocked on the meeting room door, showing in their new client. Eden looked up and shook herself when she saw the woman walking in the doorway. Long, dark hair, exposed collarbone, expensive necklace leading down to her full breasts. A slim waist and a wickedly cut suit the colour of burnt sunsets offset by a cream shirt and matching power heels. Probably Jimmy Choos.

Eden hadn't expected India Contelli at this meeting, yet here she was. The head of Stable Foods, a minor TV celebrity, and a very out and proud lesbian to boot. Eden took a deep breath before painting on a wide smile. She was going to need extra charm for this one.

Johan was already on his feet and walking over, shaking the woman's hand. "India," Eden heard their client say, smiling at Johan and revealing two rows of bright white teeth. When Eden composed herself and shook India's hand, it was firm, just as she'd expected. It also came paired with a direct stare that put Eden off balance. She gulped, dropping India's hand and pulling out a chair, before sitting down beside their guest. Heat paraded down her body. She was glad the air-con was on.

India's colleague, David, was introduced as he sat beside her. Eden immediately felt sorry for David. It was one thing to listen to client pitches; quite another to do it with your big boss.

"It's great to meet you both, and sorry I didn't warn you it was going to be me." India crossed her legs.

Eden tried not to stare.

"It's just, when I tell people, they tend to go into meltdown because I've been on the TV. Just treat me like you would any of your clients and we'll be fine."

Eden nodded, knowing she could never treat India Contelli as just another client. She was famous, for goodness sake. The daughter of Daniel Contelli, the Stable Foods billionaire. Heir to the Stable Foods throne. Her media clients weren't like India Contelli. They were well presented, sure, but they also tried a little too hard to be cool, to act like they knew it all when they didn't. India didn't need to try for cool. She oozed it.

"David's got over doing these meetings with me just about, haven't you?"

David nodded, but his face said otherwise.

"Just to let you know, we've seen two other firms today, but we want to move quick on this. We'll make a decision by the end of the week so you're not left in limbo." India appraised Eden once more, her gaze loaded, leaving a mark on Eden's skin. "I wouldn't want you to be left wondering if you're liked or not."

"Our ego's sturdier than that, isn't it, Eden?" Johan was giving them both his charming smile.

"Rock solid," Eden replied. "Plus, we've got the best presentation, I can promise you." She paused, breathing in and trying not to focus on India's tan, which she had no doubt covered her whole body. She'd only met the woman two minutes ago, but Eden could already tell she was the type to get an all-over tan, no straplines for her. Eden could just picture her striding along a nudist beach, not realising the ripples she created as she walked. A blur of smooth skin and confidence, the ultimate aphrodisiac.

Eden shook herself, coming back to the moment. A vision of Heidi and her gorgeous smile waltzed across her eyeline. Eden's body was a mass of frayed nerve endings.

What was going on? She'd managed to go years without being drawn to any women, and now she'd met two in the same week? Perhaps there was something to this midlife crisis theory. Maybe that's *exactly* what was going on here.

Somehow, she made it through her part of the presentation, before handing over to Johan. When he finished, the room fell silent.

India broke it after a few moments. "I have to say, you do stand out from the competition. Everyone else is proposing to market our chocolate spread in the usual way. But you're suggesting keeping it family-focused, but also taking it along riskier lines. For family time and for bedtime."

Eden laughed. "Exactly that. Chocolate spread is known for being sexy, so why not play on that? No other brands do apart from edible chocolate spread, but isn't all chocolate spread edible? Nail this ad and it could seriously promote your sales. We have tons of PR ideas to make it really take off, too."

India put a smooth, manicured hand on her thigh, and Eden made herself stop following it.

What was wrong with her? Maybe she was perimenopausal. She had no idea when it had started happening to her gran or her mum, and she guessed she never would. She could see Johan giving her a look, but she ignored him. She sat up straight, giving India her full attention. This was business and she was going to be business-like. Even when she was talking about getting sexy with chocolate spread.

India leaned forward and cast her gaze from Johan to Eden. "You know what, I'm not going to play games. I've already seen the other two agencies, and I like you the best. Getting on with the people I'm working with is important to me. Life's too short to work with idiots, don't you agree?"

Eden was nodding before India finished her sentence. "Totally. Completely with you." She glanced at Johan. "We're idiot-proof, aren't we?"

Johan snorted. "One hundred per cent."

India gave them a killer smile. "Glad to hear it. Plus, I like your ideas, so I'm giving you the job." She sat back in her seat, letting out a deep sigh. "I wish all business deals were as easy."

"Just like that?" Eden wished all business was as easy, too. They normally had to jump through hoops to get new clients.

"Just like that." India beamed at her. "Make this work and the sky's the limit. We're not enthused with our current team, so the door's open. All you have to do is make the whole country fall for our spread."

Johan sat forward. "We're going to do more than that. We're going to make the whole world fall in love with it."

India raised a calculated eyebrow before putting her notebook back in her bag and standing up. The meeting was over, apparently. "I like you two, did I mention that?"

But her gaze was on Eden, and only Eden.

Chapter Nine

Heidi was back at Aquababy, and wondering why she put herself through it. The answer was Maya. Her daughter loved water. Every night when Heidi gave her a bath, her daughter splashed around with glee. She was doing just the same today, as Heidi plunged her back in the pool and the water flicked up and splashed her face. Maya couldn't get enough.

It was one of the magical things about being a parent: witnessing firsts. Heidi had begun to see the world in a different light ever since Maya's birth. The first time Maya had eaten ice cream, her face had lit up like she'd just discovered the meaning of life. Being an ice-cream lover, Heidi got it.

It was a philosophy Heidi was trying to imprint on the rest of her life: seeing things for the first time, taking a fresh look. She did it in her professional life, because she had no choice. Every wedding had to be like the first; she had to bring her A-game, because the couple weren't going to get another shot at doing this. At least, not with each other. She was trying to bring the same philosophy to her personal life, too. Meeting friends with more gusto, like it was the first time. Seeing her family and not feeling like it was a chore.

The one thing she didn't need to get hyped up for was seeing Eden again. Eden had left a lasting impression on her, and she'd only been 39. Heidi had been wondering what it would be like to kiss 40-year-old Eden all week. With luck, she wouldn't have to wait long.

However, the logistics might be tricky. Eden had texted to see if she was free for a drink this weekend. But weekends were when Heidi worked. On the plus side, Heidi was thrilled Eden had made contact, that she wasn't following some weird rule-set that went out of date in the 1990s. They'd met, they'd had a firework of a kiss, they both wanted more. But this time, just the two of them. She was looking forward to getting to know Eden, seeing what made her tick.

Heidi focused back on her daughter, her tiny arms wrapped in bright yellow armbands, her face creased with delight. How could anyone be put off by this perfect little girl? If Eden was, it was set to be the shortest date in history. Not liking children was akin to not liking animals, wasn't it? Yes, Heidi was allergic to cats, but she still loved them.

"Mummy! Look me!"

Pleasure poured down Heidi like a waterfall. She scooped her daughter up and swung her in the air.

"Did you just say 'look me?' Almost a full sentence? Who's a clever girl?" She pressed her nose and lips to Maya's cheek, kissing all over her face.

Her daughter wriggled, then giggled.

Maya tended to just shoot out words like a machine gun, but lately, she was beginning to string them together. Heidi saw it as a sign of burgeoning genius.

She turned to one of the dads beside her, currently swinging his daughter around. "Isn't it fabulous when they really start talking?"

The dad — perhaps called Tim? — gave her an encouraging smile. "It's brilliant. Angel said Mama for the first time last week and my wife was thrilled, too." Then, just like always, he moved away from Heidi. Shutting the conversation down.

The elation of the moment drained away, and she glanced up at the massive clock on the swimming pool wall, its black hands stark against the bright white face. Nearly eleven. Time to get out anyway. Particularly as she was having lunch with her mum and she needed to shop for ingredients on the way home.

***

Heidi was still getting used to her new flat, mainly because she'd moved in a hurry. When she had Maya, the difficulties of living in a first-floor flat had become apparent. Seeing that, her mum had given her brochures for a new development near them in north London. Heidi had gone along to appease her mum, not thinking she'd buy anything. And she hadn't.

However, on the way home from the development, she'd spotted a Victorian terraced flat for sale on a pretty tree-lined street. She'd viewed it the same day, and put an offer in the next. Heidi moved into her two-bed garden flat in Stamford Hill four months ago. Her new home was a 20-minute drive from her parents, even less time from her sister. In her youth, Heidi had always tried to put as much distance as possible between her and her family. Now, with a family of her own, having free babysitters nearby was an outstanding draw.

Last month, with the help of her friends Cleo and Becca,

she'd painted the lounge and Maya's room. Jason had promised to come and give her a hand with the garden when he had a free weekend, but she wasn't holding her breath. Her brother-in-law had great intentions, but whenever he had a free weekend, Sarah tended to fill it for him. Sarah might not want to admit Jason was her husband all the time, but Heidi knew she loved him really.

She glanced out the patio doors. It was raining again. It didn't seem to have stopped for weeks.

The front door bell signalled her mum's arrival. 12:55: she was bang-on early. Heidi greeted her with a hug and took her coat, along with her umbrella, opening it and putting it in the bath. Her mum was still an active woman even at the age of 68, and didn't look her years at all. She barely looked 60. Heidi was glad to have her mum's blood in her veins.

"You look tired." She touched Heidi's cheek as she reappeared in the hallway. "Have you been sleeping?"

Heidi shook her head. "Trying to, but Maya has other ideas."

"Did I ever tell you that you didn't sleep for the first two years of your life?"

Heidi followed her mum through to her open-plan lounge-diner-kitchen. "Once or twice," she said. "It's payback time, I know."

"She's worth it, aren't you?"

Maya already had her arms in the air, knowing what was coming next. She'd conked out when they'd got home, but was now sat in her high chair, being entertained by a spoon. However, once her grandmother walked in, the spoon was abandoned.

"Who's Nanny's gorgeous girl?" Her mum lifted Maya out of her chair and got a half-eaten pepper smudged into her cheek for her troubles. She ignored it like a boss.

"How's business?"

Heidi nodded. "Good. We're just approaching the busy season. Once Easter is gone, then boom, wedding overload. Although February and March are more popular than you think. Which means I'm dealing with an awful lot of wet weddings."

"I can imagine. Like the rainy seasons of my childhood, only far colder and they go on forever." She paused. "Sarah said you had a good time at the festival at the weekend. I saw her at church on Sunday, and she had a sore head, I could see it behind her eyes. She tried to say otherwise, but she was fooling nobody." Her mum gave Heidi a smile. "Why you need to drink so much to have a good time is beyond me, but I know, it's a different generation." She waved her hand as she spoke, before sitting down with Maya on her lap. "We missed you at church on Sunday, too. It would be nice to see you occasionally."

Heidi's muscles tightened. Her mum wasn't messing around today, was she? Bringing up church within five minutes of her arrival? Wasn't church off limits until at least food had been served?

"You know my thoughts on that." Heidi walked over to the kitchen, starting to bring some of the food to the small dining table squashed into the corner of the room. Hummus, falafel, flatbread, olives and roasted peppers; she breathed in the aromas of cinnamon and cumin, olive oil and smoke. She'd added Manchego and a plate of Mediterranean ham from the local Italian deli, too. Her stomach growled.

She was always hungry after Aquababy, even though she never swam a stroke. She'd often thought it was mental muscle memory. Every time Heidi was in a swimming pool, she craved cheese-and-onion crisps and Coke, because that was what her dad used to buy from the vending machine after the Sunday swimming sessions of her childhood. Sundays had always followed the same routine: church in the morning, then a swim at the local pool.

Maya would never have that routine, but Heidi wasn't sad about that. When it came to church and its lack of inclusivity, she was sticking to her guns.

"But wouldn't it be good for Maya to have some spiritual guidance in her life? For her to go to the same school as her cousins, where she'll learn about God? I know you're stubborn and you have your own views, but even you must see that it's the right thing for her."

Heidi sighed. Was her mum hoping she'd suddenly change her mind and begin to take her daughter to a church that didn't welcome Heidi? She knew parents could sometimes be deluded, but this was a little beyond the norm.

"Mum, you know the score, I've told you a million times. When the church welcomes my life, I might consider coming at Christmas. But it doesn't offer me or my life anything. I'm a lesbian. It doesn't like lesbians. It doesn't like much that's not straight."

"But you've got such a sweet voice."

Was this about Maya, or about her mum showing Heidi off in the church choir? She could never be sure. "And I use it at karaoke down the local gay bar." A slight lie. "Rather, I did. Before Maya." She missed going out. She missed singing.

A thought of Eden flitted through her mind. Did Eden do karaoke? Would she entertain Heidi doing some? Perhaps not on a first date. Maybe on the third. Or the fifth. Heidi had texted her earlier, so she guessed she'd find out soon.

Sitting there in her flat, with her mum quizzing her on why she wasn't going to church, Eden seemed very far away. Saturday seemed very far away. Removed from reality. Because this was *far* more her reality than sitting in a bar at a music festival. What would Eden make of that?

Her phone beeped and she walked over to the kitchen, picking it up off the counter. Her heart picked up speed when she saw who the message was from: Eden. She was asking if she was free the following Tuesday to go out for dinner.

Heidi did a quick calculation in her head. She thought she was. She just needed a babysitter. Someone who wouldn't mind keeping Maya overnight, perhaps. She glanced over at her mum, currently with her head in Maya's stomach, blowing a raspberry into it. She put the phone down, making a mental note to answer it as soon as her mum had gone.

Heidi sat down at the table and her mum followed, putting Maya back in her chair. Heidi put some food in Maya's bowl and gave it to her daughter, fully prepared for the mess that always followed.

"Lovely spread." Her mum helped herself, clearly attempting to get the conversation back on less rocky ground. "Sarah said you might have met someone at the festival on Saturday."

Heidi was going to kill her sister next time she saw her. Possibly with her bare hands. Sarah must have been hungover if she told Mum that. Yes, Sarah was closer to their mum than Heidi was, but she wouldn't normally blab that sort of information. Perhaps she'd still been drunk. A distinct possibility.

"Was that a message from the new woman?" Her mum dropped it into conversation so casually, it was almost a throwaway comment.

"It was. How did you know?"

Her mum finished chewing before she replied, her eyes narrowing as she spoke. "Mother's intuition." She paused. "Well, that and the grin that spread across your face when you opened the message." She smiled now, too. "You know what I think about you meeting someone. It's a good thing, so there's no need to hide it from me. I'm not the church, you know that. I'm supportive of whoever you want to love, I've always made that perfectly clear."

"I know." Heidi knew she was lucky in that way. Her parents had reacted well when she came out.

"But you know as well as I do it's best for Maya to have two parents. Two points of view. Two pairs of hands to guide her."

Heidi sighed. This was where her mum stuttered. She just couldn't understand why Heidi had voluntarily become a single parent. She couldn't comprehend a tiny bit of it. That Heidi had wanted a child, that her biological clock had been ticking, that she didn't have time to wait until she met someone.

"Could this woman be a good second parent for Maya?"

Heidi's mind blanked. She had no idea, and she knew it was hardly the first question she was likely to ask any prospective partners. She'd find out soon enough when she saw Eden again.

"I need to find out if she's a match for me first, don't you think? She's asked me out for a drink next week."

"And you're going?"

Heidi nodded. "I am." The thought of going on a date with Eden midweek seemed naughty and dangerous. Precisely the reason she felt something move at her core. She shifted in her seat.

"Good. Because I don't want you bringing up Maya on her own, and I don't want *you* being alone, either." She reached across the table and covered Heidi's hand with hers. "You've got so much love to give to someone, so I hope this woman knows that."

Heidi took a deep breath, about to tell her mum not to put so much on this. Even though in the back of her mind, she was already filling out the betting slip herself.

Her mum squeezed her hand. "I know it, and God knows it. You're a beautiful creation, just like Maya. God's creation."

Heidi ground her teeth together. Her mother was a mix of sweet, well meaning and bloody infuriating all at the same time. But this time, she decided not to bite.

"Can you babysit on Tuesday if I go on this date?"

Her mum nodded, spooning a mound of hummus onto her plate. "Of course we can."

Chapter Ten

Eden's day at work had been full-on, with back-to-back meetings with clients and a final one with her boss to get up to speed on next steps for Stable Foods. She'd also had an email from India's assistant asking if Eden was free to meet for lunch next week. She assumed India had meant to include Johan, too, but she didn't want to be presumptuous. Whatever, she had a lot on her plate at the moment, and that wasn't even taking Heidi into account.

The festival seemed a long time ago now, and Eden's palms were itchy as she sat in the restaurant she'd booked for the evening in Fitzrovia. An ode to Mexican cuisine, Casa Martinez had started out life as a food truck but quickly gained a cult following. Now the chef had expanded her team and opened a space in central London, and Eden had been keen to try it for a while. She hoped Heidi liked Mexican, otherwise they were in for a long evening.

She was fidgeting with her phone when someone nearby cleared their throat. When Eden looked up, she gulped. Heidi was standing there, and she looked stunning.

She'd captured Eden's attention from the word go. However, now, away from a damp field, and with the memory of their kiss seared into Eden's brain, Heidi had taken on a very different meaning. Heidi oozed style, but also, she oozed attitude. Plus, it didn't hurt that her wavy dark brown hair matched her almond eyes with its shine. Whatever Heidi had on her side, Eden was on board.

She stood, a tingle of anticipation running down her spine as Heidi leaned in and kissed her cheek.

"It's good to see you again," she said as she drew back.

"You, too." And it was. Eden had spent last night in bed wondering how this moment would be. Because the festival had been like a mirage in her week. A floating, wet mirage. She hadn't been sure to trust everything that happened, everything she'd felt. It had been otherworldly. But now, seeing Heidi again, all the feelings came flooding back to her body. Lightness. Happiness. Air. And luckily, today was a clear day in London. One of the first for what seemed like weeks. "I didn't recognise you without water stuck to your body," Eden added as they both sat.

"I know. No umbrellas. Unheard of." Heidi shook out her napkin and spread it over her knees.

Eden was transfixed. "I hope you like Mexican."

Heidi nodded. "Love it. I went to Cancun with some friends a while ago. We had an awesome time." She tapped the table with her index finger. "I've heard about this place and been wanting to try it, so it's a good call."

"Glad you think so." Another tick in Heidi's column. Eden's muscles relaxed one by one as the tension she'd been housing ebbed away. Heidi was just as she remembered her, if not better. It was a good start. "So how have you been since the festival?"

"Busy," Heidi replied. "I'm doing four weddings this month,

but thankfully I had the foresight not to book myself the Sunday after the festival. A good plan. My mum was round for lunch last week and told me my sister rocked up at church the next day still reeking of booze." She paused. "Apparently, the Lord is very forgiving, though."

Eden sat up. "Church? Wow, that's something that doesn't cross my radar very often." She couldn't decide if she was agnostic or atheist. Whatever, she knew she didn't much like what went on in most churches across the world.

Heidi shook her head. "Mine either, much to my mother's distaste." She perused the menu. "But that's what life's about, disappointing your mother, isn't it? I make sure to do it on a regular basis."

Eden tensed up again. "I wouldn't know. My mum and I... Let's just say our relationship isn't the norm." It was too early in their fledging relationship — if that's what this turned out to be — to reveal the truth. Eden steered the conversation onto safer topics. "What were you up to the next day, if you weren't at church?"

Heidi's face flickered for a moment, an emotion crossing it Eden couldn't quite pin down. Heidi settled on a hesitant smile. "Oh, you know, the usual. Sunday brunch, PJs, coffee, bacon."

Eden nodded. "That sounds exactly like our day. I was with Lib, who you met. My flatmate." She held up her hands. "We had a lazy day, before going to the pub for a late lunch. The perfect birthday. Unlike Issy and Kath, who went home to their kids. They were up at seven, after only four hours' sleep." Eden shuddered, making a face like she'd just eaten something hideous. "Makes me glad I don't have kids."

Heidi cast her gaze down to the table, back up to Eden, then hid behind her menu.

Had Eden said something wrong? She pulled the menu down so she could see Heidi's face. It was still scrunched. "Everything okay?"

Her date shook her head. "I'm fine. Just deciding on food. I think I might go for the tacos. They're meant to be good, I read the reviews before I came here."

Heidi's words sounded anything but fine, but Eden let it slide for now. "You're booked for four weddings. No funeral mixed in, like the movie?"

That raised a smile. "No. I think that would be a whole other photography speciality, wouldn't it? I don't think I'd be up for it, either. Weddings and funerals do share the fact that everyone's stressed, but at least the overriding feeling at a wedding, once the formalities are out the way, is happiness. Funerals are the opposite."

"They certainly are." She wanted to move the topic onto brighter things, seeing as she was still picking up a weird vibe from Heidi. The mood had changed suddenly, and she was at a loss to know why. "How's your week been otherwise? I'm guessing you don't have as many weddings during the weekdays?"

Heidi shook her head. "Not as many, but they're getting more popular. Saturdays and Sundays are still the busiest days, but Thursdays and Fridays are catching up. The rest of the week is when I meet the clients, curate the photos I've done and do all my admin. If I take a day off, it's normally a Monday or Tuesday."

Eden nodded. "I've been to a couple on a Thursday and

one on a Friday. I didn't mind, but some people got very upset." She paused. "What do you do on Mondays and Tuesdays?"

"Just hang out with Maya, meet my friends, take her to Aquababy. I did that this week."

And then Heidi froze, her features stilling and something crossing over her face — the same emotion Eden had struggled to work out earlier. It looked like fear, but why would Heidi be fearful of her? This was a date they both wanted to be on.

"Who's Maya? Is she one of Sarah's children? I assume she has them, seeing as she has a secret husband?"

Heidi screwed up her face, her mouth scooting to one side of her face as she shook her head. "Actually, no." She winced. "Maya is my daughter. I might have forgotten to say the other night that I have a daughter." She paused. "She's nearly two. And pretty gorgeous."

Eden's mouth went to drop open, but she forced it to shut, then swallowed. *Fuck*. Heidi had a kid. And she'd just said what she'd said about kids. No wonder the atmosphere had turned a little chilly.

"Maya's your daughter? Wow." Eden paused. "You kept that quiet on our first night." Her stomach lurched. "You are single, right? If your daughter's still so young, I assume there's someone else in the picture, whether you're together or not?"

But Heidi was shaking her head even before Eden had finished. "There's nobody else. I had Maya on my own. I'd been single a while and wanted a child, so I decided to investigate sperm donation solo." She sighed. "Sorry, you didn't ask for the full details. It's just I'm a little embarrassed I didn't tell you the other night. Blame Sarah. She was going on about wanting to be someone different. To get rid of her responsibilities for one night. I don't want to get rid of Maya — she's the most wanted child on the planet — but for one night, it felt nice to just be me again. It hasn't happened for a while. And it hasn't happened that a gorgeous woman has hit on me. Kissed me. Just me, nobody else involved."

Eden wasn't sure what to say. This was still Heidi, and she was still attracted to her. That hadn't changed. But this wasn't what she'd expected. Heidi had a child. Children were non-negotiable.

Eden didn't want kids. Kids were fragile and impressionable. Eden didn't want to scar them with her experience. Plus, kids were chaotic. Eden didn't do chaos. She'd had enough of that in her childhood. In her adult life, control was key.

At that moment, a waiter walked up to their table, white pad in hand, a perky smile on his face. "Ladies! Can I get you some drinks?"

Eden shot him a look she hoped spoke a thousand words. She was sure he could at least pick up the tension hovering over the table. She was scared to move in case she was pulled in to its force field further. "Can you give us a few more minutes?"

The man nodded. "Sure thing. Just give me a shout when you're ready."

Eden turned back to Heidi, blowing out a breath. She still had no words that could smooth this over.

"Should I leave?" Heidi took the napkin she'd arranged so perfectly off her lap and put it on the table in front of her.

Eden's stomach lurched. She shook her head. "No! Stay, let's eat, have a drink. It's just… a shock, that's all. We were talking about things that had changed in the past decade of our lives at the festival. You've had a child. On your own. That's quite a big change."

"I told you I came with baggage. I was going to tell you, but you said we should have a little mystery between us."

"There's mystery, and there's *mystery*." Eden's words came out louder than she'd anticipated. She sat up, clearing her throat and leaning forward.

"I think it's best if I leave." Heidi pushed out her chair, but Eden covered Heidi's hands with hers, making her stay put. For now, at least.

"Sorry, I didn't mean to raise my voice." She looked into Heidi's eyes and didn't like what she saw there. She didn't want to be responsible for negative emotions. "It's just when it comes to single mums, my story is muddied. I was the child of a single mum. A bad single mum." Panic rose in her. "Not that I'm saying you're a bad single mum."

Shit, she wasn't explaining this very well. She was averse to single mums, but not for the reason Heidi thought.

"Not all single mums are feckless, you know. I've heard so much prejudice since I became one. And believe me, I have a whole new respect for them." Heidi looked Eden directly in the eye. "I did this on my own, and I'm not looking for a second parent for Maya. She's fine as she is. You don't have to worry, I wasn't trying to trap you. I was just looking to go out and have a little fun, then see where things went. Especially after *that* kiss. I had high hopes. But they're kinda blunted now."

Eden wanted to smooth out the lines on Heidi's face, to tell her she didn't care.

But she did.

She loved kids, but she didn't trust herself with them in

her life. But could she change that mindset for Heidi? Not if it meant dredging up the past and her mother. She shivered just thinking about it. Was Heidi worth that? Nobody had been up until now.

"It's just not what I expected. I love kids, but I never saw myself having any, that's all. Because of many reasons. It's complicated." Oh. My. God. She should shut up. Tonight, she clearly couldn't say the right thing.

Heidi shook off Eden's hands and stood, grabbing her jacket from the back of her chair. "I'm going to leave. I think it's for the best, because you haven't stopped looking freaked ever since I told you I had a child. That doesn't go down well with mothers, just in case you were curious." Anger crossed her features. Eden didn't like being the author of that, either. "If this isn't going to work out because of Maya, it's best to know now, because she's not going anywhere." Heidi paused. "A shame though, because I really liked you."

Heidi gave her one last defeated look, before slinging her red bag over her shoulder and walking out.

The waiter, who had taken Heidi standing up as a sign to take their order, retreated as fast as he'd arrived.

Eden couldn't think properly, her breath all jammed in her throat. "You're not the only one," she whispered.

Chapter Eleven

When the chilled evening air hit Heidi, she thought she might vomit. But she kept it together. On top of everything, she was dying for a wee. When she was doing her big walking-out speech, like she was on a made-for-TV movie, the entire time, all she could think was 'I need the loo'. But there had been no way she was going in the restaurant.

She scanned the posh, urban street with its four-storey Georgian terraces with black railings. There was a pub on the next corner down: The Crooked Hare. She walked towards it, pain throbbing in her gut. Once inside, she ignored the bright lights, shiny brass fixtures and clientele, moving swiftly to the loo. She locked the door, put the toilet seat down, then put her head in her hands. The feel of her fingers on her skull was soothing. It was the only thing that was in that moment.

It was safe to say, tonight had not gone to plan. Eden didn't do kids. Had she said that? Come right out and said those words? Heidi thought so, but she couldn't be sure.

Her stomach rumbled. She was starving, too. She hadn't eaten all day, saving her calories for tonight's restaurant food and booze. But now, she'd had neither of those. Just a healthy dollop of reality spooned onto her plate instead.

She'd read about dating with children when Maya was first born, but then had put it to one side, the enormity of parenthood being enough to cope with. This was her first experience of dating with a child, and she'd fallen at the very first hurdle. The first mention of her daughter, and Eden's face had curdled like a week-old pint of milk.

Well, fuck her. Heidi didn't need her or her judgement in her life. This was real life, not the fake version Eden clearly played in. People in their 40s had kids. Normally from previous relationships, yes, be they gay or straight, but she wasn't so unusual. Eden had made her feel like a freak and she was far from that. She was strong, capable and a great mum.

It was Eden's loss.

Heidi walked out of the pub head held high, feeling far more robust than when she'd gone in. She glanced down the road, but Eden wasn't there. She hadn't run after her to tell Heidi she'd been wrong. Heidi was on her own, just like she had been at the start of the night. Just like she always was.

But Maya was with her parents, and they were having her overnight. Heidi couldn't face going back to them and admitting what had happened. Because her mother was the same as Eden, wasn't she? She didn't think single mothers were a great idea, either. Had she inadvertently gone for a woman who represented her mother? Heidi shuddered. She was fairly sure at least that Eden would not try to make her join the church choir. But she'd also never know if Eden was a karaoke fan or not. She'd never serenade her in a gay bar.

That thought was like a bucket of cold water over her head, and Heidi slumped against the wall of the pub, weighing up what to do next.

She went with the first name that came into her head. Cleo. Even though she was still away. Her best friend picked up after three rings.

"Hello, gorgeous."

Heidi smiled at the familiar greeting. "Hi."

Cleo clearly picked up her tone. "What's up?"

"Not much. I just went out on a date and it didn't even reach the ordering stage."

"What?" Cleo cleared her throat, saying something to someone. Probably Becca. "You were on a date? Since when were you on a date?"

"Since you've been away in Boston with work, so I haven't had a chance to tell you."

"There's email, you could have told me then."

"You wouldn't have been satisfied with email. I was going to tell you after it went well. But it didn't."

Cleo was silent for a moment. "Listen, I'm out with clients at the moment so I can't speak. Can I call you tomorrow?"

Heidi nodded, already pushing herself off the wall. "Sure. No problem."

"Hang in there."

Easier said than done. Heidi came to the junction of Great Portland Street and Euston Road. Should she turn around, head back into Soho and have a drink on her own? See if she could chat someone up? But even the thought sent a chill right through her. She didn't want to do that. She wanted to still be on a date that had been promised to her, to be kissing Eden's lips after eating glorious tacos.

Cars and red buses rushed by, oblivious to her plight. She pulled her jacket closer around her and sighed. Her best friend was working; even her daughter had a date with her grandparents. Warren Street tube was just around the corner and could take her home. That seemed like a good option. A takeaway and a glass of wine were calling her name.

Chapter Twelve

Eden got back to her Camden flat unsure about what had just happened. From looking forward to going on her date, she was now stunned and didn't know what to think. Theoretically, she didn't want a partner with children. That had never been on her horizon. And yet. She *liked* Heidi. Once she got over the shock, she'd wanted to talk about it, but Heidi had hightailed it like a bat out of hell.

Maybe she shouldn't have been so blunt. Maybe she should have used some of those PR skills that people paid her good money for. Had she turned off her relationship emotions, having ducked out of them in recent years? Maybe. She'd ask Lib. She never held back on telling Eden the truth.

Her flatmate was chewing her way through a bag of Revels when she got in, her face glued to the TV. When she saw Eden, she looked up and said hi. Moments later, she paused the TV.

"What the fuck are you doing here?" Lib shouted that at Eden's back as she breezed into the kitchen like this was an everyday occurrence. They both knew it wasn't. "You should still be on a date with festival woman, or am I getting it wrong?"

Eden poured herself a glass of water, skulled it, then went

to the fridge and grabbed a beer. She hadn't even had a drink tonight. She needed something to calm her shredded nerves.

"I was meant to be," she said, walking into the lounge. She slumped down on the other end of her new sofa. Even its welcoming cushions weren't enough to soothe her. "But she forgot to mention she had a child, and when she dropped that into the conversation, I kinda froze."

Lib's mouth formed an 'O'. "She never said the other night?"

Eden shook her head. "No, and she had ample opportunity. I mean, we spent nearly a whole day together. You'd think her having a daughter would have been a high priority."

Lib tilted her head. "Maybe, maybe not. Her sister was pretty lit and doing a great impression of someone who wasn't married, even though she let it slip she actually was. So maybe Heidi was copying her for the day. It's not the crime of the century."

"No. But *kids*. You know me and kids." Eden splayed her hands like it was the most obvious thing in the world.

Lib shook her head "I've never seen you around kids. You might be great with them. But you tend to avoid them."

"Because they're *kids*. And kids are unpredictable."

"So is life, my friend."

"Not my life." She'd structured it to be just the way she liked it.

Lib snorted. "Welcome to the world." She paused. "People have kids, you know. Lesbians, too. I don't know if it's escaped your notice, but Issy and Kath have two of them."

"And look how fucked they are. They don't know what day it is, they never have any time together, they're constantly stressed. I mean, it's no sort of life, is it? They can't jet off to places whenever they like, they can't work late. Plus, they always have colds."

"I'm sure there are upsides, too." Lib sighed. "And *you* don't jet off anywhere, by the way. You're too busy working and being in control. So those might be upsides to having no kids, but you don't exploit them."

"But I could if I wanted to." Eden sat back, satisfied she'd won the argument. Even though it felt anything but. What was Heidi doing? Was her stomach rumbling as much as Eden's? Was Heidi feeling like someone had ransacked her feelings, then left them strewn on the floor of her life, too? "It's not the ending I wanted. I liked her. But I don't want to be that person to her child. I know what it feels like."

Lib studied her for a few seconds before answering. "How about this. For now, forget about the kid. Just go out with her and see how it goes. Then, if it goes well, you meet her child." Lib shook her head. "You're not dating her kid, remember. You're dating her."

"They come as a package."

"True. But you don't even know if you two are compatible yet, so you're kinda jumping the gun."

Eden shook her head. "I know. But my mother was always out, always looking for *the one*. In the process, she ignored me. I'm not going to take part in the process for another child to be hurt." She still remembered how much it hurt when she tried to win her mum's affection, but always came out second best.

Lib shuffled over, putting both hands on Eden's shoulders. "I know your history."

"Sorry, this is just a sensitive topic." Eden ground her teeth together.

"No shit." Lib sat forward, holding her gaze. "But not every mother is *your* mother, is she? My parents went out and left me with family and friends when they needed a night away and I'm glad they did. They were better parents for doing it and came back to me happier. Did you ever think that might be the case with Heidi?"

Eden said nothing, processing Lib's words. They rolled around her head, but she couldn't make sense of them quite yet.

"Parents need breaks. Especially single parents. And kids need looking after by other people because their parents might not always be there for them. Heidi was out for her sister's birthday, and she was out for a date with you. Not the crimes of the century, I'm sure you'll agree. So don't put all your parenthood issues onto her. She's probably a great parent. In fact, I'd bet my house on it. You know why?"

Eden sighed. "Because lesbian parents really want their children, they don't just happen by accident?"

Lib patted her leg. "I'm glad you remembered that part." She shook her head, smiling at Eden. "Have a drink, take a breath."

Eden did as she was told. The sharp hooks of a tension headache were already beginning to sink into her brain.

"I still don't think dating a woman with a child is for me." Beyond the mess, she wasn't sure she was ready to be in a relationship of three. She massaged her temples as she spoke.

Lib stared at her, then shook her head.

"What?" Eden hated it when she did that.

"You're smart, you know that. You've got a big job,

a nice flat. But sometimes, you're stupid. You have all these rules, and yet you forgot the most important one: do you like Heidi? The answer's yes, right?"

Eden nodded slowly. "But it's not that simple, is it?"

"It can be if you want it to be. Once you decide that you like her, then you see how you can make it work, what rule you can break. Because if you really wanted to see where it might go, you would try. Or maybe you don't. Only you know the answer."

Eden sighed. "What if I don't know the answer?"

"Try harder." Lib paused. "Because if you don't like disorder, I hate to break it to you, but kittens are not controllable and you're getting one in a few weeks. Maybe 40 is your year of messy? As your best friend, I'd support it wholly."

Chapter Thirteen

Eden had spent the last two days wondering what to do about Heidi. Could they make it work? She wasn't sure she was capable of it. Thinking about going for it felt like treading on Lego. However, now she'd woken up to the prospect of something, it had her attention. That kiss had her attention. She was in PR and marketing for fuck's sake; attention was the lifeblood of her business. Attention was what she spent her life trying to achieve.

Heidi had her attention, but she had no idea how to handle it. Eden didn't want to be responsible for passing on any residue from her upbringing onto a child. She'd never forgive herself.

"I never wanted you anyway! You're a millstone round my neck."

That had been her mother's favourite phrase.

Work was the perfect distraction. It was something Eden knew, something she was good at. Her life had routine and she liked it. However, Heidi was making her routine harder to focus on. Making her mind rush down unfamiliar roads. Heidi was beckoning her to undo her neatly tied life. Just the thought made Eden sweat.

They'd just had a campaign hit a bunch of national newspapers, which had made the client happy and would raise their company's stock that little bit higher. Eden would normally have been chuffed to bits about that, but today, her mind was clouded. At least this afternoon she was having a late lunch with India Contelli, which was welcome. Their first meeting had gone well, and India now wanted Eden's advice on a delicate matter. Eden hoped it was work-related and nothing personal. She was good at solving practical issues. It was emotion she found more tricky.

India was waiting when she arrived at Claridge's, another reason Eden hadn't minded leaving the office. Who didn't like a business meeting that involved a posh dinner? India shook her hand with gusto, before sitting down.

Eden took in her bottle-green suit and tan brogues, along with another sparkling necklace. The woman appeared to have a never-ending supply of suits and jewellery. Not for the first time, Eden wondered how much she was paid. Did she even get a salary? Perhaps she received a monthly allowance? She was so rich, it was beyond Eden's imagination. She might live in a castle for all she knew.

But, despite all of her wealth, India was surprisingly candid with Eden. Also, she was down to earth. If you discounted the bling and having lunch at Claridge's, India was remarkably normal. Having lunch with a celebrity was at least something to take her mind away from Heidi. Eden was grateful for that.

"Thanks for coming. I've ordered a bottle of champagne. From the look on your face, you seem like you could use one."

Was she that transparent? "It's certainly been a trying week so far."

India leaned back as the drinks arrived. "I hope I'm not going to add to your woes. First, the good news. The board loved your ideas, so the contract has been confirmed. Like I said, get this right and the sky's the limit with us."

"No pressure." Eden gave her a smile, pride at winning the contract making her sit up straighter. Work, she could do. This wasn't how she'd normally talk to a client, especially one with such gravitas. But somehow, she and India had clicked. Maybe it was the gay thing, but Eden felt like she could speak her mind with her, be herself. Johan had said the same when she'd left. India Contelli was a breath of fresh air.

"None at all." India laughed, then sipped her champagne. "We also have a little crisis on our hands and need your help."

Eden sat forward. "I'm all ears."

India leaned over to examine Eden's lobes. "Very delicate they are too, may I say."

A warning crept up Eden's spine as India's breath caressed her skin. She sat up, frowning. Was India coming on to her? She pushed the thought away, focusing on what India was saying.

"Anyway. Our spread, Chocolate Delight. We're producing it at a new factory with brand-new machinery. A lot of money has gone into this launch, so it has to go right."

Eden nodded. "Understood."

India tapped her delicate, long fingers on the stem of her champagne flute. "But we have a problem. Every time one of the jars is filled, a device with a metal circle pushes the spread down to make the top smooth, and then the lid is put in place. Makes sense so far?"

Eden nodded again.

"This was working like clockwork until recently, when someone stopped the line after they realised some of the metal discs were missing. Six of them, to be precise. They're changed every few hours because otherwise, they get too clogged with spread. They're cleaned and then they go back to work on the production line. But somehow, six of them have disappeared. A bit of investigation and peering at CCTV would suggest they've fallen into six jars. But we don't know which or where those jars are.

"When we're just about to launch a massive marketing campaign nationwide, we don't need some kid opening a jar of chocolate spread and cutting themselves on a metal disc. That would be the ultimate PR nightmare."

Eden clenched her fists into balls, thinking hard. "Are the discs sharp? Have they got edges that cut?"

"Not razor-sharp, but they are metal."

She nodded. "I can think of a clear solution."

India raised her eyebrows. "Which is?"

"You've got to make it a treasure hunt. Tell the public there are six discs inside the jars, and if they find one, they win a prize. Say, £5,000 to five of those who find them, and one lucky winner wins ten grand. That way, even if a child does cut their finger, the parents won't sue if you're giving them money. And they can afford plasters, too." Eden didn't take her eyes from India, taking a sip of her champagne. She was the queen of multitasking. "Happy customers, great publicity, no lawsuit. What do you think?"

India sat back, her gaze never leaving Eden. "I think I could lean across the table and kiss you."

Blood rushed to Eden's cheeks. "Just doing my job. Are you happy with that? If you are, I can get our departments working on some press releases and we can splash it everywhere so that everyone knows."

"Yes, that sounds perfect."

"What's the timeframe?"

"ASAP. The discs are out there. Could you get something rushed out tomorrow?"

Eden blew out a long breath. "If you throw enough money at it, yes. We can pull some strings with contacts, but this will cost, obviously."

India nodded. "Obviously. But it's something you can jump on quickly?"

Eden's nod was without hesitation. "Of course."

"Great." India exhaled. "You're very calm about this."

"I have experience of crisis management. It's all part of good PR. Nothing's really a crisis. More an opportunity. It's how you frame it."

India held Eden's gaze, then shook her head. "You're a little too good to be true, you know that?"

Eden squirmed under her gaze, clenching her buttocks. The blush on her cheeks reflected in the shiny cutlery. She was glad when the food arrived. The starter of quail looked incredible.

"I think only my grandmother ever thought that." Definitely not Eden's mother. Definitely not Heidi.

Eden's stomach churned anew. Heidi. At least work had taken her mind off her for a while.

"You know, I did have an ulterior motive for inviting just you here today, and not Johan too. Although I'm very glad he's on board because he seemed very capable."

Something twisted in Eden's gut. She wasn't sure where this was heading.

"Your calm and your confidence are also very appealing." A heated stare. "I wonder, would you like to go out for dinner with me?" India smiled, and for the first time, her smile wasn't quite so certain.

Eden frowned. "We're already out." She cast her gaze around the room, before bringing it back to India. "Or did I get that wrong?"

India's face gave nothing away. "We are, but I don't mean a work dinner. I'm talking about you and me going out on a date-type dinner. Although it wouldn't be for a little while, as I'm going away on business." She paused. "Or did I get it wrong in assuming you were interested in women?"

Eden shook her head. She was flattered, of course. But Eden was just Eden. Whereas India was, well, *India*. "No, I very much am interested in women."

Eden tried to control her face, even though her insides had just begun to churn. India was asking her out on a date? Fucking hell, what kind of a week was this turning into? First, she went out on her first date in years and fucked it up royally. Then, she went out for a work dinner and the gorgeous client hit on her.

India's suggestion left her in an awkward position. This woman was going to bring in a lot of business to the firm. Could she turn her down? Did the job depend on it? She'd never been put in this position before, and she had no idea what to do. Wasn't it a cardinal rule never to mix business with pleasure? All Eden knew was, India was gorgeous, rich, available, child-free. Ordinarily, she'd jump on this opportunity.

Yet all she was thinking about was Heidi.

But could she say no? She got on with India. She was attractive, there was no denying that. Would it be the worst thing in the world? After all, she wasn't exactly going out with Heidi, was she? In fact, as evidenced by Heidi's silence, things between them were over in the real world, even if they weren't quite over in Eden's head.

Maybe a date with India would shake her out of her Heidi funk. Plus, if she wanted to keep her sweet for work, it was probably wise to have at least one dinner. She didn't have to sleep with her. What could dinner hurt?

"Unless you're seeing someone?" That was India speaking again.

Heidi flashed into Eden's mind. But she wasn't seeing her, was she? They'd shared one dynamite kiss, and then, nothing. Eden's heart slumped at the thought there might be nothing more, full stop.

"No, I'm not. I'd love to have dinner with you." Eden frowned. This didn't feel right, but then, nothing had since she'd met Heidi. "So long as this would be completely separate from business?" She knew that was impossible, but she wanted to ask it all the same.

"Of course. I promise not to judge your performance at dinner against your performance at work."

Eden swallowed. Somehow, it felt like the performance clock had already started ticking.

Chapter Fourteen

Heidi had just finished her second wedding of the week and she was ready to drop. Instead, she had to pick up Maya from Kate and Meg's. Heidi loved them both, they were her sort of people: funny, and also honest about parenting and how hard it could be. Their son Finn was three and gorgeous, but a handful, too.

When Heidi had told them about her weekend childcare dilemmas, they'd volunteered to help when they could. Finn and Maya got on, so Heidi had taken them up on their offer, insisting on paying them in cash or wine. They were her fallback if family or childcare failed, and Heidi didn't know what she'd do without them.

Tonight, as she pulled up to their flat just off Hoxton Square, she stilled. There was a woman laughing with her friend on the pavement who looked just like Eden. The sway of her blond hair made Heidi catch her breath. She'd been focused all day, but now her heart lurched. It wasn't the first time this had happened since their ill-fated date.

A week had passed and she'd heard nothing. Eden had sent an apologetic text the night of the failed date and promised to follow up, but since then, tumbleweed. Heidi had thought that once Eden got over the shock, she might have contacted her.

She'd been wrong. She was wondering whether she should take the reins, but it wasn't that easy. Her ego was fragile and she didn't want to get knocked back again. Once had been enough.

She got out of the car and rapped her knuckles on Kate and Meg's door; it was shiny and red with the number 73 in chrome. Kate and Meg lived in a first-floor flat in Shoreditch, making them the coolest lesbians Heidi knew. It also meant they were only a 15-minute drive from her on a good day, another plus of her recent move.

She heard someone coming down the stairs, then the barked instruction: "Finn! Stay there!" A pause. "Meg! Can you get him!" She smiled as she waited. The door opened and Kate gave her a grin, followed by a hug. "Come in. Mind the bike." Kate said the same thing every time Heidi turned up at their house. She knew the drill.

"Can Finn undo the stair gate, now?" Heidi followed Kate up the stairs.

"I wouldn't put anything past our son. Little cunning genius, that's what he is." Kate picked him up when she was through the gate, kissing his cheek. "What are you?"

"A sodding genius!" Finn replied.

From out of sight, Heidi heard Meg laugh. "He learned that from Kate, not me!" she shouted.

"Lies, all lies," Kate replied as she walked into the lounge.

When Maya saw Heidi, she toddled over, clapping her hands. "Mummy!" It was a far cry from the pout she'd left her with this morning.

Heidi bent down to give her a kiss. No matter how tired she was, seeing Maya always lifted her mood. "How's my best girl? Have you been good for Aunty Kate and Aunty Meg?"

"She's been a little gem, haven't you?" Meg shifted on the sofa as Heidi sat down. "She's been playing with Finn and we watched *Mary Poppins*, didn't we? Apart from the bit where she fell asleep."

"Mare-wee!" Maya spun round in circles in front of Heidi, her excitement topped up.

"Was it Dick Van Dyke's terrible accent she gave up on?"

"Snored all the way through it." Meg grinned. "Let me get you a drink and you can tell me all about your day."

"Yes to the drink, but the day was pretty regular. Bride, groom, guests, cake, dinner, dancing. Just once, I'd love a different wedding. I get them occasionally, but I'd like more. People don't seem to realise photographers need variety, too."

"Sounds like working in magazines. Same shit, different day," Kate said, sitting on the brown leather couch opposite.

"How is the world of *Female Health & Fitness*?" Heidi asked.

"Hanging by a thread, like most magazines." Kate shrugged. "But we're still afloat, just. One of the only magazines that is. I'm looking into alternatives before I get pushed. Maybe I should become a wedding photographer?"

"No thanks, I'd never see you." Meg squeezed Kate's knee as she walked past her. "Plus, we can't have two people working for themselves. That would be mayhem. And a recipe for disaster." Meg paused. "Have you eaten? We've still got some spaghetti Bolognese if you want some. Kate's speciality."

Heidi shook her head. "I ate the wedding meal. Just a cup of tea would be great before I get Maya home and to bed."

Meg disappeared to get Heidi's drink.

Out of the corner of her eye, Heidi saw Finn smack Maya

on the head with a plastic brick. She waited for the wailing, but it never came. Instead, Maya simply picked up the brick and hit herself with it again. Heidi shook her head and turned her attention back to Kate.

"How did your date go the other week, by the way? You were pretty upbeat about that woman beforehand."

Heidi stuck out her bottom lip. "Not good. We didn't even order food. Once I revealed I had a child, she couldn't shut the date down fast enough. Granted, I should have told her when I met her, but still." Maya was now smacking Finn in the face with a brick. It was a game they both seemed to be loving. "It wasn't for her, so best to find that out now."

Kate frowned. "Sorry to hear that."

Meg walked in and put Heidi's tea on the bookcase, out of the reach of tiny hands. These were things Heidi hadn't understood before she had children, but now she got it fully.

"What were you talking about?"

Heidi filled her in.

Meg shook her head. "I don't get it when people do that. Kids are part of life, aren't they? You can't avoid them, even if you don't want them."

"Some people just don't. Some of our best friends don't want kids." Kate sat back. "And having had them, I completely understand it." She smirked at Meg.

"I don't know if it's the not wanting kids, me being a single mum or me lying to her that was the issue. They all seemed to blend into one by the end of the shortest date of my life. She did send a text after saying she was sorry things hadn't worked out, as she really liked me." Heidi sighed. "I really liked her, too. There was a spark and it was pretty powerful.

I'm just a bit loath to leave it, but then again, I don't want more rejection."

Maya walked over and Heidi pulled her onto her lap. She snuggled into her, and Heidi breathed in her smell. She didn't think she'd ever tire of it.

"Maybe some things just aren't meant to work out," Meg said.

"Or maybe some things need a little nudge to get them going." Kate raised an eyebrow as she spoke.

Heidi blew out a breath. "The many computations are making me dizzy. Can you pass my tea? I have a dead weight on me, now." Heidi kissed Maya's curls as she accepted the glass from Meg. Maya's breathing was slowing as she leaned into Heidi. She was tired.

"But if you did want to pursue it, send one last message to see if she fancies meeting again now all your cards are on the table. We'd be happy to watch Maya. We could even have her overnight so you could let the evening play out any way you like." Meg sat forward as she spoke, excitement creasing her face.

"Are you trying to live vicariously through me?" Heidi grinned as she asked.

"Totally." Meg flopped backwards, arms in the air. "Our lives are so set now, it's criminal. My younger self would have shot me. Florist, childcare, bath time, wine." She sat up. "But it's what we ordered, so we can't send it back." She glanced up at Kate, giving her a wink. "And I wouldn't change it for the world."

Meg glanced around the room, noticing what was missing around the same time as Heidi and Kate.

"Where's Finn? Oh god, it's too quiet for him to be up to any good." Kate took off down the hallway, and Heidi heard her groan. Seconds later, she walked in carrying Finn, whose face was now covered in something brown, which was also smeared across his hands and top. His face-splitting grin was also laced with triumph. "Before I clean him up, I just thought I'd show you the damage that can be achieved when the chocolate spread is left open on the table, especially when he can now climb onto the chairs."

Meg let out a howl of laughter. "What was I just saying about our lives? I guess it's bath time. You want to do the honours, darling?"

Kate nodded, walking out of the room.

Heidi glanced back at Meg, whose gaze was assessing her. "What do you think about our plan, anyhow? Invite this woman… what's her name?"

"Eden."

"Very biblical. Invite her out for dinner, drinks, whatever, and we'll have Maya. Your child's not part of the getting-to-know-each-other deal anyhow, so try Eden on and see how you fit. You shouldn't be worrying about kids till you're past that stage."

It wasn't anything Heidi hadn't considered, and yet, she hadn't been brave enough to do it.

"If you don't do it now, the window will close and you'll never know. And then, you'll always be wondering 'what if'?" Meg pulled her knees up to her chest as she spoke. "When Kate and I got together, there was a point where things could have gone off track."

Heidi sat up. This was news. She'd always just assumed

Kate and Meg met, knew instantly they were meant for each other, and had sailed off into the sunset of marriage and kids. Apparently not. "What happened?"

Meg pulled her lips into a thin line. "Kate's mum started seeing someone. That someone was my dad, but Kate had no idea of the link. At the time, I hadn't seen my dad for years. Our relationship was rocky.

"Kate had met him and liked him, and mentioned her mum was seeing someone. Kate's sister had a birthday, we all turned up for the party, my dad was there with Kate's mum, and the shit hit the fan. I didn't want anything to do with him. When I realised the truth, I bolted. I didn't want to be pushed into a situation I wasn't ready for."

Heidi's mouth dropped open. "That is some leftfield shit. I never knew." She couldn't imagine what that would feel like. Meg loved Kate, but not the whole package she came with.

"Why would you?" Meg shrugged. "At that point, I could have left. I mean, I *did* leave, I ran off. However, Kate wouldn't let it lie. She pursued me, because she thought we had something special. I'm glad she did, but at the time, it took a while to get my head around." Meg gave her a wry smile.

Did Kate and Meg's situation have shades of her own? It did. The chemistry between her and Eden had been incredible, but Eden had to accept the whole package, or nothing at all.

"What did Kate do, by the way?"

Meg took a few moments to respond. "She sent me flowers. Which was a pretty bold move considering I'm a florist."

Heidi nearly choked laughing, but then swallowed it down. She didn't want to wake Maya. She moved her delicately onto the cushion beside her, then turned her attention back to Meg. "She sent you flowers? Did she order them from you, too?"

Meg laughed. "She didn't, but I still remember the face of the Interflora delivery bloke when he dropped them off to my shop. Priceless. I once complained nobody ever bought me flowers because I'm a florist, but nobody had ever taken me seriously."

"I love that. Was that when you knew?"

Meg's smile was now the width of her face as she nodded. "Yep. I couldn't let her go, could I?"

"And how did it work out with your dad?" Heidi had to know. It was one thing acting on a situation, but she needed to know the outcome, too.

Meg tensed a little before she answered; that didn't go unnoticed. "Things are as good as they can be. He can't make up for some stuff, but he's certainly changed. Plus, he makes Kate's mum happy, so who am I to stand in his way? My brother gets on better with him, always has. But there's always a bit of me that feels like I'm being disloyal to my mum if I give him too much attention."

Heidi nodded. "Makes me glad my parents are still together."

"It makes it easier," Meg replied. "But for you, it shouldn't be as hard. Charm Eden on a date, and then surely she'll be charmed by Maya, too. How could she not be?"

Heidi winced. "I'm not sure it'll be that easy. I get the impression she's dragging a lot of childhood baggage along with her."

"Maybe she needs someone to help her unpack."

Heidi sat back, shaking her head at Meg. "You're very wise, you know that?"

Meg winked. "Remind my wife of that when she comes back."

Heidi smiled, standing up. "Anyway, I should go. I've got another wedding tomorrow, but it's a short one. Just four hours in the afternoon. This little one's going to my sister's for the afternoon. I should get her home so she's not too grouchy tomorrow."

"Okay." Meg jumped up and put her hands on her hips. "But you'll think about what I've said?"

Heidi nodded. "I promise. No what-ifs."

Chapter Fifteen

Eden woke up in a sweat — she'd dreamed she had a child. The child was mixed race and running towards her, arms outstretched. She didn't need a dream doctor to decipher that one.

Heidi.

She rolled over and got her phone from her bedside table, pulling up the photo of her and Heidi they'd snapped at the festival. One of many they'd taken after too much wine, but this one was the shot Eden had gone back to again and again. The one where Heidi's smile and her spirit jumped off the screen. She was pretty sure Heidi's daughter was just as cute as her mother.

In the dream, Eden had scooped up the little girl in her arms, showering her with kisses. She'd never done that to a child in her life. Was Lib right? Might Eden have something to offer kids if she gave them a chance? Eden went on adult-only holidays, and most of her friends were happily child-free. The ones who had kids, she saw less frequently. Maybe she should make more effort.

She'd always just assumed her terrible childhood meant she'd be a nightmare with kids. But was it true? Could it be she just had to give it a shot with children and maybe she might surprise herself?

She closed her eyes and pictured her gran in front of her. What would she say?

"You were a child once, you know. And what would have happened if I hadn't wanted anything to do with you?" That would never have happened, but her gran had a point. She wasn't finished, either. "Play with a child and you'll have a friend for life. Nobody forgets who plays with them when they were little."

That was true, too. Eden remembered her gran, and also her uncle Ed. Both were gone now, and she was pretty much alone. She'd thought she was happy that way, but meeting Heidi had made her question that. How had that happened in such a short space of time? She and Heidi had spent less than 12 hours in each other's company. Twelve hours. Was that really enough to reassess what you'd always thought, the rules you lived your life by?

The plain fact was, she couldn't stop thinking about Heidi, and thinking about the future date with India made her stomach churn with anxiety.

Eden had to get out of this date, didn't she? But first, she had to impress India with her advertising prowess, and then let her down gently. That would take all of Eden's PR skills. Her life wasn't normally so complicated, but strange things had happened since she met Heidi.

Heidi had unlocked a part of Eden she'd kept under strict orders not to show its face. But now the genie was out of the bottle, and she couldn't stuff it back in no matter how hard she tried. One thing was now clear. Even though Heidi had a child, Eden wanted to see her again. Now, she just had to swing into action.

What was more pressing was her need to get out of bed and get to work. The chocolate spread competition was in full swing, with the whole country talking about it and social media going mad. Two of the missing discs had already been found, and they were just waiting for the final four to be claimed before they could put that PR triumph to bed.

If only Eden's personal life could be solved so easily.

* * *

"The third and fourth people have claimed their prizes! So far, nobody's died or sliced a hand off. Job nearly done." Johan walked over to her desk, undoing the top button of his black shirt. He'd been doing it up and then undoing it all day, not quite decided on which look he liked best.

Eden held up her hand and he high-fived, their palms connecting with a satisfying thwack.

"Boom!" Johan added. "PR disaster turned into PR triumph."

She pointed a finger at him. "Leave it undone. I prefer the more relaxed look."

He raised an eyebrow and fingered his collar. "You do? Okay, I'll go with what you say, seeing as you're the office style icon."

Eden laughed. "I hardly think I'm that."

"As close as we get, anyway." He paused. "Seriously though, great work on the competition. The public are gullible, aren't they? They thought Chocolate Delight was doing them a favour, when really, it was a huge cock-up."

She shook her head. "Just goes to show that, lurking behind every supposed disaster, there's an opportunity. It's a message for life, in case you were wondering." She gave him a wink. "Thanks for coming to my TED Talk."

Johan laughed. "I don't know how I'd get through the day without you."

"You're not the only one." Eden spun in her chair, blowing out mouthfuls of air as she looked at the ceiling of their office. "But you know that's only half the job done, right? We still need to follow through with that brilliant ad campaign we promised. How do we link sexy with family life and do it in a light-hearted way that doesn't offend the nation?"

Johan plonked himself down in the chair beside her. "We're not the best two to ask, are we? Seeing as neither of us have kids."

"But you have friends who have kids, right?"

Johan nodded. "Course. Friends, family. I love kids, want some of my own one day. I just need to convince Cam that he does, too." Johan and Cameron had been together for five years, and Eden knew Johan was itching to add kids to their portfolio. Cameron, on the other hand, was yet to be convinced of the impact said kids might have on his *actual* portfolio.

Eden hoped they worked out their differences soon, because Johan was getting broodier by the week.

"Hey guys."

She spun round, as did Johan. Their boss Caroline was smiling at them. She was dressed in her regulation Cos wardrobe, all block shapes and muted colours. When she walked round the office, she was like a gentle waft of sophistication. Eden tried to keep up with style, changing with the seasons. Caroline didn't bother. Seasons came and seasons went, but Caroline was classic and cool all year round.

"You saw the email about the competition?" She leaned on Johan's desk, opposite Eden's.

Eden nodded. "Yep, Boy Wonder here was just telling me."

"Now that's nearly complete, they want the proposal for the ad by next week. Do you think you can come up with something by then? Doesn't have to be storyboarded, just the basic outline."

This was a question that had only one answer.

"Of course. We were just discussing it," Eden replied. "We'll come up with one a little out-there, like they requested, and then one a little more safe."

Caroline grinned. "You read my mind. You know what these companies are like. They say they want to push the boundaries, but when you give them what they ask for, they're normally a little weirded out by it. Best to have a Plan B to offer them, too, just in case Plan A pushes them too far out of their comfort zone."

"Leave it with us. Although we might have to go down the pub and brainstorm." Johan grinned at Caroline, who waved her hand.

"Whatever it takes. Take the company card and get pissed, just so long as you give me a winning idea next week."

Eden grinned. "You know, some people moan about their boss. Whenever they do, I always think how lucky we are to have you." She knew it was cheesy, but it was true. Caroline was the main reason Eden was still at Quote Media.

Her boss wagged a finger at her, getting up from the desk and smoothing down her top. "You know what they say, Eden. Keep the flattery coming."

Johan rolled his eyes when Caroline had gone. "You're such a suck-up, you know that?"

"You're just sad I got there first." Eden stuck out a tongue, then picked up her phone. She scrolled to the photo of her and Heidi, grinning and drunk. It had been taken before their scorching kiss. A tingle raced down her spine when she thought back to it.

Things were going well for her today, and she believed in positive energy. She should strike while she was feeling good. Before she second-guessed herself. She opened her text app, and sent Heidi a brief message asking if she fancied going out again. That was step one. She could grovel when she saw her.

She sent the message, then sat back. Her stomach lurched. All her positive energy disappeared. Eden hadn't missed this part of dating. She put her phone on her desk and checked some emails.

It only took ten minutes for a reply to appear. When Eden saw it, she exhaled deeply, then spun around, glad Johan had slipped away somewhere. This text was about to predict her mood for the rest of the day. She swallowed hard, her stomach fizzing with anticipation. She counted to three, then clicked.

The text read: 'I've been thinking the same. I think there were things left unsaid. So let's meet up.'

Eden leaned back in her chair and closed her eyes. They were on the same wavelength. Plus, Heidi had replied straight away, showing she wasn't a player. That thought warmed Eden. She hadn't been tactical, playing a game of emotional Jenga. She'd been honest. Maybe her first lie wasn't the crime of the century, after all.

Eden stared at the message, and thought about the kiss.

Then her heart boomed. She was going to reply right away and get another date in the diary.

And this time, she wasn't going to fuck it up.

Chapter Sixteen

Heidi wasn't sure having her next date with Eden on April Fool's Day was wise, but they were about to find out. Between both their work commitments and Maya, it'd taken a week till they both had a matching free day or evening. To assuage her guilt over leaving Maya on a Sunday, Heidi had taken her trampolining this morning, and Maya had loved it. Heidi had already decided that trampolining was taking the place of Aquababy. The parents there had been happy to engage in small talk while their kids bounced. She'd even exchanged phone numbers with another single mum, Denise. The experience had left Heidi feeling upbeat about the world. She hoped it continued into her date with Eden.

What to wear for such an occasion? It was a day date, so she didn't want to go overboard. She decided on a denim skirt and patterned top, with strappy sandals. Casual, but showing she'd made an effort. Plus, she knew it would be something Eden wouldn't wear. She'd only ever seen her in trousers or jeans, and got the impression she never wore skirts. Which is exactly the kind of lesbian Heidi preferred. An image of Eden strutting into the pub looking hot in jeans and a shirt dropped into her eyeline. A flash of heat left pinpricks on her skin. Yes, she was ready for this date.

She glanced at her phone and saw she had two missed calls from Kate. She was dropping Maya off to them on the way to her date, and her breathing stalled. They'd made the arrangements by text yesterday. Had something changed? Heidi winced as she opened the message.

When she read it, her heart sank.

The whole family had come down with some sort of vomiting bug, and they'd spent yesterday and today taking it in turns to be sick. Kate was apologetic, but said it was for the best that Maya didn't come round and catch it.

Disappointment ran through her, until Heidi focused her thoughts. Was there anyone else she could ask at such short notice? Not really. Her family were all away this weekend. Sarah and Jason were at his parents' place in Devon, and her mum and dad were on holiday in the Lake District.

She flopped down on her bed and stared at the ceiling. The stars were not aligning, were they? All her closest babysitting resources had been cut off. She either cancelled, which she was loath to do, or she went ahead and took Maya with her.

That thought made her swing her legs off the bed and sit up.

Could she test their fledging relationship so soon? Ideally, she wouldn't introduce Maya so early to anyone, but her daughter was young enough to not really understand what was going on. Maya was introduced to friends and family she only saw a couple of times a year all the time. Was this so different?

She grabbed her phone and fired a text to Eden, telling her the situation and the options. She sat back, a strange metallic taste settling on her tongue. If Eden really had no appetite for kids, Heidi guessed she was about to find out.

Eden's reply was swift, flashing up on Heidi's phone within five minutes.

'Sure, bring Maya. It would be lovely to meet her.'

It was time to see if Eden was telling the truth.

* * *

They met in the pub Heidi had chosen: The Pied Piper. A massive old boozer with a scuffed-up wooden bar in the centre of the action, it had five bar staff taking care of customer needs. On Sunday lunchtime it was bustling, but Heidi had snagged a table. She waited with Maya on her lap.

Was she about to commit dating suicide? Possibly. Still, at the very least, she was determined to order food this time, because she hadn't eaten today. She'd already been eyeing the fish and chips, along with the delicious apple crumble and custard she'd seen those at the table beside her devouring. Her stomach growled as she thought about it.

Eden walked in five minutes late. Had she timed it that way? Whatever, her cheeks were adorably flushed as she approached Heidi, a mix of trepidation and concern stamped across her face. Heidi could well understand it. Their relationship so far had hardly gone well, apart from a single Saturday spent in a damp field. Plus that far-from-damp kiss.

It was that kiss that had kept them tethered, she was sure. That kiss was why Eden was walking towards her, wearing a pair of jeans with artfully ripped knees. Heidi smiled inside and out when she saw them. Yep, Eden wore a pair of jeans just as well as she recalled. Her long legs filled them well, the denim close to her skin. Eden had teamed the jeans with a black shirt, Nikes and black bomber jacket.

Heidi's heart rate rocketed. Yep, she wanted to see how they could build on that kiss for sure.

"Don't get up." Eden bent down as Heidi was doing just that.

Heidi went to kiss Eden's cheek, but their mouths rushed together at speed, as if drawn by an invisible magnet. The resulting kiss was bruising. More of a kiss-punch, if that was a thing. Heidi pulled back, stunned.

"Sorry. I was going for your cheek." Her cheeks heated like a winter furnace.

A smile danced onto Eden's lips. "I was going for yours, too. But I prefer your lips." She paused. "Shall we try that again?" Eden stared at Heidi's lips, before placing her own back on them again. Lightly, briefly, but with maximum intent. Then, as if it were an everyday occurrence, she sat down next to her.

Heidi wobbled. *Fuck*. She hadn't expected that. But it wasn't a kiss she wanted to reject. When it finished, she stared at Eden's lips. Then Maya squeezed her hand and she was brought back into the room. Into the here and now. Heidi gulped, straightened up, and placed a kiss on Maya's head.

"Mummy kiss!" Blood rushed to Heidi's cheeks as she shook her head. At least Maya was young enough to not decipher the difference in that kiss to one she might give to, say, her cousin. At least, Heidi hoped she was. She gave Eden a tight smile, then turned Maya towards her.

"Maya, this is Mummy's friend Eden. You want to say hi?"

Maya glanced at Eden, frowned, then buried her head in Heidi's chest. Heidi hugged her daughter close. "She can be shy at first."

"Not a glowing initial report." Eden took off her jacket and hung it over the back of her chair. "Good job I've got an in with her mum, so perhaps we can work on it." Eden reached into her bag. "I brought some swag from work as a bribe. For you and Maya. Chocolate Delight, have you heard of it?" Eden held up a Chocolate Delight-branded bag. She opened it to reveal it held a few tubs of the spread inside, along with a soft toy wearing the Chocolate Delight emblem on its chest.

Heidi nodded. "Course I have. They've had that big competition where you could win ten grand. I bought some hoping I might get one of those winning discs, but it wasn't to be. But we'll accept those gladly. I might love it more than she does."

Eden gave her a broad grin. "I've been trying not to eat it, but seeing as I'm working on the PR and marketing campaign, it's a bit tricky when they keep giving us boxes of the stuff." She paused. "The competition was my idea, so I'm thrilled you know about it."

Heidi sat back. "Really? I'm sure they were pleased with you. You couldn't get away from it. It was on radio, TV, billboards, social media. If that was your intention, well done, you succeeded."

"Media saturation was the goal, and I think we achieved it."

Heidi laughed. "You did. The product's a hit with everyone. I was round at a friend's house recently, and their little boy got into a jar and got it all over his face. He was pretty pleased. His parents, not so much."

"Sorry, not sorry."

Heidi tilted her head. "If you ran that competition, does that mean you've met India Contelli?"

Eden's face twitched, before she gave Heidi a half-smile. "I have. A few times."

Heidi's eyes widened. "Oh my god, I love her. She's so fierce and hot. I mean, when she's on those business shows, she's always the one the camera loves. Is she as forthright and gorgeous in real life?"

Eden still looked a little pained.

"I'm not getting happy vibes from your face," Heidi said. "Don't tell me she's a nightmare. I hate when that happens."

Eden shook her head. "She's not, she's really lovely. Very easy to get on with. I wasn't sure what she'd be like, but she's surprisingly down-to-earth."

Heidi grinned. "I love that she's so out, too. How she's still single is a mystery. If she ever does get married, I want to do her wedding. You think you can slip her one of my business cards?"

Eden gave Heidi another jagged smile, nodding. "I'll see what I can do." Then she leaned forward, her eyes not leaving Heidi's face. "Enough about India Contelli and Chocolate Delight. Let's talk about us. It's good to see you again. Thanks for saying yes. I wasn't sure if I'd left it too long."

"I wasn't sure, either. But then, when you texted, my initial thought was yes. I went with that."

"I'm glad." The skin around Eden's eyes crinkled. "I'm hoping today, we can start again. Wipe off our first date as a blip." She took a breath. "Would that be okay?"

Heidi stalled for a couple of seconds before replying. "We can to a certain degree. But the issue is still sat on my lap."

On cue, Maya twisted around, putting a hand on Heidi's cheek. "Play, Mummy."

Heidi glanced out the window of the pub. The back garden housed a small kids' playground and a bouncy castle. Maya had already spotted it out the window and was pointing now, wriggling to get off Heidi's lap. If Heidi didn't want Maya to cause a scene, she was going to have to go along with her request for now.

She glanced up at Eden. "But just to be clear, I didn't mean to force the issue today. Bringing Maya couldn't be helped."

Eden shook her head. "It's fine. She's gorgeous."

Maya was on her feet now, pulling at Heidi's hand. "She's also very insistent when she wants something. Do you mind getting a drink and going outside?" Was Eden going to bail before ordering again? Heidi braced herself.

But Eden shook her head, getting to her feet. "No problem. I'll grab your bag and jackets, you grab her."

Outside, the weather had April stamped all over it. A chill wind blew, but Maya paid no attention as she raced over to the bouncy castle. Heidi paid the attendant cash and put Maya on, a knot in her stomach. She used to love playing on bouncy castles as a kid, but she was less in love with them as a parent. All she could see now were far larger children paying no heed to her daughter, their elbows at Maya's head height, there to knock her out with no notice at all.

A picnic table nearby freed up, and Eden took their coats and bags and put them on the table. "You want to sit?" She walked back to stand beside Heidi.

Heidi shook her head. "I just want to keep an eye on her for a bit. She's only little."

Eden dug her hands in her jeans pockets and watched, too. A few moments went by and neither spoke.

"Did you go on these when you were little?"

Heidi glanced to her left, before looking back. Maya was holding hands with another little girl about the same height. Heidi liked that. Safety in numbers. "All the time," she said, not turning her head. "But now I'm the parent, I find it less fun. Especially when I hear about kids being catapulted off them and dying."

"You'd have to be very unlucky for that to happen." Eden paused. "When I was a kid, my cousin fell on me when I was on one. I made sure not to get in his way again. Kids are pretty robust, and Maya looks like she's got the knack of it."

Just at that moment, her daughter let out a shriek of laughter, then promptly fell on her bum. She bounced for a bit, but then managed to get up again. Heidi flooded with pride.

"Maybe you're right She's more robust than I give her credit for."

"How about us? You think we're robust?"

Heidi turned to her. "We'll see. This is a good test, though, right? For a non-child person."

"The ultimate. I thought it might be a joke, you arranging to meet me on April 1st."

Heidi gave a throaty laugh. "Nobody wants to get married on April 1st, so that's why I'm free. I'm not superstitious. Are you?"

Eden shook her head. "Nope. I believe life is driven by action, not chance. Which is why I asked you to meet me again. I didn't want to leave that to chance."

Heidi glanced sideways and held her gaze. After a few seconds, Eden looked away, scanning the pub garden. Heidi followed her gaze, allowing herself a minute to take her eyes off Maya.

The air was shrill with the sound of children's voices, and to her left a young child was screaming, snot running down her face. It looked like she'd either fallen off the monkey bars or the swings, and Heidi felt for whom she assumed was the little girl's dad. The little girl had worked herself up into a lather of tears and there was nothing her parent could do apart from comfort her and let it play out. Patience was something you had to learn more of when you became a parent, or you'd simply never survive.

"That right there is the stuff I dread." Eden pointed at the little girl. "Because I've no idea how to handle it."

"Neither did I, but you learn to."

"I'm not good with things I'm not in control of. My work, I have a handle on. My life, it runs how I want it to."

"So meeting me wasn't in your plans then, was it?" Heidi took in her electric blue eyes; she definitely hadn't planned for those.

Eden bit her lip, before lifting her eyes to Heidi. "It wasn't, but I'm open to curve balls."

"You weren't when I dropped Maya into the conversation first."

"I know, but it was a shock. We chatted enough at the festival and I wasn't sure why you didn't tell me."

"Because I was afraid of a bad reaction?" Heidi raised an eyebrow at Eden.

She bowed her head.

Heidi hoped she took the point. "It wasn't so much a lie, more an omission of the facts. I am sorry, though. Blame my sister for her little scheme."

"She has a husband, that much I know. And kids?"

"Three kids."

"Wow. Her lie was three times as big."

"But it was mainly to herself." Heidi paused. "You said you had an issue with single mothers, too. If you do, we still have a problem."

Eden kicked the ground, looking down. She shook her head. "I don't. Not with you. Just with my mother. She was a single mum and let's just say she wasn't a great example." Eden glanced up. "I'm sorry for putting that on you, too. I hope you can forgive me."

Heidi took a moment, before she squeezed Eden's hand. The connection warmed her. "There's a good chance."

They both gazed over at Maya bouncing again.

"She's going to be bounced out today. I took her trampolining this morning. She loved it. I think it's our new thing."

Eden's face fell.

"What is it?" Heidi had no idea what she'd said. Something wrong again? This was like walking on eggshells.

Eden shook her head. "Nothing." She exhaled. "It's just, I hardly think about my mum much, then I've mentioned her twice in as many minutes with you." She frowned. "My mum used to take me trampolining. She loved it, too. It was the one thing we did together that she never begrudged." Eden's shoulders went up, then down as she sighed. "Anyway, that's my sad, sorry tale. Enough about me."

The woman in charge of the bouncy castle blew her whistle, bringing their conversation to a close. Heidi wanted to ask more, but sensed this wasn't the right moment. They moved towards the steady stream of children climbing off.

"Is Maya the end for you, or are you planning any more?"

Heidi ran her tongue along her bottom lip, wondering if this was another key question, one that might trip up their fledging relationship. But she could only answer it honestly. "I think the end, but never say never."

Eden's face gave nothing away as she nodded.

Maya was adorable as she shuffled to the edge of the castle, her movements small and precise. Her nose was snotty as Heidi held out a hand to her. Heidi wiped it, then picked her up and walked back to Eden, who was sitting at their picnic table. Had they smoothed things over? She had no idea.

"This table reminds me of our epic Saturday night." Eden flashed her an unsure smile.

Relief rolled through Heidi. Perhaps they were okay. "Apart from we're dry. A miracle." She paused. "I particularly enjoyed the end of that night. Did you?"

Now Eden's smile reached her gorgeous eyes. "It was a birthday highlight."

A worked-up Maya slapped the table with both hands.

"I think she wants some attention," Heidi said.

Eden fished in her pocket and pulled out a bag of banana sweets. She leaned in to Maya. "I'm not sure if this is your thing, Maya. But one of my favourite things to do with chocolate spread is to smear it onto a banana sweet and eat both together. Like spreading it on your toast. What do you think?" She opened the bag of sweets and offered one to Heidi's daughter.

Heidi knew just what Maya would think. "Those sweets are her favourite, so your stock might just have jumped a notch or two."

Sure enough, her daughter took the offered sweet, then dipped her hand into the chocolate spread Eden was offering. She smeared it on her banana as instructed.

"Like toast!" Maya gave Eden an impossibly cute grin, and Heidi sent up a silent note of thanks. Eden was finally getting cute, cheery Maya, not grumpy, grouchy Maya. Now she was nearing her terrible twos, Heidi was never sure what was going to happen.

"What do you say to Eden for giving you chocolate and bananas?"

"Like toast!" Maya repeated, holding out her hand for another.

Eden obliged.

"I was thinking more 'thank you', but close enough." Heidi paused. "Well played, by the way," she told Eden. "You're better at this kid stuff than you think."

Eden blushed then, and Heidi melted a little. "I hoped it might get me onside. With you and her."

Heidi raised an eyebrow. "You'll only get me onside if you give me a sweet, too."

They both laughed, as did Maya. Heidi relaxed into the moment, and for the first time, she wondered if this *could* work. Bringing her child on a date wasn't optimal, but it wasn't the end of the world. That was a revelation in itself.

Chapter Seventeen

An hour later, Heidi and Eden had fresh drinks, and they'd shared some fish and chips, which had pleased Maya no end. What Eden was taking away from this brief encounter with a toddler was that distraction was key to controlling their behaviour, and the best way to do that was with a never-ending supply of food. So far, with the mix of banana sweets, chocolate spread and ketchup-covered chips, it was working a treat.

Maya was playing with a friend from her playgroup now, setting up a tea party on a tiny picnic table in the play area, replete with mini plates, cups, a teapot and even some plastic bread.

This date was far from her usual, but being here with Heidi was just as good as she remembered. Once they'd got past the thorny issues of what had been said and done, Eden relaxed. When she was around Heidi, she couldn't help it. Somehow, Heidi made Eden click into place. Made her remember a version of herself she didn't know existed. The one her gran had tried to shine a light on, but she'd shied away. The one Lib kept banging the drum about. The one that, if she was honest, Eden was just seeing for the first time.

When Heidi had reacted so strongly to India Contelli earlier, it had thrown Eden. She'd almost come clean, but then she realised there was nothing to say. India was her client. India had asked her out, and Eden was going to turn her down. She and Heidi hadn't been a thing then, so it wasn't even connected. What's more, Eden was damn sure India Contelli wouldn't light her up the way Heidi did. Every time their eyes connected, Eden wanted to climb across the wooden table and kiss Heidi into next week.

But she didn't.

Not yet.

Heidi ate the last couple of chips, licking a spot of ketchup from her fingers.

What she'd give to be that ketchup. "The chips were a hit." She glanced at Maya, who was chatting to her friend. Yes, she was cute, but boy, was she messy. It had taken three wet wipes to clean her up.

"Chips are a hit with everyone, aren't they?" Heidi gave her a smile. "If anyone tells you different, they're lying. You know those people who ask restaurants to replace their chips with a salad? Every time they do, if you listen really carefully, you can hear their souls weeping."

Eden laughed. "I take it you've never done that?"

Heidi snorted. "If I ever do, you have permission to slap me. I can't foresee a day where I turn down chips."

"You might develop some sort of weird chip allergy."

Heidi shuddered. "Now you're talking the language of horror." She popped the last chip in her mouth, and as she stared into Eden's eyes, a flash of heat sailed down Eden's body. When her gaze landed on Heidi's mouth, it only intensified.

"I just want you to know, it's been good reconnecting. Meeting up again. I've thought about you a lot since the festival. Since that kiss."

Heidi tilted her head, wiping her hands on the final wet wipe. "That kiss was kinda special, wasn't it? Although it seems a very long time ago."

"Too long," Eden replied.

"But I've thought about it, too. About how I'd like to replicate it, and perhaps more."

"More?" Eden raised an eyebrow.

"Uh-huh."

"Maybe the more could involve chocolate spread, too?"

"Are you just trying to boost sales for your product?"

"Would it work?"

"Absolutely." Heidi smiled, gazing into Eden's eyes.

Eden could have happily frozen that moment and stayed there for a while longer. However, as she was learning from today, romantic moments were harder when you were surrounded by children, as evidenced by the sound of two kids running by, one shouting "You're going to die!" at the top of his voice. Yep, Eden could see how parents might have a hard time squeezing romance back into their lives.

"I hope we can get to more," Heidi added, gazing at Eden. "Probably not today, because I have my daughter, but sometime when it can be just the two of us?"

"I'd like that a lot." Eden licked her lips as her heart rate kicked up a notch. Heat spread through her under Heidi's intense gaze. Maybe she could kick aside all her children and single mum hang-ups. For Heidi, she was ready to do most things.

"You've got the most intense, gorgeous eyes. But I think you probably know that."

Eden smiled, squirming a little. "I also get embarrassed easily."

Heidi let out a bark of laughter. "If you're going to go out with someone with children, you have to get over that quickly." She paused. "You've never gone out with anyone with children before?"

Eden shook her head, lowering her gaze to Heidi's lips. "Nope. Never been a thing."

"And today hasn't put you off?"

Eden shook her head. "I thought it would, but I'm opening myself up to new possibilities. Your daughter is a part of you, and I want to get to know you." She still wouldn't describe herself as comfortable with it, but she was going with the flow. Which, for Eden, was a miracle. Going with the flow meant giving up control. Seeing where life took you. Was she prepared to take a deep breath and jump?

"I want to get to know you, too. But I can't change the fact that I have a child. Life with her is messy and unpredictable, so strap yourself in for the ride."

"I work with major executives, who I always say are a little like overgrown toddlers. Sometimes they throw their toys on the floor, sometimes they decide to make it about who can scream the loudest. So I've had some experience." She swallowed down hard. "I admit I don't do messy very well, but I'd like to think I can take whatever Maya throws at me."

Heidi reached across, took Eden's hand in hers and kissed it.

Eden already knew she wanted those lips planted all over her body.

"Be careful what you wish for," Heidi replied.

Eden glanced over to where Maya and her friend were smearing chocolate spread onto fake plastic pieces of bread. Good for branding was her first thought. Then she rolled her eyes at herself. She needed to impress on Heidi she was cool with her child, not pounce on her every move and use it for her own ends.

Eden nodded to where Heidi was already looking. "Isn't it cute they're using the chocolate spread? I was just thinking I should be filming it for Instagram."

Heidi glanced Maya's way, then frowned. Her movements went into overdrive as she scrabbled for the Chocolate Delight bag Eden had brought, and tipped out the tubs. "How many tubs were in the bag?" She stood up, almost shouting.

Eden frowned. "What?"

"How many tubs of the spread were in the bag?" More urgent now.

"Three."

"There are still three here. So what's she spreading on that toast?" Heidi was suddenly a blur as she sprinted over to the play area, shouting at Maya to stop doing what she was doing.

But what *was* she doing? Eden could only see she was playing still. What was wrong with that? She stood up, craning her neck to see.

The other parent had run over now, and both she and Heidi were taking the fake toast and cutlery from their children's hands, before lifting both kids by the underarms, holding them at arm's length as they walked swiftly towards Eden.

Eden stood up.

The chocolate was all over Maya's hands and down her

top and trousers, too — and just when they'd run out of wet wipes. She needed cleaning up. What was it Heidi had been saying about her being messy?

"You taking her to the bathroom?" But Eden's final word was clipped as a pungent smell hit her, causing her to stumble. She took a step back, before wrinkling her nose, and then her whole face. Oh. My. God. She breathed in again, then turned her head, before looking back at Heidi.

Maya held her hands out towards Eden, clenching and unclenching her tiny fists, which were caked in the brown stuff.

"Like toast!" Maya said with a smile.

"Do not put your hands in your mouth! Hold them out where I can see them!" Heidi told her daughter.

Maya did as she was told, her tiny fingers spread wide and in front of her.

Eden now understood the urgency with which Heidi had moved. How had she known? "That's not chocolate, is it?" Eden's stomach lurched, and she swallowed down. She was not going to be sick, but it was taking all her willpower to keep her chips in her stomach. From the colour of Heidi's face, which was set to pale grey, she was doing the same thing, too.

Heidi's face was contorted, and she was shaking her head. "I wish it was, but apparently she really wanted to smear something onto the bread, and look what present was waiting to be used on the floor of the playground. If I could get my hands on that dog owner, I'd tell them a thing or two." Heidi grimaced, then blew out a long breath. "I'm not sure what to do, apart from put her in a poo bag, but I don't have one big enough." She walked a few more steps, then stopped.

"I'm taking her to the bathroom, but then I'm going to have to go home. She stinks. And this is… more than a little embarrassing." She shook her head. "Can you keep an eye on our stuff till I get back?"

Eden ground her teeth together, not knowing what to say. "Of course. Is there anything I can do?"

Heidi shook her head. "Just tell yourself the next date we have will be better than our first two. It has to be."

Eden hoped that was true.

***

Heidi put Maya to bed and poured herself the largest glass of Malbec possible. She considered putting a straw in the bottle and to hell with the glass, but she was trying to keep a lid on her disappointment. So far, dating with kids was proving more of an issue than she'd thought possible.

Today had gone so well at first. Maya had warmed up to Eden, and they'd even started chatting and laughing. While Maya had played, they'd shared some conversation, and the one thing that stuck out to Heidi was they both wanted to take this further, to see where they might end up. They were on the same page. She so wanted to be on the same page as Eden. In the same bed would be nice, too.

However, she couldn't work out why the universe kept setting them up, then knocking them down. Tonight she'd had visions of Maya falling asleep in her arms after playing, of Eden and her sharing looks and touches, and leaving with promises of more child-free times to come. She'd envisioned a farewell kiss that promised more. A dreamlike state for this evening.

Instead, Heidi had come home, thrown all Maya's clothes straight into the bin, then plonked her in the shower, hosing her down until she was sure all trace of the day had gone. The one saving grace was that neither she nor her friend Etty had got any in their mouths. However, if she'd been trying to show Eden how wonderful children could be, it had backfired spectacularly.

Her stomach rumbled, and she got up, spying the chocolate spread bag on the counter. She opened the bread bin and took out a couple of crumpets. Some chocolate-covered crumpets to soothe her woes? It sounded perfect.

She'd left the pub in a whirl, not quite knowing what to say or do, embarrassment peaked. It couldn't get any worse than that, could it? Eden had been so sweet, but Heidi could see she was trying not to barf, trying not to run screaming from the scene, and who could blame her? It wasn't anything she'd run to, and she was a parent.

When the crumpets popped from her toaster, she fished them out with her wooden tongs — just like her mother always told her — and opened the jar of spread.

"Like toast." Her stomach lurched.

She wasn't all that hungry, after all.

Chapter Eighteen

"I don't believe that happened." Johan was sat aghast as Eden regaled the tale of yesterday to him. "The kid was spreading dog shit onto a bit of plastic bread like it was chocolate spread?"

"In the middle of a pub in broad daylight." When you didn't know the sweet little girl involved, it sounded far worse.

"And this was your date's kid?"

Eden nodded. "It was." A second date that hadn't ended well either, although it was definitely more promising than the first. Just when she was beginning to think there might be something there for her and Heidi, something else happened that made her question it all over again.

Not that any of it was Heidi's fault. What had happened was an accident. But their relationship hadn't gone smoothly so far, and it was making Eden doubt date three. Yesterday, they'd just started to talk when Maya had her incident. Then Heidi had left in more than a hurry.

Which made Eden question the whole child thing again. Was she ready for it? Her heart said yes, because Heidi had already made a strong case where her heart was concerned.

However, her head was questioning her choices. Her head

said this was the tip of the iceberg. That her original thoughts about kids still stood. Whichever way she jumped, she knew today she'd woken up with a hangover, and it had nothing to do with the amount of alcohol she'd drunk the day before. This was an emotional hangover.

"I'm sure you'll look back and laugh."

"Maybe in a year."

"Perhaps two. So how did you leave it? You were wary of the kid, anyway. Then she shits all over your date. Literally." He sat back, pleased with his joke.

Eden's smile was tight. "I said I'd call her. I'm not going to run just because her kid mistook dog poo for chocolate spread."

At least, she didn't think she was.

"Should that be our ad campaign tagline?" Johan painted his hand across the air above his head. "I can see it now, on billboards everywhere: 'Tastes much better than dog shit'!"

She rolled her eyes. "Very funny. But it did make me think about an ad campaign for Chocolate Delight. Because Maya — the name of dogshit child—"

"Cute name."

"It is, isn't it?" Eden's heart did a somersault as she thought about Maya, then Heidi. Maya might be cute, but she had nothing on her mother. "Anyway, Maya got obsessed with me telling her she could spread Chocolate Delight on toast. Also, Heidi told me about another friend whose kid got it all over his face. Maybe we could include that, too?"

Johan nodded. "Go on."

Eden clicked her tongue against the roof of her mouth. "I was thinking we could have a Chocolate Delight ad based on a story around a family with a toddler. In the morning, the toddler demands it for breakfast — because they do demand, as I now know — and we show the parent spreading it on her toast, saying something memorable, repeatable. 'Delight for you.'" Eden circled her hand. "We'll work on it, you get the gist.

"In the afternoon, we show that same parent spreading it on something for him or herself. Maybe himself to flip the expectation. He spreads it on a rice cake, and says 'Delight for me.' They kiss the child goodnight. The last scene is of the couple in bed together, naked, about to get busy. The woman smears some spread over the husband's lips and says, 'Delight for us', then kisses it off. And then we have some kind of tagline, that indicates Chocolate Delight is the spread for the whole family that will see you through the day, from morning till night." She sat back, knitting her fingers together in the shape of a steeple, resting them on her forehead. "What do you think?"

Johan frowned, his gaze questioning. "You got all that from some kid playing with dog poo?"

Eden laughed. That storyboard had been going around in her head all last night when she couldn't sleep. She'd composed a couple of messages to Heidi during the early hours of this morning, but hadn't sent them. She hadn't checked her phone in the past two hours as she'd been in meetings. Heidi had messaged last night to apologise, and Eden had sent one back right away telling her there was no need. Because there wasn't. None of it was anyone's fault, it had just happened.

For Eden even to think that showed she was changing. Pushing aside her imperfect past, taking a deep breath and opening herself up to new possibilities. One thing she was sure of: Heidi had some kind of mystical power over her.

"There's something in it. It's rough at the moment, but it could work." He pointed a finger in her direction. "I also think one of us needs to have a child for moments of inspiration like this. Maybe that's why this woman's come into your life, to show you what family life is like, then we can depict it."

"It's crossed my mind." Eden had never experienced true family life. She thought of Heidi. Of her strength, her courage to do it alone. Heidi had shown Maya more love and commitment in one lunchtime than Eden had ever got from her mum in 40 years.

Emotion lodged in Eden's throat. She had to push it down. She was at work, her in-control place. Yet since she'd met Heidi, her work and personal life were becoming intertwined. With every passing day, Eden could feel control slipping from her grasp.

She swallowed down and refocused. What would India think of the ad? Because in the end, she was the one they had to impress with their story and execution. Would she warm to it? Or did she want something way more out there?

"You know," Eden said, an image of Heidi flashing into her mind. And then Heidi was stripping off her top, beckoning Eden in with a crooked finger. She had a pot of Chocolate Delight in one hand, and proceeded to trail that suggestive finger through the spread, before licking it off her fingertip in one swift move.

Eden stopped spinning around in her chair and let that image marinade in her mind for a few minutes. She sat with it, too. She knew enough about mindfulness to understand that you were meant to notice small moments of joy in your life and be present for them. She was totally present for this.

All over it, in fact. Even if the moment was a daydream, a fabrication of her own making.

The moment broke when Johan snapped his fingers in front of her face. He stared at her, his face a question mark. "Where did you go?"

"Sorry, I was deep in thought." She paused. "I was just wondering…" She trailed off. She was just wondering whether or not she could bring her fantasy to life. Who knew if she and Heidi were ever going to get it together? But if they couldn't, she could put it in an ad. She sat up, planting both feet onto the polished wooden floorboards, pacing to the window and staring out at Soho below. April drizzle was falling again, and the streets were a blur of shuffling umbrellas.

"What if the couple they focus on isn't a man and a woman? What if it's two men or two women? I'd say two men has been done before, whereas two women isn't as common. Plus, we're pitching to India Contelli, who, as everybody knows, is one of the most eligible lesbians in the world. If anyone is going to give the green light to a lesbian-themed ad, it's her, right?"

Johan was looking at her like she'd gone mad. "Are you serious? You've got to get it past Caroline first, which would be the hardest part."

"Caroline's pro-LGBT."

"She's also pro keeping her business shipshape."

Eden shook her head. The more she thought about this idea, the more sure she was this was the moment to push. They'd toyed with putting LGBT characters in their campaigns before, but they'd always shied away. But if India wanted something different, she was going to get it.

"I'm going to take it to Caroline now." Eden stood up. "Strike while the iron's hot. Otherwise, tomorrow I might chicken out."

"And if she says yes?"

Eden grinned. "Then those rough edges are going to need to be smoothed out. And we have to hire two smokin'-hot lesbian mums for the ad." She put a finger to her chest. "I'll be in charge of casting, by the way."

Chapter Nineteen

Two days later, Heidi met Sarah in one of the local Jewish coffee shops in their area. She'd been working this morning and had just booked a new job with two lovely women for their wedding in six months' time. Maya was at nursery, and Heidi was picking her up in two hours, which gave her time to have a coffee with her sister.

She loved the community mix of this part of London. While Stoke Newington was within spitting distance, with its hipsters and Turkish community, Stamford Hill was very much a Jewish enclave. However, all the residents, whatever their nationality, lived happily together, showcasing London's ability to be the poster child for diversity. Their family was a case in point: Caribbean meets Surrey, all living in north London surrounded by Jews. As if reinforcing her point, further up the road there was a mosque on one side, a synagogue on the other. When the services collided, which happened most weekends, the various congregations smiled and walked past each other on the same pavements. There was no issue with the Jewish and Muslim communities here.

But it wasn't religion that had been clogging up Heidi's brain for the past couple of days. That honour had gone to what she was now referring to as Poo-gate.

Sarah had her hand over her eyes as Heidi finished telling the story. "Shut the fuck up. She was spreading poo on her toast?" Sarah grimaced a little more. "Was it spreadable?"

"Apparently in Maya's mind it was. But you know, I didn't really take too close a look. I was a bit busy trying not to vomit on my shoes."

"Wow, that's some hardcore dating experiences you've had there. Some would say you two don't look destined. But I think you should see it as a challenge."

"That's because you're married." Heidi held up a hand. "No more poo talk, it's time to eat." She took a bite of her pastry – light, buttery and shot through with lemon and cream cheese – and swooned. "You know what, I'm glad I moved here just to be close to these."

"I thought you moved to be closer to your nearest and dearest?"

"That was a happy coincidence." Heidi gave her a grin. "Seriously, though. Do you think there's something wrong with Maya? I mean, is what happened a bit weird?"

Sarah was shaking her head before Heidi finished her sentence. "No. Kids are grim and weird, especially when they're little. They'll pick up anything and put it in their mouths. It's part of childhood. When Albert was little, he was playing in the back garden with his friend and they found a dead baby bird. When I went out there, they were dissecting it, totally fascinated. They might have been about to grill it and add a little olive oil if I'd left it any longer."

Heidi baulked. "Were we like that when we were kids? I don't recall."

"Probably. You want to ask Mum?"

"No."

Sarah winced. "By the way, I might have kinda half-mentioned about you having a date. Sorry, it just slipped out."

Heidi recoiled. She really didn't need extra pressure. "Can you try to keep your mouth shut where Eden is concerned?"

Sarah nodded, contrite. "I'll try."

"The thing is, I've been spending the last few days putting myself in Eden's shoes. And honestly? I'm not sure I'd be bothered to make it work when everything just keeps going wrong. Look at it from her perspective. Her life's a breeze, she's got a cool job, she's gorgeous. I'm sure she could easily snag herself a woman without all the baggage I come with."

"She hasn't done so far, though, has she? Plus, don't underestimate the power of a Hughes woman." Sarah banged her finger on the table to underline her point. "When Jason met me, I was sick in his shoes the next day. But he still married me and had my children."

Heidi screwed up her forehead. "Isn't that the other way around?"

Sarah shook her head. "No, that's some male chauvinist bullshit. I let Jason put his sperm in me and then I let it produce my children."

"If you say so. My point is, puking in Jason's shoes is bad, but is it *as* bad?"

"If she really didn't want anything to do with Maya, she wouldn't have turned up the other day on date two. And yes, I grant you, it could have gone better. But did you chat?"

Heidi nodded, a slow smile ripening across her cheeks. "We did."

"Exchange cutesy smiles and looks, like the gushy one you're giving me now?"

More nodding.

"Then you're in the zone. You just have to find a way to engineer another zonal meeting where you don't have a child or a dog anywhere near. That shit doesn't happen by accident." Then she burst out laughing. "Excuse the pun, but it doesn't. And cutesy smiles and looks don't go away in a hurry, either."

"A zonal meeting? You make it sound like a painful thing. Like we have to meet at a certain point in geometry and impale ourselves on a spike to make it happen."

"Whatever it takes to get you laid." Sarah sat back, giving Heidi a wide grin. "Call it what you like but it's all true."

"How do you know? You've been married for 12 years, you're hardly what I'd call a dating lexicon. You met Jason when you were 20 and got married at 25. You haven't even suffered a broken heart."

"I have!"

"Bobby Trainer doesn't count. You were six."

"It still hurt." Sarah put on her aggrieved face. "Anyway, I watch a lot of movies, I read a lot of books. I understand the world plenty."

"I wish I did." Heidi finished her pastry, then sat back, sipping her coffee. "I didn't even mean to introduce her to Maya so early, but circumstance conspired against me." She put her head in her hands. "Am I a terrible mother?"

Sarah snorted, putting a hand on Heidi's arm. "Will you stop? Look at me."

Heidi prised her hands away from her face and sighed.

"Things go wrong with children, you can't legislate for it.

That's why it's generally better to have two adults around. It's not for the children, it's to support each other in times of need."

That raised a laugh. "I get that."

"You're doing just fine. You're muddling through, just like everyone else. Maya is a gorgeous girl who's always so happy. I don't think you've scarred her by having a drink with Eden. Unless you were humping on the table while she was playing kitchens."

Heidi rolled her eyes. "Yep, we were naked the whole time."

"Give yourself a break. And I'm sure Eden will cut you some slack, too."

"You don't think she'll want to run a mile after two false starts?"

Sarah shook her head. "I might have been drunk at the festival, but I still remember walking up to see you two kissing. That kiss was the stuff of someone who wanted to keep on kissing you indefinitely. She might be a bit hacked off that obstacles keep getting in the way, but tough titties. Jason went on a management course last week, and the trainer said obstacles are the stuff that make you inventive and, ultimately, make you stronger. I believe that. Eden works in a professional job, right?"

Heidi nodded. "She's in PR and marketing."

Sarah waved a hand. "She'll already have been processing this stuff. She'll have been sitting with her negroni, pondering if she wants to date the woman with the shit-sandwich kid. But ultimately, what she really remembers is you and your lips that she wants to kiss. Obstacles. If you really want to, you can get around them."

"Jason had to go away all week to learn this?"

Sarah snorted. "He did. He *so* owes me. Plus, he got his food cooked for him and got his bed made every single day. Bliss." She stopped, wagging a finger in Heidi's direction. "But you need to get in contact to see if she wants to meet up. Start again. Focus on the future, not on the past."

Heidi exhaled. Maybe her sister was right. She was just echoing what Meg had said the other week after disaster date one.

Sarah's finger was prodding her. "Do it now!" She checked her watch. "You've got a bit of time before you pick up Maya. That was another thing Jason brought home from his week away, which he jokingly calls working. The two-minute rule. If you can do something within two minutes of thinking of it, then do it. Then it's done and you're not thinking about it for the rest of the day. Action moves things forward."

Eden was keen on action, Heidi knew. "Makes sense."

"I told him it applies to changing the toilet roll, which he never used to do, and it's working! For now."

Heidi dug her phone out of her bag and pulled up Eden's number. That was the easy bit. Her finger hovered over her keypad, but her mind was blank.

"What should I say?"

Sarah smiled, putting a hand on her knee. "Something short, snappy, to the point. Fancy a third try at a date and I promise no kids, no dogs?"

Heidi nodded. "Good plan." She paused. "What if I can't get a babysitter?"

Sarah shook her head. "She can come to ours and stay overnight. I promise. Whatever day it is, we'll sort it out. Even if Max has to look after her."

Heidi raised an eyebrow. "My six-year-old nephew looking after his baby cousin?" She shrugged. "Sure, I don't see a problem."

Heidi typed it out, read it through, then sent it before she could second-guess herself. It was done.

Maybe she had been guilty of creating scenarios in her head when she hadn't actually asked Eden what she thought first. She was going to wipe the memories of dates one and two from her system and go again. She just hoped Eden was up for doing the same.

Chapter Twenty

Eden was wearing a new suit she'd got from an independent boutique in Camden. She'd had her eye on it for a while and been weighing up the pros and cons. But now she knew she had to impress the cool, sophisticated Caroline — as well as the sharp, tailored India — she'd decided to up her game.

When she walked into the kitchen of their shared flat, Lib glanced up from her phone and bowl of porridge. Then she did a double take.

That was when Eden was sure she'd got this one right.

"Erm, hello, Mrs Dressed-To-Kill." Lib stared. Then she stood, circling Eden, wanting a view from every angle. "Where has this gorgeously dressed goddess risen from?"

Eden felt her cheeks heat under Lib's intense stare. "I got it yesterday from that boutique down the road. The one we always gawp at but never go in." She and Lib had done just that quite a few times. But then, when they couldn't see any price tags visible on the displays, they'd decided it was probably too rich for their blood.

"You went in?"

"That's generally what you have to do when you want to buy something."

"And how was it?" If Lib's eyes could have popped out

on stalks, they would have. "I can't believe you went in. *Without me.* That's our store!"

Eden shook her head. "It can still be our store." She paused, heading over to the sink to pour herself a glass of water. She didn't want to chance anything else in this outfit. No food that might splash. She'd made sure to brush her teeth and do her makeup before getting dressed. "They were lovely in there, though. And you remember this?" She fingered the lapel of her navy blue and white chequered suit.

"Of course! It looks even better on." Lib shook her head. "I'm so borrowing it for my next power meeting."

"You have power meetings?"

"I'm going to make sure I have them now." Lib tilted her head. "So who or what is this in aid of?"

"It's for the meeting with India. I need to make an impression on her and Caroline for this project, and I hope this does it." Eden pulled up the collar of her crisp lemon shirt. "You think the shirt's okay? Not too much?" She'd tried on a white and a pink as well, but had settled for yellow. The woman in the shop had told her it complemented the colour of her eyes, and by that point, Eden had been so swept away with the look of it all, she'd have agreed to buy anything. She'd spunked up nearly £450, but she was thrilled with the end product.

"Shirt looks good." Lib gave her a thumbs-up. "And your matching Converse tone it down just that little bit. Make you look like you're trying, but not too hard. If you don't succeed today in this getup, there's no hope for anyone."

"I hope you're right."

Lib paused. "But this outfit also works the other way, too. How are you going to handle India? Because I hate to break it to you, but you look *smokin'*. Your suit, your hair." Lib waved a hand up and down Eden, just in case she was in any doubt what she was talking about. "This outfit might score you the contract, but it's not going to cool India's desire to go out with you."

Eden made a face. "Why is life so hard?"

Lib gave her a face only a close friend could. "Because you make it hard?"

"Shut up."

The truth was, Eden had been putting off thinking about letting India down. She had to get through the meeting first. Then, she'd deal with India personally. It was all the more imperative because she'd said yes to another date with Heidi. Although with all her work commitments this week and Heidi's packed weekend schedule, they'd yet to work out a date. Eden was okay with that. She could only deal with one big thing at a time. Once this meeting and India were out the way, she planned to give all her attention to Heidi.

It was the slowest take-off of a possible relationship she'd ever lived through, but maybe that was a positive. All the quick starts she'd had in her 20s had never worked out, had they? But she was back in the game, a toe dipped. Once today was over, she was ready to step into it with both feet; set sail, and see where it took her.

"My plan is for me and Johan to work our campaign magic, go for celebratory drinks, tell India it can't happen, and then arrange a date with Heidi."

Lib shook her head. "Who would have believed Mrs Sworn-Off-Relationships would be juggling two women? One of them a minor celeb?"

"I'm hardly juggling. I've only barely kissed one of them."

"You were tonsil-deep when I saw you."

Eden blushed, a warmth flooding through her at the memory. Yes, she had been. And it was something she was super-keen to do again.

"Once this week is over, I hope to be right back there again."

"Wearing that suit, I'd say anything is possible."

* * *

Johan sat down, his introductory spiel done. Now it was on Eden's shoulders, encased in a slight shoulder pad. That had been the only part of the outfit she'd been hesitant about, but the woman in the shop had told her it was essential to the shape. She was right.

Glancing down on her shoulder pads now, there was a subtle force radiating from them, transmitting down her whole body. Perhaps this truly was a power suit.

Eden took a deep breath and pulled up the first slide of the storyboard. Watching round the conference table were Caroline, India, David, and India's communications director, Adrian. Adrian looked like he worked in a food company, his suit not quite so tailored. India, on the other hand, looked like she'd just stepped out of Milan.

"As Johan said, we took you at your word that you wanted us to create something that truly pushed the envelope and made Chocolate Delight memorable to everyone. By the time this ad has aired, everyone's going to want some, and every child in the land is going to want some gorgeous lesbian parents, too."

Eden held India's gaze as she said the last bit, and saw the hint of a smile on her delicate features. It was a shameless play into her court, but if Eden couldn't do it, then who the hell could?

Caroline blurted out a shard of nervous laughter at Eden's words.

Eden turned back to the first screen of the storyboard: the mum making breakfast for the child. "Of course, you expect that, right? Mum making breakfast for her child. So far, so normal. The kid is happy about getting the crumpet with chocolate spread. What kid doesn't love that?"

She clicked to the next slide. "Then we see the progress of their day. The mum at work, the child at nursery." Click. "They get home, then we see the child on a stool getting chocolate spread all over his mouth. Mum finds him and tells him off." She'd have to remember to thank Heidi for that one when she saw her. Click. "She wipes his mouth, and puts him to bed, stopping en route to kiss his other mummy, who's just come in from work."

Eden swept her gaze across the room. Adrian looked like he'd just swallowed a litre of drain cleaner.

She carried on. Click. "The pair finally come together in the kitchen, where the just-home Mum holds up the jar of Chocolate Delight and gives her partner a sexy smile. She walks over, she smears a little spread onto her lip, and she kisses it off, giving her a loving look." Click. "Cut to the following morning with the three of them at breakfast, more relaxed, it's the weekend. The child with chocolate spread on his face, happy as a lark. The women exchange looks and drink their coffee. We finish by telling the world that your product is for the whole family. For their morning, their afternoon and their evening delight."

Eden paused. The whole way through the storyboard, India hadn't given much away. One nod, that was it. Meanwhile, Caroline's face was white as a ghost. As if she'd agreed to it in principle, but now it was getting real, she wasn't sure about any of it.

"Of course, we have the happy, bouncy, more everyone-friendly ad to fall back on with a man and a woman. But this would cause the splash you're after. If you put this ad prime-time, you'd get column inches for and against by the skipful. Look at Greggs when they launched their vegan sausage roll. The papers went mad, like it was the end of the world. The final result? Greggs sold out of vegan sausage rolls all over the country.

"No publicity is bad, which I'm sure you know. This would start a conversation, and make your spread the sexy option. Plus, it would get the gays eating it by the caseload." Eden paused, aware India still hadn't said anything. "What do you think?"

India uncrossed her legs and sat forward, taking a deep breath. "I think I love it. I've been sitting here wondering if putting on a lesbian-focused ad would be bad because I'm a lesbian." She pressed her index finger into her chest, her gaze fully on Eden. "Is it a little obvious, a bit too much? But then I realised, straight execs greenlight straight ads all the time, and they never ask themselves this question. By that token, I shouldn't either." She cupped her hands together. "We might need a little more discussion of details, but overall, let's do it. The public is ready for this, and the FMCG market won't know what's hit it."

Johan frowned. "FMCG? Isn't that a bad thing?"

"Fast-moving consumer goods," Eden whispered.

He nodded. "Of course."

India gave her a broad smile. "I'm thrilled. Thank you so much, Eden and Johan, for all your hard work, and that of the team. The treasure hunt's all wrapped up, all the discs back and customers happy. I can't wait to see the finished ad. Don't you agree, Adrian?"

Looking at Adrian's face, Eden was pretty sure he didn't agree one bit, but he couldn't say much about it, could he? Not with the company head and star of consumer TV sitting beside him. "Can't wait to see it jump from idea to screen."

Eden would love to take Adrian on at poker. She'd wipe the floor with him every time.

Johan and Caroline left the room, and Adrian excused himself to the bathroom. That left Eden, India and David. Could he feel the change in energy, the charge in the air? Perhaps, because suddenly, David had somewhere better to be, too.

Then it was just the two of them. Eden cleared her throat, hoping her makeup was doing its job of covering the blush rushing to her cheeks.

When she glanced up, India's gaze was trained on her, sweeping up and down with an approving stare.

"Great presentation." India pushed herself off the table she'd been leaning against, walking towards her. "I have to say, that suit looks incredible on you. Like it was made for you." When India drew level with Eden, she flicked something from her shoulder, her dark eyes holding Eden in place. "I was listening to every word you said. I had to. It was impossible to look away."

Eden took a step back, panic washing down her. She had to hold her nerve and just put it out there. She clutched the desk behind her for certainty.

"Are you free for dinner tonight? A little celebration of your stellar campaign, a glass of champagne to toast your stunning new look?"

Eden gulped, shaking her head. "I'm afraid I'm not going to be able to have dinner with you tonight. I hope that doesn't affect our working relationship, though. My circumstances have changed. Plus, is it a good idea to mix work with pleasure?"

"If I never mixed work with pleasure, I'd never have any pleasure." She paused, frowning at Eden. "Hang on, you're serious?"

Eden nodded. "I'm afraid so."

A gamut of emotions flashed over India's face, but she didn't say a word. Instead, she took a deep breath and composed herself, as Eden was sure she'd been taught to do in whatever finishing and then business school she'd attended. Then she flashed Eden a smile that wouldn't quite stick to her face, no matter how hard she tried.

"I didn't see that coming, but no, of course it won't affect business. If I mix them, I don't let the pleasure affect the business decisions. A shame, though, because I think we could have had quite a lot of pleasure."

Eden's stomach rolled for all the bad reasons, but she managed to keep her face stoic. She hoped India was true to her word and wasn't going to use this against them.

"You've met someone else?" Almost immediately, India held up a hand. "You know what, that's none of my business. You have your life, and I have mine. I get that. I don't need details." She paused. "But I've booked a hotel in town and I need to eat. So how about a drink before I do that. Just one drink, no strings attached? To celebrate the work we're doing, and because I like you. Friends go out with each other for drinks, right?"

Eden took a deep breath while she considered that. She was pretty sure her and India weren't going to be true friends, but you never could tell. She'd taken the news that Eden was bailing on their date with grace. One drink couldn't hurt, could it?

She nodded, ignoring the warning tap on her shoulder. It would be fine. She was a 40-year-old grown woman, for goodness sake.

"A drink would be lovely. And you can tell me all about your trip to New York."

India grinned. "It involves a lot of New Yorkers, so prepare to hear a lot of swearing." She paused. "I'm staying at the Mondrian on the river. Perhaps we could go for a drink on the South Bank?"

Chapter Twenty-One

Heidi's mum was a retired business and journalism professor. She was far better read than either of her daughters, but Heidi had picked up her love of reading and also of live theatre. Her mum had insisted on taking her to see a new play at the National Theatre for her birthday week as well as treating Heidi to an early dinner. Her dad had come over to babysit Maya, and her mum was paying, too. She'd have preferred to be going out with Eden, but at least that date was on the horizon. Tonight, she was enjoying her mum's company.

They ate at a restaurant on the South Bank in the Royal Festival Hall, overlooking the Thames. The evening was settled after a day of rain, the moonlight shimmering on the river. Nights like these reminded Heidi why she loved London, living this close to so much culture. The air in the restaurant was seared with grilled meats and fish, the volume cranked a little higher since their arrival.

On the way in, Heidi spotted posters advertising kids' activities in the summer holidays. That would be perfect for Maya. Heidi had fond memories of her mum bringing her to pantomimes and children's exhibitions at the South Bank. Heidi doing the same with Maya would please her mum. What her mum wasn't so pleased with was Heidi's increased workload while her daughter was still so young.

"She's not even two yet. She's still very impressionable, still learning. You'll never get this time back with her."

Much to her annoyance, Heidi thought the same. "You might be surprised to hear I agree with you. But it's not easy when it's just me. I'm responsible for the child-rearing and the moneymaking."

She could see her mum wanted to say 'I told you so', but kept her mouth shut. For now. Perhaps Dad had put a word in for her.

"And before you say I knew that when I got pregnant, you're right. But this is something even two parents struggle with, too."

"Of course it is. Kids are expensive and exhausting."

Heidi sat up. Her mum had never said anything like that before. "Just as an aside, were we disgusting as kids?"

Her mum gave a gentle chuckle. "Of course you were. One particular night that sticks in my memory is when you were sick in your bed. I hope Maya never does that to you. Anyway, you were sick, it woke Sarah up, then because you were crying, she got into bed to cuddle you. Thus getting covered in sick, too."

Heidi recoiled, laughing. "I'm sorry."

Her mum smiled. "It's all part of the job."

"Did Dad help you clear it up?"

Her mum let out a deep laugh. "What do you think? Your father is a lovely man, but not very hands-on when it comes to children." Her mum took a sip of her wine and sat back.

They'd eaten delicious tuna steaks tonight and Heidi had

finished with honeycomb ice cream covered in hot chocolate sauce. Which, for once, she didn't have to share. It had been divine. Heidi checked her watch. They should get the bill if they wanted to get to the theatre on time.

She hadn't told Eden it was her birthday on Friday. Their relationship was too new. She'd celebrate this one with close friends and family, but she hoped Eden might be a part of that group soon. They'd left messages on each other's phones trying to nail down a time when they could meet. Eden was busy till tonight with work. Heidi would try her again tomorrow.

"You know what you need to do with your business?" Her mum leaned back as their bill was brought. She asked for the card machine, and the waiter nodded, turning to get it. "Charge more. That way, your income doesn't go down, just your hours. Time is what you need to claw back."

Charge more. Heidi knitted her eyebrows together as a lightbulb lit in her head. Perhaps that was the answer she'd been looking for.

Her mum paid the bill, leaving her tip in cash on the silver tray. "That way, you can make more time for Maya, but also more time for yourself. Because I haven't stopped banging the drum about you meeting someone, either. You'll be a better mother if you're loved and supported by a partner, and Maya will benefit from that, too."

"Even if it takes away from time spent with her?"

"If you're happier, she'll benefit far more from the time you spend with her anyway."

Maya Snr got up, pushing her chair under the smooth wooden table and tucking her dark greying hair behind her ear. She'd had it cut short recently and it suited her. Her yellow dress was on-point, too, popping against her dark skin. Her mum always said yellow was her spirit colour. Heidi didn't doubt it.

As they walked out of the restaurant, she threaded her arm through Heidi's. "We got through that whole meal without me asking you about that new woman. Sarah said you saw her again." She glanced Heidi's way. "Is anything happening? I don't want details, I know how you are. Just a yes or no."

Heidi ground her teeth together. Why was it that anything her mum asked about her life felt like an intrusion? When Heidi had become a mother, she'd vowed to get closer to her mum, to make their relationship stronger. While they were definitely seeing more of each other since she'd moved and had Maya, Heidi wasn't sure she'd succeeded in her mission. She needed to open up a little for that to happen.

"Sort of." The words were thorny coming out of her mouth, but she ploughed on. "It's early days, but I hope something might come of it. She seems lovely, and she even met Maya last weekend after my babysitter let me down and I had no choice."

Her mum stopped in her tracks. "She's met Maya? Isn't that a bit soon?"

And there it was — the judgement. The implication it wasn't how her mother would do things. But Heidi's life wasn't her mother's, was it?

"It is what it is, Mum. It was either that or cancel the date, and that wasn't an option. I introduced her as a friend, and Maya was none the wiser. So relax, Maya's not scarred for life. Plus, she's agreed to another date with me, even after meeting Maya."

"Why wouldn't she? She's a wonderful little girl."

"She's your granddaughter, you have to say that." Heidi squeezed her mother's arm, the cue for them to start walking again.

Two women walking just ahead of them went to walk out the main door of the Royal Festival Hall, but one of them walked straight into the glass door, smacking her head with an audible thwack. Heidi stifled a laugh, but even if her mum had seen it, she kept walking. A few moments passed before she spoke again.

"You've got a lot to offer, even with a daughter. Just remember that. Both your dad and I are very proud of you."

Heidi gulped. Now it was her turn to stop walking. "You already bought me dinner. I know it's my birthday week, but there's no need to go overboard." But as soon as the words were out of her mouth, she wanted to push them back in. Their relationship wasn't one where declarations of love and pride were thrown into the air so readily. Yes, they were always there for each other, but putting it into words? That wasn't their way.

However, if Heidi wanted to change the way they communicated, perhaps it started with accepting compliments and not batting them away as she just had. That's how she wanted to bring Maya up. She should practise what she preached.

She turned and hugged her mum. She was stiff at first, and Heidi hoped she hadn't wounded her with her words. "What I meant to say was, thank you. I'm proud to have you as my mum, too."

Then her mum's arms were around her, squeezing her tight. A wave of love and warmth spread up Heidi, from the tips of her toes to her scalp. She squeezed her eyes tight shut. Heidi was grateful to have been given the parents she had. She hoped Maya felt the same way one day, too.

When her eyes sprang open, she saw a woman walking in she vaguely recognised, but her brain couldn't quite place her. A friend of a friend? Facebook friend? Recent guest at a wedding? Heidi met so many new people on a weekly basis, her brain struggled to keep up. Whoever this woman was, she was slickly dressed, with eyes that snagged Heidi's attention.

Behind her, another sharply dressed woman followed her in, smiling. The first thought that crossed Heidi's brain was 'nice suit'. Before she realised who was *in* the suit.

The name and face that had been reverberating around her brain for the past few weeks.

Eden. Who was laughing at something the other woman was saying.

Heidi had no claim on her, she knew that. Eden could dress however she wanted and walk around laughing with any woman she pleased. It was her life.

The problem was, Eden and this woman looked good together, with their tailored suits and their glossy hair. Did Heidi and Eden look so well matched?

Heidi couldn't control her response to seeing them together. She wanted to spring out of her mother's grasp and rush over to Eden, pushing her companion away.

She knew who she was now. It was India Contelli, one of the most eligible lesbians in the UK. But it wasn't the famous lesbian Heidi was interested in. Nope, her heart was pulling in the direction of Eden Price.

Yes, they were just walking and laughing. But that was

enough. Seeing Eden and India together made her stomach plummet in a way it hadn't done in years.

Heidi and Eden had kissed once, and had two terrible dates since. They hadn't exchanged vows or even slept together. Despite that, Heidi was already thinking in terms of Eden being hers. Heidi and Eden. It had a ring to it.

Even if this was a business meeting — she knew they were working together — Heidi hadn't thought they were on such good terms that they'd go for a drink together. Go for dinner. Then do whatever they might do after that. The punch of reality winded her.

Eden had said she was working tonight. This might be work. But every emotional brake Heidi had was screeching as she pressed them.

As Heidi pulled back from her mother's embrace, Eden and India walked past, oblivious. Then India put out a hand and touched Eden's arm as she said something. Eden didn't shake it off.

Heidi froze. If her heart had been soaring, Eden had just taken aim and hit it first time. Was this a work thing, or was there something more? She wanted to think it wouldn't happen, but it could. They hadn't discussed anything about being exclusive. Hell, they'd hardly managed an hour together, just the two of them. Whereas Eden and India were disappearing up the stairs to the bar now, enjoying each other's company uninterrupted.

"You've got a lot to offer, even with a daughter." Wasn't that what her mother had said? She knew it was true, but was it enough for Eden? Would her head be turned by India Contelli?

More laughter sailed down the stairs as the pair disappeared from view.

Heidi closed her eyes as her mum took hold of her arm.

"What's wrong? You look like you've just seen a ghost."

Heidi shook herself. She had to believe this was just work for Eden. Even though her stomach felt like it had been sawn in two.

Chapter Twenty-Two

As Eden walked through the glass door into the restaurant bar, a trickle of something familiar slid down her senses. What was it? She glanced around the semi-full bar, but couldn't see anyone she knew. She stopped for a moment as India walked on ahead, and then it hit her.

The smell. Or rather, *Heidi's* smell. But also, the hint of geranium.

She twisted her neck as she always did when she smelled it. Did she expect her gran to be stood there? Sometimes. More likely, someone in the restaurant was wearing Heidi's perfume, or her gran's. Eden did a final check. Definitely no Heidi. That was important. She didn't want her getting the wrong idea.

When she glanced back up, India was already sat at the bar, smiling in her direction. "Everything okay?"

Eden nodded. "Fine." She packed away her thoughts and focused on her client. "You're sitting at the bar. I would have thought you were more used to sitting at tables."

India smiled. "I guess you don't know me very well, do you?" She ordered a tequila and tonic from the barman, and Eden asked for a gin and tonic.

"You're on telly. You're a bit posh. Surely you don't like bar stools."

India laughed. "I've spent my life fighting against my background. Yes, I come from money, I can't help that. But I try to treat people well, do the right thing. Just because I was brought up with a silver spoon in my mouth, doesn't mean I'm a fan of silver." She leaned forward. "Plus, in the movies, the people who sit on bar stools are always the coolest. Everyone knows that."

The barman brought the drinks and India thanked him, slipping him a tip there and then. "Here's to us working together. A dream partnership."

Eden clinked her glass to India's and took a sip. The scent of Heidi's perfume was still clinging to her nose.

"So tell me, why the change of heart on our date? Is it because I have money? Or that I've had a snippet of fame? Because if it's either of those, they shouldn't have a bearing on us. I'm just a regular person behind it all."

Eden doubted that. Eden had been brought up by her grandmother and they'd sometimes not had enough money for food. She knew poverty far more intimately than she let on. Which was why she treasured money now, perhaps more than was healthy.

"It's not that. I met someone just before I met you, but things weren't finished. We met up again recently, and there's something there. It's not gone smoothly so far, but I can't ignore how I feel about her." Eden's heart was banging against her bones as she spoke. She wasn't sure what was going on. But *something* was. She could feel it in her heart and in her soul.

"So I was just a little bit too late." India stirred her drink. "Story of my life." She shook her head. "My last girlfriend cheated on me, so I understand complications as well as the next person."

Eden shook her head. "There's been no cheating. Just a bit of miscommunication, that's all." She paused. "If it makes you feel better, I'd say your last girlfriend was an idiot."

"Thanks." India smiled. "You're not so bad yourself." She sighed. "It's a shame, because most people want the famous me, the India they see on the TV or in the boardroom. You don't, which I like. I can just be a regular woman, too. I can be hurt." She put a hand to her face. "You know what, ignore me. This drink is clearly going to my head even after two sips. I'm being far too melancholy for a celebratory drink, aren't I?"

Eden smiled. "You can be whatever you want to be."

India put out a hand and rested it on Eden's arm. "That's the thing, I normally can't. But with you, I can." She exhaled. "Talk about wrong time, wrong place."

Eden swallowed. She had to handle this with care, she knew. "I'd say more right time for business, wrong time for love."

India looked up and held her gaze. "You're right." She drained her drink and signalled for another. After the hefty tip, the bartender didn't need telling twice. "If nothing else, I'm excited about what this campaign might achieve. It's about time we shook up middle England, isn't it?" Then she wound her fingers around Eden's wrist and held on tight, leaning in until her lips were inches from Eden's. "But if things don't work out with this woman, let me know, okay?"

Chapter Twenty-Three

"And how acrobatic do you like to be? Do you like shots where you're jumping?"

The groom was called Stuart and his face told Heidi he wasn't a jumper. "Not really what we had in mind." He glanced at Tiffany, the bride, for confirmation of that. She nodded her head more than she needed to.

Heidi tapped her keyboard and smiled. "No to action shots, got it. It's just that they're very popular right now." Heidi had spent countless minutes getting brides, grooms and their wedding parties jumping in time. She had a fool-proof system.

"I was thinking more classic. Like the ones on your website. Looking into each other's eyes, holding hands, standing in front of our wedding cars. Just the regular kind of stuff." That was Tiffany again, who was looking at Stuart for reassurance. These two were a match made in vanilla heaven.

"Classic shots. Got it. I think that's everything. Looking forward to capturing the perfect memories of your big day."

Stuart and Tiffany beamed. They loved that last line, couples always did. It spoke to the heart. Today, her heart was the very last thing Heidi wanted to think about. Not when India Contelli might be vying with her. She wasn't sure she could compete with a celebrity.

As Heidi got on the tube to pick Maya up from nursery, she settled into her seat and read the ads overhead. But the first one her eyes settled on was for a dating website.

She closed her eyes. It was only four stops to home.

The nursery was situated a five-minute walk from her house, right beside a kids' playground. Heidi was 15 minutes early, so decided to wait. She walked across the deserted space and sat down on one of the swings, the metal ropes digging into her sides. They weren't built for adults. The playground was laid with springy outdoor flooring, daffodils lining its edges.

This afternoon, she was going to draw with Maya, and do some gardening with her. Quality time, as her mother would say. How she'd be impressed with Heidi's parenting skills today. Heidi was looking forward to some time with her daughter. To focus on something that wasn't Eden.

Her phone buzzing in her pocket broke her thoughts and she pulled it out. A message from her sister. Heidi clicked. When she read the message, her stomach lurched.

'I think you should have a look at these pics. I hate to be the bearer of bad tidings, but this is your Eden, right?'

Something cold slithered down Heidi's back. She didn't want to click, but she did anyway.

An image of Eden and India filled her screen. They were sitting at the bar at the same restaurant she and her mother had gone to last night. The caption read: 'India Contelli, enjoying a drink with a mystery woman.' Nothing more, just a statement of fact.

Heidi pushed her foot on the ground, pocketing her phone. Then she gripped the metal chains, closed her eyes, tucked her legs under, then out, until she began to swing. With the sun on her face and the sound of traffic in her ears, she tuned out the noise in her head. The noise telling her to believe her thoughts. She was successful for a couple of minutes.

But when she opened her eyes again, the imprint of India's and Eden's faces were all she saw floating in the sky above. The picture was grainy, but showed India leaning in, and Eden laughing. One thing was for sure, they didn't look like they were talking business.

Heidi pumped her legs some more, going higher and higher. Kids never had thoughts like these on swings, did they? Kids were in the moment, happy. She could learn a lot from them.

Heidi needed to speak to Eden, if Eden still wanted to talk to her.

She hadn't missed this part about dating.

The uncertainty.

The part that made you feel like you were going mad.

Chapter Twenty-Four

Eden shook her head at the photo. Someone at the bar must have snapped it. Eden's first taste of secondhand fame left a nasty taste in her mouth. India wasn't a face everyone would recognise, but she was a public figure. She'd had two TV series that had garnered a cult following on BBC2. Plus, she was outspoken, and constantly on news debates about LGBT issues. India was news.

But holy fuck, Eden and Heidi were still too fragile for this. Had she seen the photos? Would she be reading more into it? Eden would be if the shoe was on the other foot.

Eden had tried to call her earlier, but it had gone to voicemail.

Her gut twisted. She'd sent a text instead, telling Heidi she hoped they could arrange a date soon. That she'd call her tonight.

However, Eden wouldn't rest until she'd spoken to her. She would deal with this the only way she knew how — with the truth. She wasn't playing Heidi, and the sooner she could let her know that, the better. Eden wasn't her mother, who led people on and let them down. Who played with people's emotions. But she'd be the first to admit that with Heidi and India in her life, it was getting more unpredictable by the day. She was holding onto control, but only just.

She was just glad she was working from home today. She couldn't take the scrutiny of everybody in the office thinking there was something going on with her and India. They should be happy she was taking time for a client. But Eden knew what they'd really be thinking.

Lib appeared half an hour later, bags under her eyes. Her mum being ill was taking it out of her. Eden got up and put the kettle on, then sat back down at her desk in the corner of the living room.

"How did you sleep?"

Lib grabbed a bowl from the cupboard, followed by a box of Shreddies. Lib had recently watched a show on Netflix about tidying up, and had rearranged their cupboards so they housed items that made sense together. Now the cereal bowls were with the cereal; the tea bags with the mugs. It had been a revelation to Eden.

"Like the dead." Lib yawned, stretching her arms above her head. "You?"

"Fitful." Eden paused. "Some photos of me and India have appeared online."

Lib tilted her head. "Doing what?"

"Having drinks."

Lib sat down on the sofa, spoon paused over her food. "You can have drinks. You work with her."

"But what if Heidi sees it?"

Lib smiled. "If she does, you explain it. You're not married, you haven't even shagged yet."

Eden got up to make them both a cup of tea. "Since when did you get so sanguine about shit like this?"

Lib sighed. "Since I deal with my dying mother every day.

Death puts things into perspective. I've been listening to a lot of cancer podcasts lately, to see if they can help my mum. You know what they all say?"

Eden shook her head. "Tell me."

"That you shouldn't sweat the small stuff. Because the small stuff leads to knots in your body, which leads to toxins being released, which leads to stress, which leads to cancer. It's just some innocent photos. Call her and tell her." Lib began to munch.

Eden waited to see if she had any more words, but that appeared to be it.

"You can't tell me this wouldn't bother you."

Lib finished her mouthful before she replied. "Of course it would. But I'm too busy observing your weird life. You've gone from being eternally single, to having two women fighting over you. One of them being a TV star. That you're choosing the single mother over the TV star is the hilarious thing. But it's the right move. You're opting for the one that's likely got a chance to succeed. India Contelli and you would never work." She paused. "Also, we've run out of chocolate spread, so you think you could tap up your contact and get us some more? Or will she not be delivering now you didn't do the decent thing and sleep with her?"

"Good to see you've got my best interests at heart."

"Always," Lib said, giving her a grin. "I'm not saying there won't be work to do. But if you've done nothing wrong, then you just need to tell Heidi that. No drama. At least, in an ideal world there would be no drama. But we don't live there, do we?" Lib finished her cereal and put down her bowl. "After this fuck-up, you just need to show her she means more to you than TV lady."

Eden sat down at her desk, then spun around to face her friend. "How do I do that?"

"I dunno. Do something that would mean a lot to her. But sort it out, please. This thing between you two has been going on too long. One of you needs to make a proper move. You did it at the festival, so why you've waited this long to make your next move is beyond me."

"We have been trying. The universe keeps conspiring against us."

Lib rolled her eyes. "If you want to make this work, you'll find a way. If Maya means a lot to Heidi, arrange something that involves both of them."

Eden tilted her head. "You're a little genius. Children *do* mean a lot to their parents. Normal parents, that is."

Lib smiled. "That's generally the case."

Eden was pumped now. "I'm going to suggest doing something with Maya. That should go down well."

"So long as it's not sending her to boarding school, all good." Lib yawned again, arms over her head. "And if you're not keen on India Contelli, ask her how she feels about dating an estate agent."

"Who do you know who's an estate agent?"

Lib grinned. "Me. I'm doing some part-time work to help a friend. Who knows, I might not go back to web developing. I might truly find my calling."

Eden laughed. "I'll be sure to ask her first thing, next time I see her."

"After you've got some more chocolate spread from her first. Priorities."

Chapter Twenty-Five

Eden had bullet points written on a notepad. She'd done more preparation for this phone call with Heidi than she sometimes did for appraisals with Caroline. Mainly because, when it came to her work, she knew what she was doing.

Phone calls to prospective girlfriends were a different ballgame. Eden took a deep breath, then pressed the green button. Here went nothing. As the call connected and the ringing began, a spiky heat crept up her spine. She was half hoping Heidi picked up, half hoping it went to voicemail. Either way, when she swallowed, she could taste dread.

After three rings, Heidi picked up.

"Hi." There was already a sigh in her voice.

Eden gritted her teeth. "Hi. How are you?" Terrible first line. What happened to her notes? Hearing Heidi's voice, all her plans had flown out the window.

"I've had better days."

Eden bet she had. "I just thought I'd call because I don't know if you've seen the photos in the press today?"

"I have. My sister sent them through. She recognised you from the festival."

"Right." Eden paused. "I miss the us that was at the festival."

A slight temperature shift as Heidi gave a gentle laugh. "With everything that's happened since, it's almost as if it never happened."

Eden's voice dropped an octave. "It did. I remember. Plus, I've got photos, just to prove I'm not going mad."

A pause. Was Heidi smiling on the other end of the phone? Even a glimmer of a smile? Eden decided she was. "I wanted to let you know those photos last night were strictly work."

"It's not just the photos, Eden. I saw you last night. I was out for my birthday with my mum—"

"It was your birthday?" Eden's heart slumped.

"It's on Friday, but that doesn't matter."

"It kinda does. Your birthday's in two days and you didn't tell me?"

"We haven't really shared all the details of our lives, have we? You being out for drinks with India Contelli, for instance? You mentioned in passing she was involved in the campaign, but not that you were on having-drinks terms."

Yep, Heidi was pissed off. "I didn't realise we'd be photographed. It was just work. She's actually really lovely." Why had she said that? Hadn't she scrubbed out any mention of India being lovely from her notes? Heidi didn't need to hear that. She needed to hear that she was the one Eden had been imagining kissing. Not India Contelli. Who, frankly, despite all her fame, was a bit of a hot mess. Particularly after a few tequilas. "Anyway, off topic. I didn't call you to tell you about my work and who I've been for drinks with."

"Good, because I know. It's all over the internet."

Direct, to the point. "I'm calling to see if you wanted to meet up again. I know we said the next time would be without kids and dogs, but now it's your birthday this week, I'd love it to be soon. Tomorrow or Friday? If it involves Maya, that's all good."

There was a pause on the other end of the line. All Eden could hear was her heartbeat, and her fractured breathing. If this was it and she was going to flunk out of both of her possible dates within the space of 24 hours, she would probably become a confirmed singleton. She could totally understand why every book, film or TV show revolved around relationships, because there was so much drama attached. The only relationships that meant anything to her were her friendships. Making this phone call was so out of character, but Heidi didn't know that. She wasn't to know she was the architect behind the new Eden.

Heidi cleared her throat. "I'm working tomorrow, and I already have family plans for my birthday. Plus, I'm meeting a friend for lunch. So you're a little late."

Eden wasn't so easily defeated. "What about breakfast?"

Heidi laughed. "You're keen. I'm taking Maya trampolining on my birthday morning."

Noise filled Eden's head. Trampolining. She used to be good at it. With her mum. Could she brave a trampoline park, knowing it might open up old wounds? If it meant seeing Heidi, she had to try. "I bet they serve breakfast there."

"You seriously want to come trampolining with us?"

Eden wasn't at all sure. She hadn't stepped foot on a trampoline in years. She hadn't dared. It might uncover too much. "Yes. I used to do trampolining in my summer holidays. I could teach you a few moves."

"I hate to break it to you, but the trampolining is for the

kids." She paused. "Plus, don't you have to be in work for all these big deals you've got on?"

"I can take a break for a few hours. I'd *like* to take a break for a few hours. What do you say?"

Heidi took a few moments to reply. "I'll be at the trampoline park at Stratford on Friday morning from 10am. If you're serious, be there then. We can have a coffee while Maya has her lesson."

"And I can wish you a happy birthday." Eden exhaled. "Are you free this weekend for a more grown-up date? I'd love to cook for you."

Heidi paused for just a moment. "I booked the weekend off to spend with my family. I'll let you know tomorrow."

Eden had to be happy with that. It wasn't a flat-out no. "I'll see you Friday to wish you a happy birthday. And Heidi?"

"Yes?"

"I'm looking forward to it already."

When the line went dead, Eden stared at her phone.

Now, on top of everything else, she had to get Heidi something impressive for her birthday. She knew just what that was going to be.

Chapter Twenty-Six

If you'd told Eden a couple of months ago she'd be at a trampoline park at 9.45am on a weekday morning, she'd have thought you were crazy. Yet, here she was. It even smelt like the hall she used to go to: excitement and adrenaline. Emotion swirled in the pit of her stomach, memories flooding her frontal cortex.

Eden didn't have many happy childhood memories created with her mum, but trampolining was one of them. School holidays and Saturday mornings had been punctuated with trampolining. Her mum had known the teacher and he'd always let her have a go when she came to pick up Eden.

Her mother had been good, too. Graceful. The only time in Eden's life she'd known that. Graceful wasn't a word you associated with Debbie Price. Hurried. Fractured. Forgetful. Crazy. These were all words Eden recalled from her childhood, words that could scar for life. Her mother hadn't been like the others. Troubled was the word her gran had used the most.

If Debbie Price had been a young mum in the 21st century, she'd probably have got the help or the drugs she needed. However, the world had been very different when Debbie was growing up in Croydon in the '70s. Then, Debbie had been categorised as a loose cannon, someone who did things her own way. Whatever things her mum had chosen, they'd never included Eden. Apart from trampolining.

Eden sucked in a breath. She was a little unsteady on her feet. Hot tears threatened to sting the back of her eyes. Oh fuck. She hadn't expected this reaction. When Heidi had mentioned trampolining, Eden had taken it as a sign. She knew trampolining. She remembered the moves, and might even be able to show them to Maya. Eden had suggested coming to show Heidi she was fine including Maya as a part of their relationship.

Now though, she was questioning that decision. She swallowed down hard. Far from impressing Heidi, she feared she might unravel. All Heidi had to do was pull on her emotional thread, and her nightmare might come true. Eden took a deep breath and walked through to the cafe where they'd arranged to meet.

Heidi was already at one of the white plastic tables with Maya, whose feet didn't reach the edge of her cream plastic chair.

Eden walked up to them, trying to control her breathing. She wasn't 13 anymore. She was a 40-year-old woman with a successful career. Eden was capable, assured.

"Hey." Shit, her voice was already wobbling.

Heidi looked up, giving her a weak smile. "You came." She got up to hug her.

Eden clung on a little too hard. "I said I would. Plus, this is the kind of date we do, right? A little weird, brightly lit, absolutely no chance of getting too close."

"Describing this as a date is stretching the definition.

You invited yourself to my daughter's trampoline session." She paused. "Now who's weird?"

Eden smiled. "Guilty as charged." She pulled out a chair and sat down. "Although I had an ulterior motive. I wanted to see you on your birthday and give you this." She pulled Heidi's present out of her bag and handed it over. The shape gave it away, square and flat. "Happy birthday."

Maya knelt up in her chair, her interest piqued. "Present!"

"It is." Heidi gave Eden a puzzled look. "What is it?"

"Open it and find out."

Heidi ripped off the paper, then grinned. "Oh my god, I love it." She glanced up at Eden. "You remembered."

Eden nodded. "Open it up."

Heidi flipped open the gatefold edition of PJ Harvey's first album. And then she gasped. "It's signed!" She clutched her chest. "How did you get this? I only told you it was my birthday two days ago."

Eden smiled. "We've done a lot of PR work with her record label, so I had an in. After you told me your mum threw your old signed copy away, I was going to see if I could replace it. This just sped up the request. I hope you like it." She also hoped it told Heidi exactly how she felt about her.

"I absolutely love it." She stared into Eden's eyes. "Thank you so much."

The sudden flash of chemistry almost punched the breath from her lungs. Eden leaned in, placing a gentle kiss on Heidi's lips. The charge of electricity it sparked nearly floored her. Eden opened her eyes and focused on Heidi, who was still staring at her lips. Eden's whole body shook.

"I really want to do that again, but the aforementioned

bright lights and toddler are holding me back." Heidi did it again anyway.

Desire crashed through Eden like a wave. With Heidi's lips on hers, she couldn't think straight.

Heidi pulled back, her breathing sketchy. She reached out a hand, her fingers gripping Eden's wrist. "Happy birthday to me." A wry smile crept onto her face. "Let's give it a repeat tomorrow, if you're free?"

Eden's grin couldn't have been any wider. "I'm free all day long."

"Perfect."

Clapping interrupted the moment. When Eden glanced up, a woman dressed in bright blue sports gear was telling them that trampolining for toddlers was about to start. Eden saw her speaking words, but couldn't quite make sense of them. Heidi's kisses had scrambled her brain.

Luckily, Heidi understood them. She grabbed Maya like she weighed nothing, motioning for Eden to follow. She did as she was told. Once Maya was safely placed on the trampoline and her bottom-lip quiver dealt with, Heidi walked back to Eden, sat in a row of chairs lined up along a wall.

"You look sad." Heidi sat beside her, glancing up at her daughter, then back to Eden. "Is the trampoline park not living up to your expected highs?"

Eden shook her head. "It's way more fancy than the one I used to attend. There was no such thing as a trampoline park in my day. When I learned the moves, I did it on a single trampoline in the middle of a sports hall, with no net around it. Not in a complex like this with so many trampolines all pushed together. You could break a bone in my day."

Heidi sat back, not taking her eyes from Maya, but talking to Eden. "No nets. I remember that. Did you also get squashed into the boots of cars with no seatbelts?"

Eden shook her head. "I was an only child. Besides, my mum didn't drive, so we didn't have a car."

Heidi turned her head. "How did your mum cope with a child and no car?"

Eden shrugged. "We got lifts or took a bus."

Heidi kept her eyes on Eden this time, the bright strip-lighting overhead making her squint. "So is this bringing it all back for you, even if it is on a far bigger scale?"

Eden let out a strangled laugh. "Kinda." She exhaled. "It's making me feel a bit emotional, actually." She put a hand on her heart. "The last time I had a trampoline lesson, I was 13. My mum disappeared that day and I didn't see her again for two years." Eden sat with her head down, not quite knowing what to do with all the feelings swirling within her.

"You were 13 and your mum walked out? Wow."

Eden moved her mouth one way, then the other. She still hadn't looked up. "It was hard at the time, but it made me into who I am today. Stronger. More capable. Independent. Life events shape us like that, don't they?" But in her case, it had left her misshapen.

She still recalled her gran picking her up from the lesson, which was unusual. Not knowing how to break it to her. The crack in Eden's heart had mended over the years, but the scar was still visible.

Eden looked up. Two teenage girls walked in, climbing onto the trampolines to their right. They could have been her all those years ago. They were babies. Only, she bet they had parents who would wonder where they were if they didn't come home.

And then, it was all too much. As her panic rose, Eden fought to gain control of her emotions, but she was fighting a losing battle. Right there in the middle of the trampoline park, with the screech of children in her ears, tears began to leak from her eyes. Closely followed by screeching alarm.

No. No. No.

This couldn't happen now.

Eden put her head down to try to disguise what was happening, but she had no control over this. Soon, her body was shaking with the force of the sobs.

She heard movement, then there was an arm around her, fingers squeezing her shoulders. "I've got you." Heidi's voice was like honey, soothing her woes. Also, her lips were dangerously close to Eden's earlobe, making her body come alive even though she was crying. How arousal and hurt could be alive in the same moment was a mystery to her, but they were.

However, mixed in with all her crazy emotions was also embarrassment. She'd come here to impress Heidi with her child-friendly trampolining ways, and ended up blubbing on her shoulder. She wasn't about to run a master class anytime soon on how to seduce a woman.

Eden pulled back, missing the heat of Heidi's embrace as soon as it left her body.

"I'm sorry, this wasn't in my plans." Eden shook her head, blowing her nose on a tissue Heidi had just given her.

"Don't be silly. I think if something that big had happened in my life, I might be a little shaky around a trampoline, too."

Eden gave her a sad smile. "And yet, some of my happiest memories of my mum involve trampolines, too." She paused. "That's a weird sentence, isn't it? I'm sorry for sobbing on your birthday. Should I go before I ruin it completely?"

Heidi shook her head, holding out her hand. "I don't invite many people on my kid's playdates. Turns out, you're not many people. Plus, your sobbing has made me forget all about being pissed off at you about India Contelli. If that was the plan, it worked."

Eden blew her nose again, giving Heidi a tired smile. "I hope the present might have done that, too."

"And the kiss." Heidi squeezed her hand.

"It really was just a work drink, not something I thought the papers would pick up. But that's what happens when you go out with a minor celebrity."

"A lesbian celebrity, no less. If you wanted to make me insecure, it worked."

"That was the last thing I wanted. In a shoot-out between you and her, you win. Every time."

Heidi stared at Eden. "I hoped you'd think that." Her brown eyes swallowed Eden whole. Heidi brought Eden's hand to her mouth and kissed it.

That simple action shocked Eden out of her funk, and brought her back from her childhood to the here and now. To the present day. To beautiful Heidi, being so kind to her when she dumped all her baggage into her lap with no warning. Yes, Heidi came with baggage, but hers was currently jumping on a trampoline. Eden's baggage was far more hidden, and likely to spring out of nowhere at any moment.

Eden gave her a pained smile. "We've got history, me and you. We've snogged at a festival, we've had a terrible date, and we've lived through Poo-gate. When you think about it, we've already gone through far more than most couples manage in their first few years. I'm not going to trade that in for a TV star, am I?" She paused. "Especially with my stunning display of tears to add to the impressive roster this morning."

She was babbling. She was aware of that. Just like she'd done at the festival. But that was probably because Heidi was still holding her hand, having kissed it. Their skin was still touching and she longed for more of it. *So much more of it.*

Heidi glanced over at Maya, but she was happily playing with the other kids. She turned her attention back to Eden, shielding her eyes. "It's bright in here, isn't it?"

"Maybe the harsh lighting made me feel like I had to spill my emotions. Like being interrogated."

Heidi was silent for a few moments. "So did your mum come back?"

Eden chewed her bottom lip, nodding. "She did eventually. But then she left again. In the end, my gran cared for me. She took me in, because we lost the flat when Mum didn't pay the rent." Eden sighed. "It was all a very long time ago. I don't think about it much, because there's not much point. It was a pattern for Mum. She'd come back, get some money off my gran, promise me things, and then disappear. She was an actor, and she got work wherever. But I think more than anything, she just wanted to be free. But I was the casualty in her dreams. I was never in them in the first place."

Heidi's face was stricken. "What an awful thing for you to know. Do you still see her? Is she still alive?"

Eden nodded. "She is, but not really. I mean, she sometimes pops up in my life, but rarely. She's my Facebook friend."

"Which says everything that needs to be said about Facebook." Heidi frowned. "What about your gran? Is she still alive?"

Eden wiped her eye before she spoke. "She died seven years ago. She was a good age, but it was still hard. Now she's gone, I'm family-less. My uncle was my other anchor, but he died, too."

Heidi's mouth moved back and forth. "You've had a shit time, but things are going to get better. Starting with this place. We're going to come back when it's adults-only and do some trampolining, make some new memories to sit alongside the old ones. Plus, you can show me your moves." She raised a single eyebrow. "You do have the moves, right?"

Eden allowed herself a smile, feeling the lightness trying to break through. "I used to do a whole routine. I haven't done it for 25 years though, so I might be a little rusty."

"Like riding a bike." Heidi blinked. "You and me, sometime soon?"

Eden nodded. "I'd like that a lot. Let's make a date tomorrow night when I cook you dinner."

"I haven't had a woman cook me dinner in a very long time. I'm looking forward to that already."

The lust pooled in Eden's belly began to simmer. Heidi had that effect on her. They locked eyes, and for a moment, the bright lights overhead dimmed. It was just the two of them, sitting in their rocky relationship, both willing it to move to the next level. Eden was amazed they were still here, determined to outsmart all the obstacles they'd faced.

Heidi was leaning forward now, till her lips were inches from Eden's. Her tongue moistened her bottom lip before she spoke. "You know, I've kissed women in some odd places before, but never in a trampoline park." Her smiled inched up her face. "You make me do strange things, Eden Price."

Chapter Twenty-Seven

Heidi took a deep breath and knocked on Eden's red front door. This was it, wasn't it? The night to move things forward. They'd been dancing around each other for so long, making too many false starts. But now, she was at Eden's for dinner, and the ending of this evening didn't seem in doubt.

Maya was staying with her parents. If all went well, Heidi wouldn't be home tonight. She hadn't been naked with anybody since she was three months pregnant. That was a long time out of the game, and now she had stretch marks to add to the mix. How would Eden react to those?

She wasn't going to think about that just yet. First, she had food to eat. Hopefully followed by Eden for dessert. Goddammit, she wanted to fuck her. That was the thought running through her mind when Eden opened the door moments later. She tried to block out the thought of pressing Eden up against the hallway wall and kissing her hot lips, but Eden wasn't making it easy. In her fitted mustard trousers and baby blue short-sleeved shirt, she was presenting as the ideal candidate for Heidi's plans. Plus, her hair was like an art installation on her head.

Eden ran her gaze up and down Heidi, before it settled on her face. Her cheeks were slightly flushed as she leaned forward, taking Heidi's hand in hers, before planting a kiss on her lips. A brief kiss, but it helped to put a capital letter on this moment of doorstep reconnection. Eden pulled her inside, a hesitancy in her steps, a darkness in her normally crystal blue eyes.

Chemistry swirled between them, brushing over Heidi's skin and darting through her body, sharp and direct. It drew her in, drew her to Eden. The source of their attraction was more than physical, but that was all Heidi could see. She breathed in the aroma of garlic, onions and tomato from the kitchen. But she wasn't hungry anymore. The only thing she was hungry for was Eden. She'd waited long enough.

Heidi was about to tell Eden that when she felt something brush against her calf. She glanced down to see a tiny black-and-white kitten scampering down the hall. Eden smiled, pulling Heidi into the lounge, before scooping up her pet.

Alarm slithered through Heidi, because she knew how this went.

This was not in the script for tonight.

"Let me introduce you to Dusty, named for her penchant for being an impromptu hoover on our laminate floors." Eden waggled one of Dusty's paw in Heidi's direction. "Dusty, meet Heidi."

In response, Heidi braced herself, then began sneezing. Once, twice, three times. "Sorry." She tried to compose herself. "You didn't mention you had a kitten."

"I only picked her up last week. She's ten weeks old." Eden narrowed her eyes. "Are you not a cat fan? Because they can revoke your lesbian membership if you're not."

Heidi winced, before sneezing again. "I'm allergic, as you

can probably tell. We had a cat when I was growing up, but my body isn't used to them anymore. So while I like them, my body has other ideas." She glanced around, her eyes glazing over with tears. "Do you have a tissue?"

Eden frowned, putting Dusty on the floor and grabbing a handful of tissues. "This is going to be an issue, isn't it?" She put her hands on Heidi's waist as she dabbed her eyes. "And you're going to smear your carefully done makeup now, too."

"Did you see it when I walked in? Because I spent a lot of time on it." Heidi was glad she could smell the delicious aromas circling the flat, because she couldn't see anything. Her eyes were just a river of cat-induced tears.

"I did. And it looked gorgeous." Eden paused. "Okay, this is the universe throwing us another curve ball. I had grand plans for tonight. I was going to amaze you with my culinary skills, then wow you in the bedroom. But we can't do that if you're a streaming mess." She cleared her throat. "And now I really shouldn't touch you because I've been holding Dusty." She took her hands away from Heidi.

Heidi missed the contact as soon as it was gone. "It's fine. If you have allergy pills, I could take them and hope it sorts itself out." It would still take a while for her body to acclimatise, and even then, it might not work. The lust inside her was now stamping its feet. She exhaled, putting her hands on her hips.

Eden raised an eyebrow. "I have an idea. What if we get an Uber and go to your place? Did you say Maya was with your parents?"

Heidi nodded, blinking away her tears. "Don't you need to stay here with Dusty?"

Eden frowned again. "Let me text Lib. She should be home

soon. If she's coming back, I'll call a cab?" Eden was staring into her eyes, concentration creasing her face.

Heidi hesitated. Had she changed the bedsheets recently? Had she left anything incriminating lying around? She had no idea. "If we want to salvage this evening, I'd say getting a cab to mine might be the only option available." Heidi screwed up her face as tears still fell. "So long as you ignore the stuff covering the floor, including toys and clothes."

Eden chuckled. "So long as the clothes on the floor include the ones you're wearing at some point tonight, I don't much care what else is there."

That sentence was all Heidi needed to hear. "In that case, pack up the damn food and let's go."

Chapter Twenty-Eight

Heidi didn't say much when they pulled up. She was still blowing her nose and recomposing herself.

Eden got the bag of food, but her stomach was already turning cartwheels. Would she be able to stomach much food tonight? Maybe she wouldn't need to. She'd wanted to rip Heidi's clothes off ever since she'd opened her front door over an hour ago.

When she stepped into Heidi's flat, Eden immediately felt at home. It was on the ground floor of an old Victorian terrace, with ceiling height in its favour, as well as period features. But its greatest asset tonight was that it had Heidi in it. Just Eden, Heidi and nobody else. No kids, no animals, just them. It felt like she should tiptoe round this moment, in case anything else went wrong.

Eden followed Heidi into the main room with her kitchen at one end, her lounge at the other. She gave it an approving nod. "Nice place." She dumped the Tupperware containers on the kitchen counter before walking to the sofa, where Heidi was picking up magazines and plumping cushions.

Eden took her hand in hers. "You don't have to tidy up. I know you weren't expecting company. I'm not here to judge your cushions."

Heidi smiled. "Reflex reaction. Blame my mother. It's her influence."

"She doesn't sound like such a bad influence." Eden's gaze settled on a photo framed on the waist-height bookcase to her right. "Is that your family?" She recognised Heidi, Maya and Sarah in it.

Heidi picked it up, nodding. "This is all of us. Mum gets it done every year in February. This is this year's edition." She wiped her cheek. "My eyes are red because of an allergic reaction to cats that day, too." She winced. "Talking of which, I need to go and redo my makeup. I must look a bloody state."

Eden gave her a slow smile. "You look gorgeous, but if you'd feel better, go and do it. I'll get the food going again. Just show me where your pans are." She stepped forward, cupping Heidi's face with her hands, kissing first her cheeks, then her lips.

When that happened again, Eden immediately felt calmed. This hadn't been the ideal start to the evening, but it was going to be plain sailing from here on in. With her lips on Heidi's, anything seemed possible. She hoped Heidi felt it, too. When she pulled back and saw how wide her pupils were, she was pretty sure she had.

"Give me five minutes, okay?"

Eden nodded and walked back to the kitchen. She was cooking homemade meatballs and spaghetti with garlic bread; it wasn't fancy, but it was a crowd-pleaser. She had a bottle of Cabernet Sauvignon to accompany it, which she opened now to breathe. She figured they could both use a glass of wine to settle their nerves.

When Heidi appeared a few minutes later, Eden had the kettle on and the meatballs heating, the garlic bread poised to go in the oven. When she glanced up, she was relieved to see Heidi's face free of tears, almost back to date-ready Heidi.

"Feeling better?"

Heidi nodded. "Much better. Plus, I have a gorgeous woman in my kitchen cooking me dinner. That hasn't happened in a long time."

Eden studied her as she walked over, stopping when she reached the bench at the end of the kitchen counter. "Have you dated since you had Maya?"

Heidi shook her head. "You're the first. I've been focusing on being a parent." She got some wine glasses from the cupboard above the cooker. "That, and growing my business. They're both full-time jobs." She poured a glass of red for each of them and handed one to Eden. "What about you? Have you dated much?"

Eden gulped. Should she come clean? She answered before she had time to think about it. "Not at all since my gran died. I don't date. I hope you realise the effect you've had on me. I'm doing things I never thought I'd do."

Heidi stilled, staring at Eden. Her rich hazel eyes were scorched with want. "I'd love to have even more of an effect, if you'll let me."

Eden nodded, lust stripping off and racing through her body. Oh god, she wanted Heidi to fuck her now, up against this cooker. She had to calm down. It'd been far too long since she'd had sex with someone else, hadn't it?

Heidi held her gaze with her dangerous stare and Eden could have drowned in it. She forgot the bubbling pan of sauce and meatballs beside her. The low hum of the oven. Forgot everything except Heidi. Still she looked at her until Eden's heart kicked in her chest.

The stillness was both sweet and torturous.

Heidi broke first, licking her lips. "Should we turn the stove off and eat dinner later?" She squeezed Eden's hand. "I don't think I can wait to taste you any longer."

"That's the best idea you've had all night." Eden did as instructed. When she turned, Heidi was staring at her, hesitancy on her face.

"What is it?"

She twisted her foot. "I just want to warn you. I've had a baby. My body reflects that."

Eden gave a strangled laugh. "I want everything your body has to offer." She pressed her lips back to Heidi's. "Now, which way to your bedroom?"

Heidi picked up the chocolate spread in one hand, beckoning Eden with the other.

It was just like the scene Eden had imagined in her office when she was planning the campaign. She knew she was wet. Her insides clenched as she followed Heidi, a grin covering her face.

"I plan on keeping that smile on your face for a very long time tonight."

When they got to the bedroom door, Heidi backed her up against the doorframe. She brought her head to within inches of Eden's lips, enough to turn Eden's internal frenzy up another notch. If Heidi wanted her to be out of control, she was going about it the right way. Eden couldn't remember feeling this way, *this loose*, in a very long time.

Heidi stroked her cheek. "Have I told you you're beautiful?"

Eden quivered. "No." Her fingers gripped Heidi's belt. Her gaze was too intense, too personal. She squirmed under it, had to break it. "Are you going to kiss me?"

Heidi moved her lips so they were almost on Eden's. "You need to relax. Unwind." Eden's breathing hitched as Heidi's hand connected with the base of her spine, her other tugging her into the bedroom.

"Relaxing isn't my strong suit." She was good at planning and control. A girlfriend with a child and a cat allergy hadn't been in her plans.

"I never would have guessed." Heidi's hand was inside Eden's top, the warmth of her palm on Eden's bare skin. Eden ached liked she'd never ached before. It hadn't just been Heidi who hadn't slept with anyone for a while. Eden could match her, stride for stride.

Heidi's hands were sliding up her back, making Eden's brain tilt. She wanted those hands elsewhere. When they slid round to her breasts, Eden stilled. This was almost too much already, and she was still fully dressed. They weren't even kissing. If she flashed forward too hard, she might short-circuit.

"I have another problem." Heidi's voice was low and barely audible. "You're wearing too much." Her fingers set to work adjusting that, snapping open Eden's trousers, unbuttoning her shirt. Heidi made short work of Eden's clothes, before easing back her bra, taking in her full breasts with hungry eyes. Then suddenly, the temperature changed and time sped up.

Their mouths clashed together, sensation shooting through Eden. There was no more slow, steady. No more careful. Instead, Eden was ripping off Heidi's clothes, one part of her brain telling her to slow down, take her time; the other part wanting to take everything Heidi had to give.

Eden moved Heidi's pants down her legs, then stopped to admire her. She was lithe and toned, her light brown skin covering her deliciously. Heidi's gaze was fixed on Eden's mouth, dropping to her breasts and then back up. Eden knew what Heidi was thinking, because she was thinking it, too. But she wanted to take a moment to drink her in, because it had taken so long to get here.

"You're stunning with clothes on, even better without." Eden swept a hand over Heidi's bum cheek, moving into her space and kissing along her shoulder. Cool air prickled up her skin, and as she stepped forward another pace, their bodies touched. Both of them let out a groan.

Flesh against flesh ignited Eden's desire once more. The flames of it licked at her, and when Heidi pulled her close, it only drove it higher. She held Eden locked in place, a thigh jammed between her legs, kissing intensely, slowly. She took her time, driving Eden crazy till she thought she might explode.

When they eventually tumbled onto the bed, they fought for control. Somehow, Eden knew she wasn't going to win this one. When she gave up and Heidi rolled on top of her, she gazed into her dark eyes, emotion bubbling inside.

Heidi put a finger to Eden's lips, her smile crooked on her face. "Well done on letting me take control. I know it's not your natural thing. You'll get your turn." Her eyes sparkled as she dropped her lips to Eden's earlobe. "But for now, let me drive. You just have to enjoy the ride." Her words sent a torrent of fresh lust tumbling through Eden.

When Heidi's mouth closed over her nipple, building arousal with every skilled flick of her tongue, Eden gave in and let her. It wasn't a hardship. She wasn't sure how she'd come to meet this incredible woman, but she was going to do everything she could to keep her. This was the sort of Saturday night that had been missing in her calendar for quite a long time.

Heidi raised her head, then an eyebrow and jumped off Eden.

"Where you going?" That wasn't what she'd been expecting. But Heidi was back in seconds, unscrewing the jar of Chocolate Delight. Then she proceeded to dip a finger into it, and smear it onto both of Eden's nipples. "I just thought I'd give this a try."

Eden's brain short-circuited.

Heidi flicked her tongue and began licking with slow, skilled moves.

Below her, Eden thought she might die from pleasure, but she was determined to hang in there. Electricity crackled and sparked within her as Heidi finished her breasts, then spread some more on her stomach, an inviting line down to her navel. Eden's breathing sped up as Heidi's mouth crushed hers once again. She tasted chocolate and desire. It was a heady combination.

The next step was to let Heidi lick chocolate from her stomach, driving her crazy as she moved lower, her breast between Eden's legs, her nipple nudging her clit. Eden's head swam.

Heidi didn't stop for any more chocolate. Instead, she carried on going south, easing a hand under Eden's thigh, spreading her legs gently. With Heidi's hot breath over her pussy, Eden closed her eyes, allowing her head to sink into

Heidi's pillow. Heidi's tongue slid inside Eden, tracing sensitive flesh with knowing skill.

Eden moaned and writhed, but Heidi held her in place, her tongue doing its work. When she arrived at her clit, Eden bucked, and Heidi pulled back, adjusting her position. She took the opportunity to slide in a single finger, and Eden thought she might pass out. When Heidi sucked Eden back into her mouth and added a second finger, all thoughts receded from Eden's mind; there was only here and now.

Need simmered inside her as she allowed herself to be completely pulled under Heidi's spell. She raised her hips as Heidi's tongue worked with devastating accuracy, her fingers thrusting in and out of her wetness. Her orgasm began to thrum within her. She knew she was close.

Her body tightened around Heidi, and for a moment, it felt too intimate, too much. But when she looked down to Heidi's head between her legs, she was gazing up at her, too. When their gazes locked, Heidi stopped. Then she gave her a delicious wink, followed by a slow, firm stroke of her tongue.

Eden's fingers were tangled in Heidi's curls as her body tensed. With every thrust and flick, she climbed higher, until everything inside her tightened and she was balanced on that dangerous edge, held in place by Heidi's skill and her need to be in control. It was futile, though. As Heidi changed gears, Eden fell, tumbling over the edge, a thick sound emerging from her throat. In seconds, Heidi was on top of her, fingers still buried inside her, kissing her lips.

Eden groaned into her mouth as she came again to Heidi's thrusts, kaleidoscopic patterns dancing on her eyelids. All the while, Heidi kissed her. Eden didn't just feel her climax, she breathed it, tasted it.

Some moments later, they were still.

Eventually, Eden's surroundings seeped back into her consciousness. She wasn't at home where she'd intended to be; she was at Heidi's flat, in her bed. But it was quiet. Far quieter than her flat. There was minimal traffic noise, no flatmate. Just the sound of her heartbeat in her ears, the sound of her body applauding.

Heidi kissed her again, rolling sideways, eyeing her with a languid stare. "That was…" she said. "You were…" She didn't finish.

"Chocolatey?" Eden grinned as she rolled towards her, kissing her lips, leaving her face inches from hers.

Heidi's face was perfect, her skin smooth and soft. When their eyes locked, Eden knew this was one of those moments. She snapped it in her mind. A perfect moment of post-coital bliss. They were in the zone.

But these moments were fleeting. They didn't last. Because relationships didn't last, did they? But this moment could. If she allowed herself, she might even enjoy it. Weren't relationships just a series of these moments, all strung together? She concentrated on staying there, not casting her mind forward to the future.

Heidi narrowed her gaze. "What's going on in your brain? Because I'd like to think what just happened would leave you with only smiles. Yet every emotion under the sun just seemed to pass over your face."

Eden bit her lip, shaking her head. She thought she'd been more subtle. "It was amazing, really." She kissed Heidi's lips and the fuzzy edges returned. The cocoon-like state. Her landing was cushioned. When they drew back, Heidi's gaze was still questioning.

"Are you sure?" She put a hand to Eden's face, and the gesture was so tender, she gulped down tears. She wasn't used to such intimacy anymore.

Eden nodded. "Positive." She tried to roll away, but Heidi rolled with her, kissing her cheek, turning her face towards her.

"You know, whatever it is you're worried about, you can talk to me."

Eden tucked her chin into her neck, suddenly exposed. Yes, they'd just had sex, but talking was far more personal than that.

Talking uncovered topics it was far harder to run away from.

Chapter Twenty-Nine

The following morning, Eden woke with a start. She wasn't sure where she was until she turned her head and remembered.

Heidi.

Then she recalled her near post-sex meltdown and closed her eyes. The sex had been incredible and had lasted half the night. Plus, she *hadn't* melted down. Perhaps that was why she'd been avoiding such intimacy for so long.

She checked her phone. She'd only had four hours' sleep, but it had been worth it. She slid out of bed, careful not to wake a still-sleeping Heidi. Then she tiptoed to the toilet, stopping to throw on a T-shirt as she did. It smelt of Heidi. She pulled the material close. She passed Maya's room on the way, peering in to see pictures of Elsa on the wall, along with a row of teddy bears lined up along a tiny bed.

This was Heidi's life. She had a daughter. She had two smiling, happy parents. Eden gulped. She'd had none of that. It had often just been her, home alone. Could she cope with an instant family?

On the loo, Eden scrolled through Facebook. Johan had uploaded a photo from the Chocolate Delight competition that showed an image of the two of them, the winner and

India Contelli with a broad smile on her face. A contented glow lit her up. That competition had gone better than Eden could ever have imagined, and it had a whole lot of likes attached to the photo, too. She clicked on the likes. Her thumb froze.

It had been liked by Debbie Price. Her mother.

Eden stared at her phone like it was a bomb. She ground her teeth together. Her mum hadn't liked anything in at least a year. Why had she chosen this morning, of all mornings, to infiltrate her life? It was like she had a sixth sense.

Lib had told her to block her mum on Facebook. Even her gran had told her to. But Eden couldn't quite bring herself to do it. Every now and again, she liked something or commented. Every time it happened, Eden stalled.

She swallowed down hard, closing the Facebook app on her phone and giving herself a stern look in the mirror as she washed her hands. Heidi's handwash smelt like Love Hearts, which made her smile inside, if not externally.

Eden had read enough to know her mum didn't have to impact her day. She could carry on, go back to bed and deal with it later. She couldn't change her mother. She'd tried over the years. However, she could change her reaction to her. Her gran had always told her that. Her friends had told her, too. Now would be a good time. She took a deep breath, gave herself a firm nod of the head and walked back through to the bedroom, where Heidi was now awake.

"I thought you'd run off." Heidi gave her a lazy smile as she climbed back into bed. As soon as Eden was under the covers, Heidi's hands were underneath her top, stroking her back before landing on her breasts. She followed it up by pressing her warm, wet lips onto Eden's, and kissing her with slow, gentle precision.

Eden was immediately brought back to the here and now, her mind dizzy with pleasure. She was disorientated. Heidi dazzled her. Plus, she'd never known anyone who could switch off the power of her mother with a single kiss.

However, once Heidi's lips left hers, her mother began to inch back to the forefront of her mind.

"You look good in my T-shirt." Heidi gave her a sleepy grin, before yawning, stretching her arms above her head. "You find the loo okay?"

Eden nodded, doubt swirling in her mind like a looming cloud. "I got A grades in geography in school. I think that came in handy."

Heidi grinned. "Good." She scooted closer.

Eden tensed.

Heidi's face fell. "Are you okay this morning? You seem... preoccupied. Like you're in my bed, but not actually here."

Eden bit her lip and nodded. "I'm fine."

Heidi raised an eyebrow. "Fine. You do know that's not a decent enough response, don't you? Fine never means fine." She raised herself up on a single elbow and assessed Eden. "You look the opposite of fine. And you should look mighty fine. I take it as a personal slight, you know. You're in my bed. We had great sex all night long. The chocolate spread jar is depleted."

That drew a smile from Eden, and she let out a shallow laugh, before rolling onto her back and staring at the ceiling. Then she covered her face with her hands, before rolling back to Heidi. "That was all mighty fine. It's just... something came up this morning." She paused, blowing out a long breath. "My mother's come up this morning."

Heidi frowned. "Your mother? I thought she was out of the picture?"

Eden nodded. "She was. She is. But sometimes she creeps back in just to mess with me." She rolled onto her back, her muscles a tangled, tense mess. "I know I shouldn't let it get to me, but it does." She peered out through her fingers. She couldn't believe this was happening.

Heidi leaned over, took Eden's hands from her face and kissed her lips, before pulling back. "Talk to me. I don't scare easily."

Eden sighed. She'd started, so she should finish. "My mum just liked a post on Facebook. Which on the face of it doesn't seem like much, but I haven't seen her in over five years." Eden sighed. "I thought by the time I was 40 I'd be over this, past it. But it seems like I'm not."

"The trampoline park yesterday might have opened something up, too."

Eden gulped, forcing down the surge of emotion that swelled in her throat. "Maybe you're right."

"Tell me a little more about your mum and what happened." Heidi reached down and took Eden's hand in hers.

Eden looked at it for a while, then at Heidi, then began to speak.

"My mum was young when she had me: 18. So she's only 58 now. Which makes me sad, as there's still time. But it's pointless getting my hopes up, because she always lets me down. She didn't have a father, either; my grandad was killed in the war. But that doesn't explain who she became because my gran was the best. However, she was never enough for my mum.

"Debbie Price was never there for anyone. Not for my gran, not for me. She ran off when she got pregnant, came back when she was a month from having me. She never said who my father was, so I never knew."

Heidi squeezed her hand as she continued.

"My gran was fantastic, but there's always been an ache inside. An ache for something more solid and reliable. A mother, a strong relationship, I'm not sure. But I'm also scared of it. I hold people at arm's length, I don't give relationships a chance. Because why should I? My mum ran off and came back intermittently, and my gran did her best, but she was old. She went back to work when I came to live with her so she could support me. She died when I was 33."

Heidi brought Eden's hand to her lips and kissed it. "I'm sorry about your gran."

Eden exhaled a long breath. "Thanks. I was with someone when Gran died, but it didn't work out." She shook her head. "I'm not good at relationships, so I wouldn't get your hopes up. I've had others try and fail."

Heidi stared at her with her steady gaze. "I'm not other people though, am I?"

Eden was getting that impression.

"When you freaked out at the Mexican restaurant, was that more to do with your lack of faith in relationships, or to do with me having Maya?" Heidi's cool stare was trained on her now.

"A bit of both. As you might be able to see, my upbringing wasn't the best. Relationships fail. Plus, I don't want to risk putting any of my issues onto a child. I've always thought it's best if I steer clear." She took a deep breath. "I don't think I've ever admitted that to anyone out loud."

Heidi leaned over and kissed her cheek, taking hold of her hand. "That's progress, then. For the record, you can be great with kids without having experienced it yourself. They show you how if you let them."

She turned her intense stare back on Eden.

But this time, Eden held it with her own.

"The barriers you put up are in your own head, nowhere else. Just because your mother wasn't there for you, doesn't mean you'd make a bad mother. Your gran sounds like she was a fabulous role model."

Eden nodded. "She was the best. But she didn't think she was. She blamed herself for her daughter's behaviour."

"I get that. But sometimes, someone's a force bigger than anyone or anything."

"That's Debbie Price." Eden's voice was a whisper. Like if she said it any louder, her mother might appear in the room, as if by magic.

"If she's commenting on Facebook, where is she?"

"No idea. She was living in Yorkshire, then in Scotland. She says London's too expensive to live in."

"She's not wrong there," Heidi said. "Do you have any urge to get in contact with her?"

Eden shook her head. If there was one thing she was positive on when it came to her mother, it was that. "I've been down that road before, and nothing good comes from it."

"So why do you keep her as a friend on Facebook?"

Eden exhaled. "I don't know. I guess for my gran? I don't

want to cut the very last ties I have with her. Just in case something happens. If she dies, I guess I'll have to go to her funeral."

Heidi lay down beside her, never letting go of Eden's hand. "Makes my issues with my family seem trivial."

"What are your issues?"

Heidi shrugged. "My mum wasn't thrilled when I got pregnant, but she loves it now Maya's here. But I'll always be the black sheep of the family when it comes to daughters, simply because I'm not married. Marriage and children go hand in hand, according to my mother."

"They're fine with the gay thing?"

"Pretty much. They were shocked at first, but it's been over 20 years, so they're used to that. The baby thing was the bigger shock, and now my mum thinks Maya needs two mummies, not just one." She turned her head. "My mother's words, not mine. If you ask Maya, she's pretty content."

"Looks to me like you're doing an amazing job. Single parents can be great parents, too. I know that now." Eden kissed Heidi's fingers, before turning to face her. "I'm sorry again for falling apart on our Sunday morning. I haven't freaked you out, have I?"

Heidi shook her head. "I'm glad you can be honest with me. But I meant what I said, too. You could be great with kids."

"I'm not sure about that."

"I am." Heidi rolled on top of Eden, kissing her lips. "What about relationships? You think you might want to give this one a go? Push your limits further than they've been pushed in a while?"

Eden looked up into her eyes, all thoughts of anything

or anyone but Heidi having now evaporated. "When you're lying on top of me naked with your thigh pressed between mine, I'd agree to anything." She paused, licking her lips. "All I can tell you is this is a first. Me telling someone about my mum and my gran, so you're doing well." She really was. Heidi had broken down Eden's defences. That was the biggest hurdle of all.

"Glad to hear it. But if I wasn't pinning you to my bed, would you have already run out the door?"

Eden gave her a slow grin. Heidi was already reading her far too well. "The more pressing question is, what about Dusty? I can handle Maya, but can you handle her?"

Heidi let out a bark of laughter that made Eden's heart sing. "Industrial-strength allergy pills and a whole lot of exposure is the only way forward on that one. Maya comes with me. Dusty comes with you. I don't have a choice really, do I?"

"You always have a choice."

Heidi leaned down till their noses were touching. "Do I? Then I choose you."

Chapter Thirty

Eden shouted something at Heidi from the bedroom, but she couldn't hear. She had the radio on, currently blasting out the UK's number one. Heidi knew every word. Which, of course, was mainly down to Maya. She'd been amazed at the amount of toddler activities that used the latest pop songs as their soundtrack. Heidi had gone from being an old-school indie kid who loved PJ Harvey and the Yeah Yeah Yeahs to knowing all the latest hits. She had to admit, some of them were pretty catchy.

But whatever was on the radio today, it couldn't be louder than the song in her heart, which was deafening her with its relentless up-tempo beat. Eden had put the needle on it, and now Heidi was walking on sunshine.

They'd spent the morning getting to know each other's bodies better. Heidi was going to ache in places she'd forgotten existed tomorrow. The last 24 hours had been a ride. Yes, it had a false start, but they'd rectified it. Eden had cooked a delicious dinner, and they'd eaten it at midnight, on the sofa, staring at each other with dreamy grins.

They'd connected in a way Heidi didn't remember doing with anyone for years. *Literally, years.* Eden had also opened up about her past. When it came to relationships, children and families, Eden was a mass of doubt. Heidi represented all three. Had she done enough to convince Eden to try the very things she was scared of? And if she hadn't, what then?

She tried to steer her mind back to the wonderful, wild sex, but it kept coming back to the chat. She was allergic to Eden's cat. Eden was allergic to family and relationships. Nothing but exposure and time were going to heal either issue, although one could be solved with pills. The other? If only it was so easy.

She wasn't going to think about it now, though. They had two hours before her parents returned with Maya, and she was going to enjoy her final moments with Eden before she made her getaway. When Heidi had mentioned her parents were turning up, Eden had gone very green and said she had to get home. Heidi didn't blame her. Meeting anyone's family was stressful, even when you didn't have family issues.

As she put the third scoop of ground coffee into her French press, Eden appeared. Her hair was still wet from the shower. She was dressed, too, which caused a swarm of disappointment inside Heidi. Eden naked was her new favourite dish. To eat, to touch, to stare at. Her favourite thing? Eden's bum, which was surprisingly firm. Heidi had joked she could probably bounce pound coins off it.

"Hey gorgeous. Coffee?"

"Yes please, goddess of caffeine." Eden walked over and nuzzled her neck. "I missed you in the shower."

Heidi turned, kissing her lips. "You had enough of me this morning. I think you can cope."

Eden gave her a grin and sat at her breakfast bar. "What are you whipping me up for breakfast?"

"I wasn't expecting you, remember? I don't have anything fancy. How does scrambled eggs on toast sound? I can do you Chocolate Delight on toast, but I'm guessing you already ate enough of that last night."

A wicked cackle. "I was still washing it out of my crevices this morning." Eden turned up her sexy smile. "But scrambled eggs on toast sounds perfect."

Heidi got the carton of eggs out of the fridge, then put the coffee pot on the table, along with two mugs. Eden pulled her into her lap as she walked back to the kitchen. "Or I could just have you on toast."

"I don't spread very well," Heidi replied.

"I disagree."

Heidi's laughter echoed round the room, just as the doorbell rang. She kissed Eden, then held her at arm's length. "Let me just get that. I'm expecting a package, and they deliver on Sunday now, don't they?" She walked to the door with joy bubbling up inside her. Eden's hands on her body had that effect.

However, when Heidi opened the front door, the joy lodged in her throat, closely followed by dread and fear. Because her mum was standing there, carrying what looked like a tray of fairy cakes.

"Morning." Her mum didn't wait to be invited in, breezing past her like she owned the place. A waft of her geranium perfume hit Heidi's airwaves. However, its usual comforting sense wasn't there this morning.

Heidi couldn't formulate the words in time to stop her. "Mum, hang on!" Her voice had gone up at least an octave. But just as those words were out, her dad's voice carried through the air, something about going straight to the door. Then Maya ran up the garden path, a beaming smile on her face. Just for a second, Heidi forgot the impending disaster that was about to unfurl.

Maya held out her arms. "Mummy!" Her smile was infectious.

Heidi bent down and picked her up, breathing in her scent. Sometimes Heidi longed to have a break from her, but she was always pleased to see her when she came back. She couldn't imagine there being a time when that was any different. But it hadn't been the case with Eden's mum, had it? Clutching her daughter now, she couldn't imagine how much that must have hurt.

Which brought her mind back to Eden. Currently in the kitchen, which her mother was heading towards.

Fucking hell.

Heidi turned and sprinted, with Maya still in her arms. Her daughter gave a squeal of delight at this turn of events, wrapping her arms around Heidi's neck.

Too late.

When Heidi arrived in the kitchen, Eden was standing like she was about to be inspected in an army line-up, hands by her side, her face sheet-white.

Meanwhile, her mother turned to Heidi, giving her a look Heidi couldn't decipher. She didn't stop to ponder, diving straight into damage-limitation mode. For Eden, not for her mum.

"Mum, this is Eden."

If Heidi had to pick an emotion to ascribe to her mother, she'd pick mild amusement. Her mum was enjoying this, wasn't she?

"Eden." Her mum walked to the kitchen counter and put down the cake box. Then she approached Eden, holding out a hand. "Pleased to meet you, dear. Sorry to interrupt your breakfast. I know we're a little early, but Heidi's dad has some stuff to do at the allotment and he wanted to make a start." Her mum was still shaking Eden's hand.

Eden visibly tensed and took a step back, her face set to freaked. This wasn't going well.

Maya wriggled in Heidi's arms and she put her down. She ran over to the counter and pointed up at the Chocolate Delight. "Spread!" Maya's voice was demanding. "Choc-lit spread!"

Heidi avoided Eden's gaze as her cheeks heated. Damn her bodily responses. A vision of licking that spread from Eden's pussy last night landed in her eyeline, and she closed her eyes briefly. When she opened them again, Eden was giving her a flushed stare. Was she thinking the same thing? Or was she thinking this situation was exactly what she was trying to avoid? Heidi had no idea. They hadn't reached the mind-reading stage yet.

Right then, her dad walked in, putting his car keys in his pocket. "Have you got a visitor parking permit, Heids? I know what they're like around here." He stopped when he saw Eden, freezing in place. "Oh, hello. Didn't know you had company."

"And I thought we said two o'clock."

"We sent you a text." Her mum raised an eyebrow. "But maybe you were too busy to read your phone."

Oh god, please make this stop. Heidi glanced at Eden, who was rubbing her hands, looking around the room. Perhaps she was looking for an exit? She wasn't going to find an easy one.

"I'm Heidi's dad, Robert." That was to Eden.

Eden shook his hand, giving him a pained smile. "Eden. Nice to meet you." It wasn't the most sincere greeting Heidi had ever heard, but she couldn't really blame her. Eden had laid out her family fears. And now, here they were. Standing in the kitchen in three-dimensional Technicolor.

"Spread!" Maya stamped her feet.

If she went into one of her recent funks that had started to creep in, Heidi was going to demand a do-over of this day. Well, perhaps not the first few hours, but definitely the past ten minutes. Didn't she deserve a break? Why weren't the gods of love smiling down on her?

"Mummeeeeeeeee! Choc-lit!"

Heidi threw Eden an apologetic look, then went over to the counter, putting the Chocolate Delight in the cupboard to take it out of Maya's sightline.

Big mistake.

Maya's lip trembled. Heidi picked her up to offset what might be coming. Heidi was the lynchpin in this situation, the manager of this moment. And yet, every single part of this conundrum needed her full attention. Eden, her parents, Maya. She couldn't split herself in three, no matter how hard she wanted to.

As if on cue, Maya flung herself backwards like she was in training for the Olympic gymnastics squad and began to wail. Not in a cute way. But in that particular way that made grown adults cover their ears and wince.

Just like now.

"Choc-lit!"

Heidi blew out a breath, trying to placate Maya, but it was too late. She'd been warned by Meg and Kate that two-year-olds were drama queens, but she was just beginning to appreciate just how much. The last few weeks, Maya had been in training, but now, it was opening night. She wasn't going to let anybody down. Her screams filled the air.

This was *so* not how she'd wanted her parents to meet Eden. And it certainly wasn't how she'd wanted this time with Eden to end.

"I should get going, I've got a bunch of stuff to do." With that, Eden was on the move, almost sprinting to get to Heidi's bedroom, away from prying eyes. Great. So now she had a toddler freaking out about chocolate spread and a lover freaking out about family. She'd look back and laugh one day. Maybe.

"Choc-lit!" Maya sobbed, kicking her legs, waving her arms, almost choking on her words and tears.

Eventually, Heidi's mum sprang to her rescue, taking Maya from Heidi's arms. "Go and see to your guest, I think we might have spooked her." She paused, grappling with her granddaughter. "Stop being so silly, Maya. You can have a cake soon if you're good."

"No! Want choc-lit!"

Heidi left her catastrophising daughter to it, running to her room and to Eden. If she'd been child-free, there's no way her mother would ever have been anywhere near her front doorstep the morning after the night before. But as Meg and Kate had told her, having a baby was like dropping a bomb on your normal life and your relationship. The challenge afterwards was to see how you coped putting your life back together again, because it could never be the same as before. She'd smiled when they'd told her that, but now she knew it was nothing but the truth.

They almost crashed into each other at the bedroom door, where it had all started last night. Heidi held out her hands to stop the on-rushing Eden. Damn, she was keener than Heidi had thought to get out of there.

"Hey." She put a hand on Eden's shoulder.

Eden almost shook it off.

Heidi cast her eyes down, then exhaled a long breath. "I came to see how you are."

In the kitchen, Maya was still wailing. Heidi tried to carry on as if it wasn't happening. "I'm sorry about my family just crashing the party, but that's my family." She shrugged, knowing it was true. But also knowing it was completely the wrong thing to say.

However, she couldn't second-guess everything she was going to say when it came to her family. They were what they were: infuriating, annoying, wonderful, her rock. They were her family, and they weren't going anywhere. But could Eden handle that? Was she going to let a Maya meltdown railroad them?

"It's fine," Eden replied.

There was that word again. So innocent, and yet, so loaded.

"But I really should go. Leave you to sort out Maya and your parents."

"You don't have to run. You could still stay for breakfast." It wasn't the most alluring offer, but it was all Heidi had.

Eden was already shaking her head. "I was going anyway. You can cook me scrambled eggs another time."

Heidi stepped a little closer. "I hope so." She pressed her lips to Eden's. Heidi felt the push and pull of Eden's fight or flight. But in the end, Eden kissed her back. It was short, and not all that sweet, but it was a kiss. Heidi would take that for now. She pulled back, searching Eden's eyes. For what, she wasn't sure.

She sighed, moved her mouth left, then right, then took Eden's hand. "I'll walk you to the door."

Heidi tugged her down the corridor, loving the feel of her hand in hers. Not wanting to let go, but knowing she had to.

Damn her parents and their timing. Of course she hadn't checked her fucking phone. She'd been too busy having sex.

They stopped at the door of the main space, hovering. Maya was still screaming, Heidi's mum now sitting with her on the sofa. Maya was lying prone, her face tear-strewn, her legs still pumping. When she got an idea in her head, her daughter was stubborn as hell. Heidi had no idea where she got it from.

Eden raised an awkward hand. "Nice to meet you both." Then, not waiting for an answer, she scuttled towards the front door. Heidi could almost feel her holding her breath. Eden opened the front door, then turned to her. She went to say something, then stopped.

"See you again soon? Let's try to get a date in the diary." Heidi put a hand on the side of Eden's face, holding it as if it were a piece of the world's most important china. Handle with care. Those three words pretty much described Eden. "Because apart from the past 15 minutes, I've loved the past 24 hours a hell of a lot."

Eden nodded, a hint of a smile crossing her face. "Me, too." She paused, then leaned forward for a quick kiss.

Her lips were warm, sexy, delicate. Heidi didn't want to let them go. But if she wanted Eden to come back, she had to do so of her own accord. That was the hardest fact to swallow as she pulled away. "Call me?"

Eden gave her a firm nod, then walked down the path. She didn't look back.

Heidi shut the front door, then pressed her back against it, closing her eyes. Maya's cries had calmed a little. Heidi needed a minute before she went back in there.

Eden was a complex case. Even without Maya in the picture, she might have bolted just because Heidi was suggesting a relationship. To Eden, they didn't last, whereas no matter what happened in Heidi's world, she always had a sure-fire belief that she'd find love and be happy. She knew that was because of her stable background, her upbringing. Because she'd always loved herself, never doubted her ability to warrant love. Whereas Eden had never had that. She'd always second-guessed herself, wondered if the problem was her. Her mum had left, so why wouldn't everyone else?

Heidi had seen the pain in her eyes, on her face, in her every movement this morning. She'd gone from being relaxed, to being hesitant, unsure. Heidi wanted to help, to reach inside and reset Eden. But she knew it was going to take a whole lot more than a few platitudes from her. Where Eden was concerned, she had years of behaviour and thought patterns to unpick. Heidi hoped she was willing to give it a try.

Because despite all the obstacles past and present, Heidi liked Eden. A lot. She loved her laugh. She loved her eyes.

But most of all, she loved her strength. Eden was a tower of strength, and that was her problem. She needed to let her guard down, be vulnerable. To open herself up and not expect the worst. It wasn't going to happen overnight. But Heidi was ready to try to help her, and in the process, burrow into Eden's life. She was worth it. Especially after last night.

She chose her.

Heidi hoped Eden felt the same.

Chapter Thirty-One

Today was filming day for the Chocolate Delight ad, India insistent they strike now and rush it into production while the treasure-hunt promotion was still fresh in the public's mind. They also had people handing out trial packs at every major London train and tube station, grabbing the attention of not just Londoners but also commuters coming in from the surrounding counties and suburbs. India texted this morning to congratulate the team on getting the commercial into production so quickly. Eden and Caroline had pulled in a glut of favours to meet the tight deadline, and Eden hoped it went smoothly. With that off her plate, she could turn her attention back to Heidi. If Heidi was still talking to her.

Eden had behaved badly when Heidi's parents had turned up, but Eden and parents were like oil and water: they didn't gel. She'd spent her entire life working out what parents *should* do, because her mum had never been a good example. Heidi had picture-book parents. Like the parents from a Hallmark movie. Eden had no time for those movies, because she couldn't make sense of them.

When Heidi's parents had turned up early, she'd panicked. Plus, Heidi's mum had been wearing something with geranium in it. That smell had been enough to make Eden struggle to keep it together, and then want to run. She couldn't stay and play happy families with Heidi's parents and daughter when the scent of her gran was lingering in the air. It had been too much. Heidi had let her go, but even as she was leaving, Eden knew running wasn't the answer. However, it was her default, and she didn't know how to change it.

When she got home on Sunday, Eden sent Heidi a couple of messages apologising about leaving so soon. She was holding back. She knew that.

However, she hadn't held back when they were in bed. When Heidi touched her, Eden felt it in her very core, in her heart and in her soul. When the two of them were together, she couldn't be anywhere but in the moment. There was nowhere to hide.

What's more, against the odds, Heidi had got Eden talking about her mum. Had Heidi judged her? She hoped not. Heidi had tried to tell Eden her upbringing didn't dictate her actions now. But Eden knew Heidi's did. She came from a stable, loving home, and that's what she wanted to give her daughter. It made sense.

Until she met Heidi, Eden had always dealt with her dating life by shutting down, retreating. If you didn't open yourself up, you couldn't get hurt. Eden had experienced enough hurt to last a lifetime. Her life was fine.

But there was that word again. The one Heidi had picked out, sat on its own and shone a spotlight on.

Eden's life *was* fine. It was *absolutely fine*. But could it be better? More than she'd ever dreamed of? What would happen if she opened up? Could she have more nights and mornings like the one she'd had with Heidi? Because despite being scared and exposed, she hadn't felt more alive in years. Was Eden prepared to sacrifice her golden rule and put her heart on the line? She was beginning to think she might be. However, to do that, she had to see Heidi again.

Her thoughts were interrupted when a folder landed on her desk with a loud thwack. Caroline folded her arms across her chest, then leaned against Eden's desk, smiling sweetly.

"What do you want?" Eden knew that smile well.

Caroline's smile got even wider. "Your genius, your charisma and your love."

"I've told you before, work relationships are rarely a good idea."

"Okay, I'll settle for the first two. Massive contract just landed." She pointed at the folder. "Literally. There's more in your inbox. If we can nail the presentation — which I know you can — then we can secure the deal. But it's got to be done by Friday, because the company they were dealing with just fell through and they need a replacement asap."

What was it with all these last-minute companies? "I don't have time to do this. Not with the other three projects I'm already handling." She paused. "Plus, I have some personal things I need to take care of."

The surprise on Caroline's face was epic. "Personal things? You don't have a personal life, do you?"

That floored Eden. "I might be starting to."

Caroline took that in. "Okay, and I have to respect that. You've given me so much of your own time over the years."

Eden nodded. She'd given her plenty.

"Only, you're the only one with the skills to really nail the pitch. So pretty please? For me? I'll take everything else off your plate if you'll at least look at this and give us your opinion. Maybe just a teeny-tiny pitch. How's that?" She gave Eden her most pathetic, needy face. "I'll make it worth your while, too. Give you time off in lieu." Even though she knew Eden never took the holiday she already had.

Eden frowned at the folder. She took up challenges like this, Caroline knew that. But her boss was playing on her good will. However, maybe this week, she could do with a project to get her teeth into. Something to completely absorb her. So long as she could see Heidi, too. Because she wanted to.

That fact made her sit up. Things really were changing on Planet Eden.

"Okay, I'll look at it and give you preliminary feedback. I'll get Johan to help, too. Be warned, though — I might shock you and take you up on that time in lieu, too." A vision of her and Heidi enjoying the summer flashed through her mind. "But can I make a request?"

"Whatever you like."

"Please hire someone if you're taking on more clients. You're going to need them."

"I know that." Caroline's face was contrite. "Thank you. I owe you."

Chapter Thirty-Two

Heidi had her sunglasses on today; spring was finally giving the relentless rain a run for its money. May was her very favourite month, and she was looking forward to its arrival. Heidi plunged Maya down the slide for the umpteenth time when she heard a voice in her ear.

"Boo!"

She jumped, turned, then thumped Cleo on the arm. "Don't you know it's wrong to do that to unsuspecting mothers in parks? You could be a psychopath."

"I could be, but I'm not. I'm just your best friend back from Boston, finally!" She gave Heidi a grin, then picked up Maya from the bottom of the slide and swung her around. "How's my favourite little girl in the whole world?"

"Don't let Becca's nieces hear you say that."

"Maya will always be my favourite. I saw her being born. You can't beat that." Cleo kissed Maya's cheek. "We saw you pop out of your mummy's vagina, didn't we?"

"Gi-na!" Maya mimicked.

"That's still not funny, by the way." But Heidi smiled, just like always.

Heidi sat Maya in her buggy, then set off round Clissold Park.

Cleo put an arm around her as they walked. "Don't take this the wrong way, but you look knackered."

"Is there a right way to take that comment?" Heidi bumped Cleo with her hip as they strolled. Even though the weather was heating up, it was nothing like the scorching spring Maya was born. "But you're right, I'm exhausted. Late nights, lots of work, birthdays."

"How did the date go on Saturday?"

"The date itself went well." It was just the handful of days since that stumped Heidi.

"Is there a but?"

"Let's just say she's worth pursuing. I think. But you know I was worried I came with baggage?"

Cleo nodded.

"Small fry. She hasn't dated anyone in seven years."

"Fucking hell. You sure she's not past her sell-by date?"

Heidi smiled. "No. We slept together, and she's definitely not." Of all the parts she was worried about, that wasn't one of them. The sex hadn't just been sex. It had been sex to write home about. Sex to write a letter to the editor about. Sex to make her heart yearn for more.

Cleo held up her hand to high-five Heidi. "So how was it? First time having sex since Maya was born?"

"It all still works, so that's a plus. And I didn't pee myself with my weaker pelvic floor. I'm calling it a win."

"And they say romance is dead."

Heidi inhaled, breathing in the moist spring day. She wasn't going to fill Cleo in on everything that had gone on. Eden's story had been too personal for that. "We're taking it slow, which is kinda necessitated by me having a kid and having to work weekends, and her having to work all the time. But I'm looking on it as a positive. I can't afford to rush into anything anymore, and she needs to take it slow, too, seeing as she has an issue with family. But it was a promising start. Until my parents gate-crashed our breakfast together and she bolted faster than Usain Bolt himself. Reminded me of our first meeting in Waitrose, actually."

"I've met your mum, she can be quite intimidating."

"I think Maya was the scarier part. She had a breakdown because I wouldn't give her chocolate spread. The speed it went from sexy morning in bed with my new lover to a bad family farce was frightening."

"Yikes."

"I'd like to say those were Eden's words, but I think she was dumbstruck." Heidi shook her head, the memory causing goosebumps to break out on her arm. "Turns out, dating with children is different."

Cleo kicked a stone off the park path as she walked. "When are you seeing her again?"

"We've still got to work it out." It was something Heidi hadn't pushed. Eden messaged her on Monday to say she had a full-on week ahead with a new project having landed on her desk. Heidi thought that sounded very convenient. Whenever life got too hard, Eden had a tendency to bury herself in work. Still, she had a busy week, too, so she was letting it lie. For now.

"How's the world of wedding photography?"

"Would you believe since I raised my prices, my enquiries have gone up? It's that age-old thing of people attaching high price to value. I'm deluged with enquiries, which really wasn't the point of doing it. But it does mean now I can turn down some Sundays, take up a few more weekday gigs, which I prefer. I'm going to make a rule I only do one weekend day, which means I can spend the other one with Maya. Or with Eden if she's still around. Or with both."

"Awesome. So as well as getting laid, you're also getting paid. I'd say that's a good week for you."

Heidi nodded. She hoped it would be, once Eden worked out her issues. "I've had worse."

"And what are you doing for Maya's birthday? You should do a trampolining party, seeing as she loves it so much. We could all come, it'd be a hoot."

That took Heidi right back to last Friday, to trampolining with Eden. To Eden breaking down, the start of her story seeping out. How was she feeling this week? Exposed and raw, Heidi was sure. Which was why she was hiding behind work.

"Eden and I took Maya trampolining last week. It was quite eventful."

Cleo stopped walking. "You took her trampolining before you had sex with her? That seems like a really strange order to do things in."

Heidi agreed. "I was going anyway, and she kinda invited herself." She paused. "I think I'll just do something at the flat for Maya's birthday. She's two. As long as she's got cake, she's happy."

Cleo didn't budge, keeping her eyes on Heidi. "And will you invite Eden? I'd like to meet her."

Heidi's breathing stalled. Would she? "I guess I will. I'll have to see how this week goes, first."

Cleo studied her as they walked. "You're a little uncertain about this woman, aren't you?"

Heidi didn't like being unsure, but she couldn't deny it. "I am. I don't know which way she's going to jump. And it's nothing to do with me and what I do. It's all about her and what she's prepared to do."

"Tread carefully, then. I might joke around, but you're my best friend, and I don't want to see you get hurt."

Chapter Thirty-Three

Eden buried herself in work right up until Wednesday. Once she turned her initial proposal in to Caroline, she took the afternoon off to meet with Heidi. The shock on Caroline's face when Eden told her she was leaving early made her smile. Everyone knew Eden wasn't behaving like Eden at all. Heidi was bringing out a whole other side of her.

Eden had tried to focus on work, but it hadn't done the trick. If she couldn't stop thinking about Heidi, she decided to give in to it. That perhaps instead of simply thinking about her, she should take action and see her. Follow her heart, see where it led. Eden had told Heidi she didn't believe in fate, she believed in action. It was about time she lived up to her billing.

The thing that drew her to Heidi was her realness. There was no hiding. All of which meant when Eden was with her, she couldn't be anything else but real, either. Heidi demanded it. Heidi made her sentences stumble, her feelings sprawl on the ground. She had to see her again. She didn't have a choice.

So now, here they were on Wednesday afternoon, walking through Soho, the sunshine casting a golden glow across the bustling streets. Eden had taken Heidi to her favourite tapas bar on Greek Street, and they'd eaten delicious tortilla, iberico ham, prawns and padron peppers. Every time Heidi had licked juice from her fingers, Eden had sat transfixed. Being with Heidi in public was all well and good, but Eden yearned to be with her in private. Behind closed doors. Her thoughts had been Heidi-flavoured all week long. Sitting beside her and keeping a polite distance had been a new level of exquisite torture.

Eden wanted to sweep Heidi off her feet. To leave her in no doubt that she was what she wanted. But having never swept anyone off their feet before, Eden wasn't sure how to do it. This was new territory.

Eden took Heidi's hand as they passed a perfume shop, Heidi stopping in front of it. "Remind me, I need to get some new perfume. I'm nearly out."

Eden's heart glowed red. "I like that. You're asking me to remind you of things. Like I'm going to be around for a while."

Heidi frowned. "I hope so. Was that not in your plans?"

Eden shook her head. "That came out wrong. It certainly is. It's just new for me, that's all." She bowed her head as she said the last part, blood flushing her cheeks. She could give massive presentations to boards, but when it came to Heidi, Eden stuttered. She was determined to smooth out her transitions.

Heidi squeezed her hand. "You're infuriating and adorable, all at the same time, you know that?"

Eden smiled. "I was hoping for sexy, but we can work up to that."

"I'll look forward to it."

Eden swallowed down. "I know I apologised for running out on Sunday morning, and I am sorry. But another contributor was your mum's perfume. Does she wear Diptyque Geranium?"

Heidi nodded. "She does. You have an impressive nose."

"Not really. It was the one my gran wore. Smelling it so up close and personal freaked me out. It's not a common scent."

Heidi glanced at Eden, her steps faltering. "No wonder it freaked you out." She squeezed Eden's hand again. "But maybe it's a good sign. You loved your gran; I hope my mum and her perfume grow on you."

"Her daughter already has, so she's already earned brownie points from me." Eden kissed her, leaving her lips inches from Heidi's as she spoke. "Your mum's not at the forefront of my mind right now, though. That honour goes to kissing you some more, getting you naked." As she said the words, lust slid down her, making her clit throb. She shivered, even though it was a warm day.

Heidi stared at her, then hesitated. "I'm desperate to go somewhere I can kiss you, too."

Eden sucked in a breath as a thought hit her. Could she suggest it? Be so bold? She stared at Heidi's red lips and decided it was the only thing she could do. Their time together was short. She wanted to make it count. "This might be a little out there, but this relationship is a little different to most I've had. In fact, so far, it's been unique."

Heidi smiled. "Agreed."

Eden kissed Heidi's hand, and was pleased to see she shivered. "But I'm not running away, which is such a huge step forward. You made me miss you." She checked her watch. "We've got a few hours till you have to get home to pick Maya up. I don't want to go to a bar. I want to get naked with you. What do you think about getting a hotel room?" Eden stared into Heidi's eyes. "I know a place we put our clients up. We could go there and make the most of today. Do what we both want to do." She paused. "Only if that is what you want to do, too?"

Eden had everything crossed that it was. If it wasn't, she was going to bawl. Right here on this Soho street.

A slow, sure smile spread over Heidi's features. Thick, charged air settled between them. "You want to get naked with me?"

Eden kissed Heidi's fingers. "More than anything in the world." Someone jostled her as they walked past, but Eden was oblivious.

In response, Heidi's lips pressed against hers. Candyfloss-flavoured thoughts swirled round Eden's brain as she melted into Heidi's kiss.

A few moments later, Heidi pulled back. "Come on then, stud," she said, her tongue trailing along her bottom lip. "Let's hustle."

Eden didn't need telling twice.

Chapter Thirty-Four

The walk through Soho's narrow, clogged streets to the hotel was one of the weirdest Heidi had ever experienced. It was late afternoon, and some people were just finishing work or shopping. Yet here they were, about to go and have sex. It was like some kind of delicious secret only she and Eden knew. Every time she caught her eye, Heidi knew Eden felt it too. It was in Eden's smile, in her walk. Eden's shoulders were pulled back, her chest high. She was pleased with herself, Heidi could tell. Truth be told, Heidi was pleased with her, too.

She'd been a mother first for the past two years, but Eden had made her come alive sexually again. She was beyond grateful for that. She'd always associated mothers with mothering, not with having a sex life. However, now she knew she was capable of both. It might take a little more organisation, and it might mean having sex in the afternoon, but it was something she could do. What's more, it was something a hot woman wanted to do with her. That was a revelation.

There was a lot they could have spoken about, but once they were in the door of the glitzy hotel, all Heidi could think about was Eden. In her normal life, she might have mentioned the deep red seats in reception, the sleek Japanese-styled lobby desk, the inviting-looking bar she could see through a silver-framed doorway. In the lift, she might have registered the soothing piped music, or how polished the mirrors were. Instead, all she registered was the width of Eden's smile, the depth of Eden's stare, and the thud of her heartbeat in her chest.

When Eden flashed the door key over the fob, the click it made was definite, final; a little like Heidi's mood. How had Eden read her so well? She would never have been so bold, so brazen to do this, and yet Eden had. Eden, who was hesitant of lurching into a relationship. Did this mean her worries about doing so were lessening? Did it mean they were moving forward? Heidi had everything crossed.

What was in no doubt, though, was Eden's intent. Once they dropped their bags, she came to Heidi. No hesitation, no stutter. Their mouths came together in a clash of teeth and lips as Eden clawed at Heidi's jacket, then her clothing. Heidi was dressed smartly today, having been to a client meeting. It wasn't destined to last. Eden popped the buttons on her shirt, and the rip of Heidi's zipper filled the air. Then her trousers were on the floor, her bra removed. Eden's hands and mouth were everywhere as Heidi gave in to the moment. This was Eden taking charge, and Heidi wasn't going to stand in her way.

A waft of Eden's musky perfume trailed into her airwaves as she guided Heidi gently towards the edge of the room. It had sleek, sophisticated decor, but Heidi was oblivious. All she saw was Eden, and all she knew was how much she wanted her.

With the cool, hard wall behind Heidi, Eden pressed her lips to Heidi's neck. Her hands slid to the curve of Heidi's hip.

A flash of electricity shot through Heidi. She dropped her head to the side, the rush of desire filling her. Eden was driving, and she was happy to let her go wherever her GPS took her.

Eden's lips slipped up to Heidi's earlobe, and she shuddered. Eden's hand trailed down her back, before sweeping between Heidi's legs. Nerves fluttered low in her belly. Then Eden's thigh was parting her legs, a firm hand grazing Heidi's centre.

"I promised myself I'd go slow, but you're too tempting." There was a rough note to Eden's voice that made Heidi's stomach flip and heat rush across her skin.

"Fuck slow." Heidi caught Eden's mouth with hers, plunging her tongue into it.

When she pulled back, panting, Eden gazed at her, a weird look in her eyes. "I could really fall for you. In fact, I think I already have."

Heidi's breathing stilled. "Show me."

The words stopped. Action began.

Eden's teeth grazed Heidi's nipples, making her gasp. Her hand latched onto Heidi's bum cheek. A squeeze.

Heidi brought her right leg up and around Eden, locking her in place. She never wanted Eden to be anywhere else but here.

Within seconds, Eden angled herself, then trailed a finger slowly, deliberately through Heidi's liquid heat.

Heidi let out a deep moan.

When Eden slipped two fingers into her, Heidi squeezed her eyes tight shut.

Fuck.

Eden's mouth claimed hers once more, her fingers sliding in and out like this was their natural home. With every touch, Heidi was taken higher. She dug her fingers into Eden's strong shoulders, hitched herself up, opened herself to whatever Eden was offering.

It wasn't just Eden who was risking it all by giving in to their feelings. Heidi was, too. Eden was a risk, but she was too hot to turn down, their chemistry off the charts. As Eden hit her G-spot, Heidi clutched her harder, sinking into her bliss point, never wanting this to end. The intensity of it, the sweet desperation, was new to her. But she gave in to it freely.

They moved to the bed, Heidi grateful to truly be able to fall into the moment. Eden lay beside her, kissing her with crazy heat. Wonder streaked through Heidi, as Eden's fingers slid all over her, circling her, mesmerising her.

Heidi pulled her close, kissing her lips, the need for them to be skin-tight everywhere overwhelming. She caught Eden's gaze, and they stilled. Right then, something swelled inside Heidi, so big she could hardly breathe. The flicker of something beginning. Something so *them*, so personal, she almost looked away. But she didn't. Neither did Eden. Together, they paused, locked eyes, traded ragged breaths. Then with a silent, still acknowledgement they were taking a bow on the same glorious stage, they continued the journey together.

As Eden's rhythm gathered and Heidi's insides twisted and turned till she wasn't sure which way was up, heat prickled all over her. She held on tight. Finally, as Eden coaxed her to her limits, Heidi's muscles tensed, her heartbeat pulsed, then her climax popped. Pleasure surged through her like the perfect pop song, making her want to sing the chorus again and again. Every time Eden squeezed a little more out of her, she clung to her, feeling what she was giving, tasting the sweetness on her tongue and in her heart.

When their gazes locked one more time, Heidi felt something shift. Yes, this was the culmination of physical attraction, but this was something deeper, too. The tumbling down of defence walls that had been built over years. Eden finally giving her something more.

Suddenly, even though she was still flying, she didn't want this to be just her. She wanted this to be the two of them together. It seemed important, because it was. This was their second time together, and after all the obstacles, could this be the start that stuck? The one that didn't scare Eden half to death? If Heidi wanted it to be, she had to make it memorable.

She rolled a stunned Eden to her side, and reached down, her orgasm still sparking within her. Then Heidi's fingers were inside Eden. She was so wet, Heidi had to pause to take it in.

"I'm so ready for you," Eden gasped.

"I know." Heidi kissed her, preparing to write the longest love letter to Eden's body.

Heidi rolled on top of her, then began to fuck Eden with such passion, she had no idea where she started and Eden ended. It was a glorious place to be. Eden was already tightening around her, already on the edge. Heidi smiled, plugging into the power of them.

Eden rolled, hands grappling. "I want to be inside you, too."

Heidi stilled. They inched left, then right, angles adjusted. Heidi clenched as Eden's fingers connected with her once more. "Fucking hell." Her eyes fluttered open, and they shared a look of raw desire. It was still there, pulsing between them. That indescribable something. She was ready to rock Eden's world, and Eden was ready to rock hers.

Heidi thrust, as did Eden, their mouths clashing together,

then apart. There was a primal nature to their sex now, rocking together, Eden's face creased as she fought to stay in control. But if this was going to work, she had to let go. Let everything she ever knew fall away, and start again from fresh.

Could Eden do it? With her help, Heidi hoped the answer was yes.

Heidi's breathing was shredded as she leaned over, circling Eden's swollen clit with her thumb.

She put her lips as close as she could get to Eden's ear, and whispered, "Let it go. I wanna feel you come all over me."

Eden's muscles tensed as Heidi spoke, and then with a shudder and a final flourish from Heidi, Eden's orgasm hit.

Heidi was spellbound.

Eden in climax was beyond beautiful.

But then Eden's fingers sprang back to life, knowing just where to go. Heidi kept her momentum going, riding Eden. As she came, so did Eden once more, Heidi grasping her round the shoulder and letting out a piercing cry. They kept their rhythms going for a few moments more, muscles spasming, minds blank, until gravity took over and they toppled back onto the bed together, skin slick with sweat and lust.

Moments later, Eden's arm was around her, pulling her tight. She leaned down, kissing Heidi's stomach, and then coming back up, adjusting their bodies until they were lying against each other, breast to breast. Eden kissed Heidi's lips slow and long, before pulling back, regarding her.

"Holy fucking hell," Eden said, finally.

"You could say that."

"You think we could do this every week?"

Heidi laughed and it came out croaky. She wasn't surprised.

Her head throbbed and her throat was sore. All her blood, all her body's juices, had sailed down her body to where it was needed most. She wasn't complaining. "I'd be happy to, but I'm not sure I'd get much work done."

Eden ran a hand up and down her back. "I've always said work is overrated."

Heidi let out a cackle of laughter. "Hello, Mrs Workaholic. What have you done with Eden? If you find her, can you let her know I'm looking for her?"

Eden grinned. "I think I've finally found my ultimate calling, and it turns out it's not creating advertising and branding. It's having sex with you." She rolled onto her back. "It's something I have no trouble focusing on, and I'm pretty good at it, too."

"You're fucking amazing at it." Heidi pulled Eden back towards her, kissing her lips. Fresh flourishes of desire scampered down her body.

"I wish I'd worked this out earlier. I could have saved myself so much time."

"If you create the post, maybe we could job share. Perhaps get some crowd-funding to back us? We could stream our sex live on the internet in return." Heidi put her weight on one elbow, a delicious smile creeping onto her face. "Did I just describe how the sex industry works?"

Eden laughed. "Yes, but if you're working in that, you don't normally get to have sex with someone you love."

Eden stilled, frozen, a deer in the headlights.

Knowing this was a delicate moment, Heidi dimmed her beams. "You love me?" It took everything she had not to punch the air.

Eden's face still didn't move. Instead, there was just a faint hint of a nod, her cheeks flushing pillar-box red. "I do. I can't stop thinking about you. But I didn't mean to blurt it out. My heart's thumping in my chest." She put a hand there, as if checking it.

Heidi kissed her hand, and then gathered her in her arms. Eden melted into her embrace.

"If it helps, I love you, too." She pulled her tighter. "But promise me we won't have to do live sex on the internet. My mum would get very cross for starters."

Eden began to laugh. "Okay, I promise. We might have to keep our day jobs for now."

Heidi pulled back, and they stared at each other for a few long moments. "You really love me?" The words were bright in her mind, lit up.

Eden nodded. "I think I do. In fact, I know I do. I'm doing weird things, behaving in weird ways. Hell, I took an afternoon off to have sex with you."

"I know." Heidi grinned. "Good decision, by the way." She kissed Eden's lips again, wanting more of them every time she did. She was like a drug.

"I agree." Eden sighed. "I really am sorry about everything. About bolting. About being an idiot. I'm amazed you stuck with me."

"I figured you were an intelligent woman, and that you'd figure out I was worth keeping eventually."

"And if I hadn't?"

"Then I'd have been forced to play you at your own game and take out an ad in the national media, telling you to wise up or else."

Eden grinned. "I'd have liked that. Although I'm not sure if it would have been good for my brand."

"Lucky you wised up then, isn't it?"

Eden ran a hand down the side of Heidi's face.

Heidi shuddered. Her breath quickened, as pops of pleasure roamed her body, making her swoon. The tips of Eden's fingers held magic, of that she was sure.

"So now we've both declared love for each other, we should see how that affects our sex, right? How long do we have?"

Heidi rolled over, missing the heat of Eden's skin. She grabbed her phone, squinting at the brightness of the screen. Her world over the past hour had taken on a sepia filter, and letting the real world back in was a jolt. "It's just gone five thirty, so I'd say we've got a couple of hours yet. I need to leave by eight at the latest. You can accomplish a lot in two and a half hours."

"I agree." Eden pulled her back into her embrace, kissing her roughly.

Heidi's desire was instantly turned right back to top speed. She pushed Eden down on the bed, climbing on top of her, pinning her arms either side of her head. "Let me give you a lesson in focus and application." She crushed Eden's lips with her own, desire making her wet all over again. "Ready?"

Chapter Thirty-Five

Eden took a deep breath and knocked on Heidi's black wooden door. Even though it was early May, the rain was rattling down on her umbrella like it was tap dancing in a West End show. She'd got an Uber — it was her weakness — but even in the short few steps from the pavement to Heidi's front door, her fresh white trainers had taken on a little dirt. The day was still warm, and the air was coated with the smell of rain as it hit hot tarmac. She took another deep breath, the flowers in Heidi's front garden mixing into the air, too. Heidi had talked about getting a canopy for the garden if the weather was good, but she was guessing the weather had put paid to that.

She recalled the last time she'd been here and someone had knocked on the front door. Heidi's mum. Nothing had changed on the other side of the door: Heidi's family were still there. The only thing that had changed was Eden and how she coped. She'd lain in bed this morning working up the courage for today. Now it was time to face the music, and more importantly, a two-year-old's birthday party.

Heidi opened the front door, a slow smile spreading across her face as she saw Eden. She pulled her inside, taking her umbrella. Eden's escape routes were all cut off. She was here to stay.

"Hello, my favourite guest." Heidi stood, the water from the umbrella dripping silently at her side. She didn't seem to mind.

"Hello yourself."

Heidi kissed her, and it extinguished any morsels of panic inside Eden, threatening to bubble up. When she pulled back, she put a finger to Eden's lips. "Just remember, my family are nice people. Most of the time. And they're going to love you, so don't worry. Just relax and be yourself."

How could she read her so well already? "Relaxing around family. I'll give it my best shot." Eden gave her another quick kiss on the lips, then allowed herself to be pulled through to the main room.

***

"Honestly, you should have seen them at this festival. Snogging like their lives depended on it. It was a little much on my birthday." Heidi's sister Sarah was filling the assorted crowd in on the first time they kissed. Heidi's friends, Kate and Meg, along with Cleo and Becca, were captivated.

It was only three months ago, but it seemed so much longer. Eden still remembered the eye-opening feelings of lust and curiosity. The feelings she'd thought had died in her, along with her gran. But Heidi had prodded Eden, woken her from her romantic slumber.

Heidi rolled her eyes. "No more wine for you. This is a two-year-old's party, remember?"

Her sister grinned, holding up her glass of white. "Maya poured it for me, so I figured it was okay. She wants me to have a good time, even if her puritanical mother doesn't." She paused, leaning into Eden. "She's been like this my whole life, you know. Just so you know what you're letting yourself in for."

Eden rubbed the small of Heidi's back, belatedly realising how natural that felt. Even in front of friends and family. Maybe she was better at this shit than she gave herself credit for. "I'll take my chances. Besides, I don't mind a bossy woman in the right circumstances."

Sarah held up a hand. "Pur-lease. Married lady here. No need for such talk on a two-year-old's birthday."

"Shame we didn't come to this festival. I quite fancy snogging you in a field." That was Heidi's friend, Cleo, talking to her girlfriend Becca. They'd arrived just after Eden, carrying in a mini motorbike for Maya. Maya was currently riding it around the kitchen, making super-loud engine noises, being shepherded by her grandad. Eden had bought Maya some books, along with more Chocolate Delight. It wasn't as popular as the motorbike.

"You hate fields. You're far more five-star," Becca replied. "Remember the yurt two years ago?"

"We had fun in the yurt," Cleo said with a grin.

"Not what you were saying the morning after. When your boss walked in on us and your brother got arrested."

Eden furrowed her brow. "That sounds like a juicy story."

"I'll tell you another time," Cleo replied.

Kate and Meg's son Finn arrived, banging into Kate's leg with no warning. She remained steady, showing she was completely used to it. Eden had been quietly admiring Kate's artfully styled platinum-blond look ever since they were introduced.

"Mummy, I won the parcel!" He was holding up a plastic

figure that Eden had never seen before, but was probably very familiar to all the parents in the room.

Kate squatted next to him. "You did? Wow, that's brilliant! What's his name?"

As Finn chatted excitedly to his mother, Eden's toddler-heart ached for the same. Parental love and attention like that was something she'd always yearned for, but never had. Like Maya, Finn would never have to ask himself the question, "What can I do to make my mum love me?" These kids were loved and cared for, and she was so warmed by that. Perhaps that was why she'd always shielded herself from kids, too. Because the small one still inside her needed love she'd never received.

Eden blew out a breath as that thought invaded her brain. The solution was right in front of her. Being around these kids and spending time with them was the way forward. Maybe she could learn a lot from these tiny people.

"Want to get another drink?" Heidi steered Eden towards the kitchen, where her mum was chatting to her sister's husband, Jason.

"Just the woman." Jason grabbed Heidi's arm. He was a 40-year-old hipster, clinging to his youth by still wearing skinny jeans and sporting a styled beard. Eden felt a kindred spirit instantly.

"I was just telling your mum that the England women's cricket team are the best we've ever had. In with a chance of beating the West Indies. What do you think?"

"There's a chance, but always remember Caribbean countries are cricket-mad. They get more coverage, so it matters more."

Jason and Heidi were soon lost in conversation, which left Heidi's mum smiling at Eden. They'd shaken hands earlier, but beyond small talk, they'd kept their communication on need-to-happen basis. Now, there was nowhere to hide.

"Are you a cricket fan, Eden?"

She shook her head. "No. Me and sport don't really mix. I played hockey at school, but only because they made me. I prefer running."

"How are you coping with all the children around? Heidi tells me you don't have a big family. This must be a shock." As if backing up Heidi's mum's statement, Maya and two other similar-aged girls whizzed through the kitchen at speed. There were around eight small children and their parents at the party, along with Heidi's family. Games had been played and cake had been cut. Now, all the kids were high on E numbers, and all the adults were draining the wine to cope with the volume levels.

"A toddler's birthday party is certainly a new experience for me," Eden replied. "Although, after a while, their behaviour is probably the same as most adults after a few drinks in a bar. Only they've got more energy."

Heidi's mum laughed, and Eden recognised Heidi's smile in her face, along with Heidi's eyes. Those same ones, still the colour of her gran's afternoon sherry. Eden inhaled, just to make sure it was still there. It was. Maya Snr was still wearing her gran's perfume, too. But this time, rather than freaking her out, it was comforting. Almost like her gran was still with her.

"And you and Heidi are getting on well I hear?" She didn't stop for Eden to reply. "I'm pleased. I know Heidi thinks I only wanted her to have a partner so that Maya had a second parent. While that's true, it's a lot to put on one person. Plus, Heidi does a great job as a single parent."

"No arguments there."

"But I don't want her to be a single parent, because having someone to share life with makes it that much better." She eyed Eden directly, putting a hand on her arm. "All of that to say, I'm glad she's met someone who makes her smile again. She always smiled, but now she glows. My eldest is very independent, always has been. She doesn't need anyone else to be happy, but she deserves it." She squeezed Eden's arm. "Thanks for coming along and being that person."

Eden shook her head. "I'm the lucky one with your daughter coming into my life. I'm going to do all I can to make her smile."

Heidi's mum beamed at her. "That's all a mother can ask."

Eden breathed in Heidi's mum's scent, and swallowed down. "My gran would have said exactly the same."

Chapter Thirty-Six

Heidi saw the last person out at just after 8pm, then walked back into the main room, sagging against the doorframe. Maya was conked out on the couch, letting out tiny snores. Heidi walked over to Eden and kissed her lips, pulling back to look into her eyes. She was still here, she'd survived, and that was the main thing.

She glanced out the window, grabbing a tea towel from the kitchen drawer. The weather had cleared up and the sun was now low in the sky. Heidi opened the patio doors and wiped down her metal table and chairs. Then she grabbed two cold beers from the fridge, popping their caps before raising an eyebrow at Eden. "Join me?"

"Love to."

They sat down, enjoying the silence for a few moments. Heidi took a swig from the bottle, before snagging Eden's gaze. "How was round one of the Hughes family?" She sat forward. "Or should I say, Hughes family plus toddler overload?"

Eden shrugged, batting a hand through the air. "Piece of cake. Go hard or go home, I say. Family? Tick. Toddlers everywhere screaming at the tops of their lungs? That could take some getting used to."

Heidi laughed. "If it helps, I think all the parents would say the same thing, too."

"Kate and Meg were lovely. As were Cleo and Becca. I approve of all your friends. That's a good start, right?"

Heidi nodded. "Excellent. Kate and Meg have been one of the best things to happen because of Maya. And they've got a fabulous group of friends, too. Becca knows them through her sister. It's the usual thing: six degrees of separation in the lesbian world."

"Some things never change." Eden drank some beer, glancing around Heidi's garden. "And your mum was sweet, too. Told me she was pleased I'd come into your life and made you smile again."

Heidi put a hand to her mouth. "Parents never stop being embarrassing, do they?" But then she winced. Was Eden embarrassed by her mum? Or just ashamed? "Sorry, that was insensitive."

Eden shook her head. "Never think that. Just because my mum is a waste of space, don't ever think you can't talk about yours. Because she's really lovely." She pointed to the flowerbeds on either side of Heidi's paved back garden. "Talking of lovely, this garden reminds me of my gran's. Paving, decking, and carefully tended flowers either side."

Heidi smiled. "This was all planted when I moved here, so I can't take the credit. But my mum is a keen gardener, and as I get older, I find I'm turning into her. I'm glad you liked her, because that's my future." She hoped she wouldn't scare Eden, talking like that.

But when she looked back up, Eden was smiling. "Good that I have a gauge. You don't have that, so my future is a mystery."

"You're a mystery I'm happy to unravel and solve at my leisure." Heidi got up, wrapped an arm around Eden's neck and sat in her lap. Their closeness made her smile right away. She kissed Eden's lips, losing herself in the moment. When she pulled back, Heidi stared into Eden's blue eyes till she was lost at sea.

"Are you sure I'm not too much?"

Heidi shook her head, holding Eden's gaze. "You're perfect. I've got everything I could possibly want right here. Maya, my family, you." She pressed her lips to Eden's. "It's enough." She kissed her again. "You're enough. I don't know if I've said, but I love kissing you."

Eden's eyes grew darker. "I love kissing you, too." She paused, before kissing her again. This time, it left Heidi shipwrecked. But somehow, she knew Eden would save her. She already had.

"I even enjoyed chatting with your mum today. Even smelling her perfume. It was comforting more than freaky today, which was good."

"That's amazing."

Eden nodded. "It is. My gran was my world, and I miss her every day. But maybe meeting you and your family has helped me turn a corner in my grief, too. I wasn't aware I needed to, but apparently I did." She glanced up. "Your eyes remind me of my gran. Did I tell you that?"

Heidi's heart boomed as she shook her head. "You didn't, but I'm honoured."

"It's fitting, too. She was the only good thing in my life for so long. My rock. Now, you're here." She buried her head in Heidi's waist. "I hope that doesn't scare you."

Heidi squeezed her shoulder. "Sweetheart, we're way beyond that. I'm in this for the long haul. I hope you are, too?"

Eden met her stare. "One hundred per cent," she replied. "You know what else I realised today?"

Heidi shook her head. "Tell me."

"That you're a brilliant single mum. That some mums can be enough. That's a change for me, too. I met your friend Denise and she was brilliant with her son, too. I guess it's all about the people involved, not about the amount of people involved. You can have two great parents, or two shit parents. Or one brilliant one, just like Maya's got."

Heidi beamed. She hadn't expected today to work its magic that quickly, but she was beyond happy it had. "You're saying that even *after* all the children."

Eden laughed. "Even then." She cleared her throat. "Your life is unpredictable, but it's full. Your family drive you mad, but they're also there for you. You've never doubted that, have you?"

Heidi replied in a heartbeat. "Not for one single second of my life."

Eden was quiet for a moment. "Always remember what a gift that is. After my upbringing, and after gran died, I thought the easiest thing was to push everyone away. Be self-sufficient. Throw myself into work. If you don't open yourself up, you can't get hurt. But I get it now. I get why you might want to have a child. In your case, to spread the love. To carry on your great family tradition of support. Because what a gift that is."

Heidi kissed her cheek. "Whatever you suffered in the past, I can't change that. But I want you to be part of our family now. Me, you and Maya. And that means you're part of the extended Hughes clan, too. You think you're ready for that?"

Eden took a deep breath, raising her crystal-blue gaze to Heidi. "Let's give it a go, shall we?"

Chapter Thirty-Seven

Eden couldn't quite believe what she was reading. *The Daily Mail* — or *The Daily Fail*, as she called it — had done a double-page spread on their 'deviant' Chocolate Delight ad. Apparently, the brand, having wooed the public with its brilliant competition, was now revealed to be in on the LGBT agenda to turn the public into a mass of sexual deviants. All via the power of chocolate spread. Even Eden was impressed with their warped logic.

Johan couldn't stop laughing. "What the fuck do they think this is going to do? We couldn't have engineered this any better, could we? Two pages in the biggest national newspaper in the land, and one that's read all over the world." He paused, glancing at Eden. "It's online, too, right?"

She nodded. It was one of the first things she'd checked this morning. "Uh-huh. The whole country is now waking up to the fact that lesbians and their children love chocolate spread, and lesbians are going to rule the world. Or something."

"This literally couldn't have gone any better. They took the bait and they hung themselves. I absolutely love it." Johan shook his head, putting the paper down. "Have you heard from India?"

"I have." Eden had received a message earlier, telling her

sales had gone through the roof because of the ad, and this coverage could only make things better. "I wondered if she'd be worried about family groups boycotting, but she said she doesn't give a rat's arse. Actual quote. She only wants morally upstanding people enjoying her spread, and she doesn't class homophobes or haters under that heading. As she told me in her email, 'other brands of chocolate spread are available'."

"Ha! Go India!" Johan kicked the case of Chocolate Delight at his feet. "You know we've got a glut of food brands lining up for us to do similar with their products, now."

Caroline had told them both this morning that their achievement had opened other avenues for the firm, ones she was pretty pleased with.

"I know. I'm hoping for something I really love to eat or drink this time. Something like a champagne brand."

That tickled Johan's taste buds. "Laurent Perrier would be good. Even Lanson. I'm not fussy about champagne if it's free."

"What would you say if Blossom Hill came calling?"

Johan screwed up his face. "I've got standards."

"We could make it cool."

"I'm always up for a challenge." He smiled. "But the success of this is down to you. Bringing in the family angle, having the guts to make it gay. Who knows what else might happen now you're almost a parent."

It'd been three weeks since Maya's birthday, and she was slowly getting used to Eden, and vice versa. "I've got a long way to go before I'm a parent, but I've got a window on family life now, that's for sure. So much so, I might be taking some time off."

Johan clutched his chest. "You're having a baby?" She could hear the smile in his voice.

"Or Heidi and I have talked about taking a holiday."

"You're taking holiday. You, who never takes holiday?"

"Heidi's the same. She works for herself, plus going away solo with a kid is hard. Seeing each other even when we both live in the same city is hard. So we've decided, maybe a holiday is in order. I told Caroline, and she almost fell off her chair."

"I'm not surprised."

"But she agreed. It won't be till late September when Heidi's bookings have died down a little, but we've made a plan. I'm finally going to be taking some of my holiday, rather than taking it in financial terms."

"When am I going to get to meet the amazing Heidi, who has so turned your life around in a matter of a few short months?"

"We're going out tomorrow if you want to come. Gay karaoke. Can you handle it?"

Johan's mouth dropped open. "Gay karaoke is the best. I do a mean George Michael."

Eden looked at him. "This is news."

"Only because you never listen to what I tell you about my weekends." He paused. "Tomorrow night? I think we're free. I'll bring Cameron. It'll be epic. What's your song?"

Eden shook her head. "I don't have a song. My contribution is to clap all you brave souls."

Johan raised a single eyebrow. "We'll see about that."

Chapter Thirty-Eight

"Now then, I want you to make a good impression. This woman's very important to me, okay? So try not to shed so much hair that she's a streaming mess, okay? Plus, I'd like to get laid tonight and not have to decamp to hers. You think you could manage that?"

Dusty yawned in response.

Behind her, Lib laughed. "She doesn't know what you're saying, you know that, right?"

Eden scoffed. "Of course she does, she's a super-intelligent cat. Everyone who meets her says so, don't they, Dusty?" She tickled the kitten's stomach. "What time are you going out?"

Lib sat down on the couch opposite, rolling her eyes. "Subtlety has never been your strong suit, you know that?" She tapped her Fitbit. "In about half an hour. I'll stay to watch Heidi crack under the cat pressure, then I'll leave. Although she lasted longer last time, didn't she?"

This was Heidi's third evening of Dusty exposure since they'd begun seeing each other, and Eden was hoping it wouldn't be a total wipeout. They'd both agreed they were going to ride this time out. Plus, Maya was coming, too, which meant leaving wasn't an option. Heidi had told her that once Maya saw the cat, they wouldn't be going anywhere. Then, it was just a case of whether or not Dusty could cope with Maya.

"Have you heard from the hospice?" Eden glanced up at her friend, knowing she hadn't had it easy the past few months. Her mum had now reached a stage in her illness where the nurses had advised hospice care, and Lib was finally listening. She'd been trying to be a hero, but she'd finally seen sense. Still, Eden knew it hadn't been an easy task. They'd shared a bottle of wine talking about it last night, and Lib was going to a friend's birthday today. A night out had never been a more welcome distraction.

Lib nodded. "Yeah, and she's doing okay. They're being very good. They've got an app I can check, and they update her progress every couple of hours. That's amazing, isn't it?"

"It is. But tonight, promise me you'll have fun. There were enough tears last night."

Lib gave her a sad smile. "I'm trying, it's just not easy. I feel guilty going out when Mum only has so long to live."

Eden put Dusty on the couch next to her and sat forward. "You've sat with her for months. You've paused your job. You're allowed a night out."

"I know. It's just hard to remember that sometimes."

Eden got that. Losing your mum at any time was a hard lesson in life. She'd learned it early. Lib was just coming to terms with it now. "If you're feeling up to it tomorrow, we're going trampolining. Heidi has the day off, and Maya loves it. I've even started to love it again, and you said you'd like to come."

Lib nodded. "I would. You can teach me all your moves. So long as I'm not too hungover, it's a date." She paused. "And don't forget we still need to book our weekend away. I know you're going away with Heidi, but it doesn't mean you get out of your 40th birthday trip with your friends."

"I know. And I'm happy to go wherever you want. Let's book it this weekend. I've heard Lithuania is nice this time of year. Apparently the wine is less than a quid a bottle, someone wise told me."

A knock on the door interrupted their chat. Eden grinned, then jumped up to let Heidi and Maya in. It was still weird to think she was now a part of this little girl's life, but she was adjusting at an alarming rate. What she'd found out in the past month was that children were just small people. If you wanted to find out about them, all you had to do was chat to them. Nobody had ever done that to Eden when she was little, so maybe that's why it was a revelation when Heidi had told her.

When she opened the door, she made sure to kiss Heidi hello — that part was easy — but also to drop down and greet Maya. In return, she got a broad grin and a pair of tiny arms around her neck. Emotion swelled inside Eden as she untangled herself. She glanced up at Heidi, whose sure gaze was watching her.

"You're getting good, you know. Before you know it, you'll be reading child-rearing books."

Eden stood up and kissed her again. "I feel like I need to."

Heidi shook her head. "I think you're doing just fine learning on the job. Although tonight might be a steep learning curve. Especially when she sees the cat."

On hearing the 'c' word, Maya jumped in the air. "Cat!"

"You think your mummy's as excited to see the cat?" Eden gave Heidi a wry smile.

"Mummy can't wait," Heidi replied, taking Maya's hand.

"I've got a gaming coffee table too, Maya. You want to play on that?"

"Cat!" came Maya's reply.

"I guess that's a no." Heidi took a deep breath. "Come on then, let's go and meet Dusty. You've overcome your allergy. It's time for me to overcome mine."

Epilogue
The following February

"I thought I was meant to be the nervous one?" Eden sat in the front, glancing right when she spoke. She was dressed to kill in her blue-and-white chequered power suit. When she'd put it on earlier, Heidi had taken it off just as quickly and fucked her. Now, Heidi wasn't feeling quite so relaxed, her fingers clutching the white leather seat.

She gave Eden a tight smile. "I know, just stop looking at me." This was Eden's first family photo. Yet, somehow, Heidi was the one whose insides were alight with nerves, every muscle she possessed taught. She wasn't quite sure why. After all, her family all loved Eden.

In the back, Maya was strapped into her car seat, straining her neck having just seen a dog. Heidi was currently fighting the battle of getting one for them.

"Doggy, Mummy!"

Heidi eyed her daughter in her rear-view mirror. "Yes, sweetheart."

Heidi tapped her fingers on the steering wheel as the traffic slowed again. She didn't want to be late for a second year in a row.

She caught Eden's stare and followed it to the steering wheel. "What are you staring at?"

"Your fingers," Eden replied. "I can't help it. My mind is still stuck on this morning and what they did to me. Under all this makeup, I'm blushing."

Heidi raised an eyebrow and gave her a smile. "I was pretty good, I'll give you that. But enough sex talk with Maya in the car. We don't want her picking up anything she can then repeat to my mother, do we?"

Eden spread her hands on her thighs, her legs jigging up and down in time with the music on the radio. "Is there anything I need to know about today? Apart from that I shouldn't try to trip up Sarah or Jason, and I need to charm the photographer."

Heidi pumped the brakes as they pulled up at some traffic lights, turning around to check on Maya. Her eyes were closing. Typical. "Hey, no falling asleep, Maya! We've got to stay awake for the photograph, remember Mummy told you?"

Maya opened her eyes. "Doggy!" she said, pointing to a Boston Terrier currently waiting to cross the road.

Heidi turned her attention back to Eden. "All you need to do is be yourself and smile when Pippa says so. That's it. Couldn't be simpler." But Heidi knew it was bigger than that. "Just be yourself. Casual but cool. You're good at that. You're the first partner I've ever had in a photo, no biggie." She began to drum her fingers again.

"I promise not to swear or embarrass you, okay?"

Heidi placed her hand over Eden's. "More than okay. A thousand times okay." She exhaled, emotion bubbling up in her. "Today just means a lot. It's always just been me, you know? And now, you're here. I honestly couldn't be happier, but I'm feeling a little emotional. But let's not dwell on it, because I do not want to cry and have panda eyes for the photo. Not for the second year running."

Eden shook her head. "Nope, you do not. Let's think of something the opposite of panda eyes." She turned around to Maya. "What's the opposite of panda eyes, Maya?"

Heidi's daughter cocked her head. "Elephant eyes!" she replied.

Eden turned back to Heidi. "There you go. From the mouths of babes."

Heidi burst out laughing as she pulled into the studio's car park. For the first time, she had a feeling today was going to be okay.

***

"You look knackered. What were you doing last night?"

Sarah shook her head, burying her face in her husband's shoulder. "Don't ask. Somebody who shall remain nameless decided it would be a good idea to drink whisky."

Heidi winced. "Is it ever a good idea to drink whisky?"

"I've tried to cover it up. Has it worked?" Sarah's makeup was thickly applied, and to the untrained eye, you'd never know.

"You might fool Mum, but you won't fool me."

"At least I look better than you this time last year. Remember? You were a mess thanks to that shoot you'd done that came with a side order of cats."

"Don't remind me."

Heidi's parents walked over, kissing Heidi and Eden. "Lovely to see you both. And my gorgeous Maya, of course!" Her mum picked up her granddaughter. "What have you done today?"

"Doggy, Nanny!" Maya snaked an arm around her grandma's shoulders.

Her mum shot Heidi a look. "Are you getting a dog?"

Heidi shook her head. "Maya would love one, but it's her current favourite word. I'm riding it out. Last week it was casserole, so I'm hoping this one will pass, too."

Maya Snr laughed. "And you look wonderful, Eden. The lemon of your shirt really brings out the colour of your eyes."

Eden blushed. "Thank you. You look lovely, too."

Heidi's heart popped, and her nerves settled. She should never have doubted that her family or Eden could handle today. Together, they were a formidable team.

"Right, I'm going to see if Pippa's ready, and then we can get started. I've booked the pub as usual, so you're all good to come afterwards?"

Heidi nodded, glancing at Eden. "Yes, just like always."

Her mum scuttled off, putting Maya on the floor. Heidi leaned in to kiss Eden. "I think my mum loves you. She's not the only one."

Moments later, Pippa was clapping her hands, waving them all over to the spot in front of all the lighting.

"Show time." Heidi gave Eden a smile, then took her hand. "You ready to come and be immortalised in the Hughes family photo? Because once you're in, it's hard to escape. Ask Jason."

Eden gave her a smile. "Looks like I'll have to stick around then, doesn't it?" She glanced down. "What do you think, Maya? You want me to stick around?"

Maya glanced up with her big brown eyes, before putting her hand in Eden's.

Heidi's heart melted. "Looks like you're a hit with all the Hughes women."

Eden squeezed Heidi's hand. "Lucky me."

THE END

Want more from me? Sign up to join my VIP Readers' Group and get a FREE lesbian romance, **It Had To Be You!** *Claim your free book here: www.clarelydon.co.uk/it-had-to-be-you*

Would You Leave Me A Review?

If you enjoyed this slice of sapphic London life, I wonder if you'd consider leaving me a review wherever you bought it. Just a line or two is fine, and could really make the difference for someone else when they're wondering whether or not to take a chance on me and my writing. If you enjoyed the book and tell them why, it's possible your words will make them click the buy button, too! Just hop on over to wherever you bought this book — Amazon, Apple Books, Kobo, Bella Books, Barnes & Noble or any of the other digital outlets — and say what's in your heart. I always appreciate honest reviews.

Thank you, you're the best.

Love,
Clare x

Also By Clare Lydon

London Romance Series
London Calling (Book One)
This London Love (Book Two)
A Girl Called London (Book Three)
The London Of Us (Book Four)
London, Actually (Book Five)
Made In London (Book Six)
Hot London Nights (Book Seven)
Big London Dreams (Book Eight)
London Ever After (Book Nine)

Standalone Novels
A Taste Of Love
Before You Say I Do
Change Of Heart
Christmas In Mistletoe
Hotshot
It Started With A Kiss
Nothing To Lose: A Lesbian Romance
Once Upon A Princess
One Golden Summer
The Christmas Catch
The Long Weekend
Twice In A Lifetime
You're My Kind

All I Want Series
Two novels and four novellas chart the course
of one relationship over two years.

Boxsets
Available for both the London Romance series and the
All I Want series for ultimate value. Check out my
website for more: www.clarelydon.co.uk/books

Printed in Great Britain
by Amazon

48618307R10152